Praise for
A Scandalous Journey

"A well-wrought winner. Enjoy, and welcome this new star to the Regency galaxy." —Barbara Metzger

"Susannah Carleton joins the list of my favorite Regency authors. . . . An impressive debut." —Emma Jensen

"*A Scandalous Journey* is a very fine example of the traditional Regency romance, and one that shouldn't be missed. With her first book, Ms. Carleton joins the ranks of the highly recommended."

—Romance Reviews Today

Praise for
The Marriage Campaign

"[As with] Susannah Carleton's enthusiastically received debut Regency, *A Scandalous Journey* . . . *The Marriage Campaign* is an excellent read in itself [but] I strongly suggest [reading] *A Scandalous Journey*, if you haven't yet had the pleasure." —Romance Reviews Today

"In *The Marriage Campaign*, Susannah Carleton creates realistic and sympathetic characters who touch our hearts [in] this sensitive tale."

—*Romantic Times* (4½ stars)

A Twist of Fate

Susannah Carleton

A SIGNET BOOK

SIGNET
Published by New American Library, a division of
Penguin Group (USA) Inc., 375 Hudson Street,
New York, New York 10014, U.S.A.
Penguin Books Ltd, 80 Strand,
London WC2R 0RL, England
Penguin Books Australia Ltd, 250 Camberwell Road,
Camberwell, Victoria 3124, Australia
Penguin Books Canada Ltd, 10 Alcorn Avenue,
Toronto, Ontario, Canada M4V 3B2
Penguin Books (N.Z.) Ltd, Cnr Rosedale and Airborne Roads,
Albany, Auckland 1310, New Zealand

Penguin Books Ltd, Registered Offices:
80 Strand, London WC2R 0RL, England

First published by Signet, an imprint of New American Library,
a division of Penguin Group (USA) Inc.

First Printing, September 2003
10 9 8 7 6 5 4 3 2 1

 REGISTERED TRADEMARK—MARCA REGISTRADA

Printed in the United States of America

PUBLISHER'S NOTE
This is a work of fiction. Names, characters, places, and incidents either are the
product of the author's imagination or are used fictitiously, and any resemblance
to actual persons, living or dead, business establishments, events, or locales is
entirely coincidental.

To Hilary Ross, editor extraordinaire,
a patient, understanding lady
and a staunch supporter of
Regency romances and their authors.

And to Rhonda Woodward, with many thanks
for her insightful comments, late-night phone calls,
supportive e-mails, and friendship,
all of which made writing this book easier—and a lot
more fun.

Acknowledgments

I am indebted to several organizations and their very helpful employees for assistance in obtaining specific information about the weather in Oxfordshire and London during January and February of 1814. Mr. Graham Bartlett, Library Information Manager of the (British) National Meteorological Library and Archive, sent me an article on the weather in January 1814. Mr. Steve Jebson, Information Officer and Visual Aids Manager of the National Meteorological Library and Archive, combed the library archives for daily weather information and provided data from the diary of Mr. F. Doxat of Ealing. Mrs. Linda Atkinson, Librarian of the School of Geography and Earth Sciences at the University of Oxford, sent photocopies of the manuscript tables of the Records of the Radcliffe Meteorological Observer from the School of Geography and the Environment Archive Collection at the University of Oxford. Dr. Lance Tufnell, Senior Lecturer in the Division of Geographical Sciences of the School of Applied Sciences at the University of Huddersfield, contributed general information on weather patterns and phenomena.

This book would have been much more difficult to write, and much less accurate, without the contributions of these four wonderfully helpful people.

Chapter One

*L*ord David Winterbrook was lost. Not in the wilds of Africa, nor in the vastness of the Americas. He was lost somewhere in southeastern Berkshire or southern Oxfordshire, not more than twenty-five miles from home.

It was laughable really, or would be under other circumstances. In his current situation, with snow falling merrily and no habitation in sight, it was lamentable. David had left a friend's home this morning in high spirits after a two-day visit, but eager to return home to his daughter. So eager, in fact, that he'd eschewed his comfortable traveling coach and the post roads in favor of a cross-country ride. He could only hope he, and little Isabelle, too, would not suffer too much for his folly.

With the unwavering optimism that had carried him through twenty-six years of life, David told his mount, "There will be something around the next curve in the road." Then he kicked the roan gelding into a canter, hastening to assure that he was correct.

There was, indeed, something ahead, although not the cozy inn for which he'd hoped. Instead, there was a woman, bundled into a collection of rather shabby but warm-looking clothes, trying to convince an ancient nag to pull an even older gig from the ditch back onto the road. David sighed, knowing he was about to get very wet, and very cold. Then, assuming the road to be icy beneath the rapidly accumulating snow, he slowed his mount to a walk.

Dismounting several feet away from the woman and her antiquated conveyance, he tied his horse's reins to a rather thorny bush. Walking carefully—the road was quite icy—he approached her.

"May I be of assistance, ma'am?"

She either did not hear him or chose to ignore him, for she made no response. Puzzled, but too much the gentleman to leave her stranded, he walked closer and spoke again.

"May I assist you, ma'am?"

She turned toward him. David felt a shiver up his spine that had nothing to do with the cold. One look at her and he knew, instantly and with absolute surety, that she was the woman he had been searching for, the lady he would love for the rest of his life.

Three generations of Winterbrooks had recognized their loves at first sight. David had begun to wonder if his ill-fated first marriage had doomed him to live without love, and was pleased to know that was not to be his destiny.

He bowed and introduced himself. "David Winterbrook, at your service, ma'am."

She stared at him for a long moment as if judging his intentions. Or his sincerity and strength. "Thank you. I would welcome your assistance."

Her accent was that of an educated member of the upper class, but there was something unusual about the tone of her voice. David put the thought aside for later consideration and turned toward the gig. And the ditch, which contained about a foot of water. Repressing a sigh at the imminent ruination of his favorite pair of boots, he climbed down the bank to inspect the wheels of the gig.

Fortunately, they appeared undamaged. He was also pleased to note that the vehicle was not heavily laden, containing a box of what appeared to be foodstuffs: a bag of flour, a tin of tea, a jar of preserves, and other such items. The lady, apparently, had been to market. Which meant there must be a town or village nearby. David's spirits lightened at the thought.

"If you will lead the horse forward, ma'am, I will push the gig. We will soon have you back on the road again."

When she neither responded nor reached for the reins, he scrambled up the muddy bank and repeated his instruction, then climbed back down into the ditch.

A quarter of an hour later, the gig was back on the road,

and David was mud-splattered from head to foot. When she turned to thank him, the lady—*he did not even know her name!*—gaped at him. And not, he was certain, for the same reason he gazed at her face.

"Oh, look at you! Mr. Winterbrook, I am most grateful to you for your assistance, but I fear you will regret your good deed. You are muddy from head to toe."

Biting her lip, she subjected him to a long look. Since her attention was focused on his face, which he knew was not mud-splattered, he had the feeling that she was judging him in some way, although he could not imagine why. "I think, sir, that you had best follow me home and allow me to try to clean your greatcoat and boots before you continue your journey."

"It is kind of you to offer, Mrs. . . . ah, ma'am." He made the error deliberately, hoping to learn her name.

"Forgive my rag-manners, Mr. Winterbrook. I am Mrs. Graves."

She was married? Surely fate could not be so unkind! "I imagine your husband would object to a stranger accompanying you home."

"I am a widow and, thus, need please only myself. And it would not please me to have you arrive at your destination covered in mud when you were kind enough to stop and help me."

"Thank you, Mrs. Graves, but you need not worry about my appearance. I intend to travel only to the nearest inn, and can have my coat cleaned there."

She glanced at the sky, then back at him. The way she stared at him as they spoke was rather disconcerting. "The nearest inn is more than twelve miles from here—"

"Twelve miles?" He looked at the rapidly accumulating snow. "Is there no town or village closer?"

"Little Twigham is about six miles from here, but it is a very small village, scarcely larger than a bump in the road."

"If it is large enough to have a market, surely it must have an inn. Or even a tavern where a stranded traveler might find a bed."

The widow shook her head. "There is neither market nor tavern in Little Twigham."

"Is that not where you did your shopping?" He pointed at the box in the back of the gig.

"No. The squire's housekeeper was kind enough to pick up a few things for me Saturday when she went to Tidmarsh."

David could not help but wonder if the squire was one of her suitors. Not that it mattered. The snow was falling so heavily that riding twelve miles was impossible. He would have to accept her offer, and to hope that, once he looked more presentable, he could beg a night's shelter in a nearby house. Perhaps from the squire himself.

"Mrs. Graves, who are the local landowners? Perhaps I am acquainted with one or more of them and can request a bed and a meal."

"Squire Patterson owns most of the land hereabouts. Sir Brian Fifer has an estate not too far from Tidmarsh, but . . ." She gestured at the snow.

"How far is it to the squire's home? Would he give a stranger a bed for the night?"

"Nearly five miles, but I doubt that his charity would extend to giving a stranger bed and board. Especially not in your present condition."

Although he thought the squire would be pleased to host the Marquess of Bellingham's younger son for the night, mud-splattered or not, David doubted that his horse could travel half that distance in the rapidly accumulating snow.

"What houses are between here and the squire's?"

"Larkspur Cottage—my home—is about half a mile away. The only house between my cottage and the squire's home belongs to one of his tenants. It is about two miles beyond the cottage."

Two and a half miles was not impossible. It would be a damned difficult journey, but it was not completely beyond the realm of probability. But once he left her cottage, there would be no fallback position. And no margin for error.

Mrs. Graves obviously shared his concern. "At the rate the snow is falling, I wonder if you can make it even that far. Especially since it is nearly dusk."

"I have no choice but to try, ma'am."

Biting her lip again, she took another long look at him, the snow on the road, and the sky. "Yes, you do have a choice. And I think you'd best come with me. My home is not as comfortable or as commodious as the squire's, but I can offer you a good meal and a warm, dry bed for the night."

"Thank you, ma'am. It is very kind of you to offer." Very unusual as well, although it did explain her intense scrutiny. She *had* been judging him, and he, it seemed, had passed the test.

"One good turn deserves another, they say."

He wondered at her attempt to make light of her offer. *Was she already regretting her invitation?* He did not. She was the woman he would love for the rest of his life, and he welcomed the opportunity to get to know her a bit.

"Can you tie your horse to the back of the gig? I have never driven on such an icy road, and I fear I will land in the ditch again."

He did as she bade, then helped her into the gig and climbed in himself. A few minutes later, she pointed to a gatepost on the right side of the road. "Turn there."

The drive was mercifully short. David was not sure what he expected her home to be like—having any expectations at all seemed rather ludicrous under the circumstances—but he was reasonably certain the little cottage nestled under the trees was not the proper setting for the lady. No one came running from the small stable behind the house to greet them. Nor from the cottage. Just when he would have turned toward the front door, she said, "Pull up to the stable. The boy who cares for the horses probably went home when the snow began falling so heavily, so I will have to unharness the horse."

"*I* will stable the horse, ma'am, if you will show me where to find the tack and feed. And where to park the gig."

She turned toward him. "What did you say?"

"I said that I will stable the horse if you show me where the tack and feed are." David halted the vehicle outside the stable and jumped down to open the door.

The widow climbed down behind him, then led the horse inside and parked the gig in what appeared to be its designated spot on the left side of the aisle. "It is kind of you to offer, sir, but I am quite capable of caring for the horse."

"I am sure you are, Mrs. Graves, but I could not call myself a gentleman if I allowed you to do so."

Madeline Graves looked at her unexpected guest and wondered if she had made a terrible mistake in inviting him to her home. She had assumed Mr. Winterbrook to be a solicitor or a man of business, possibly even a merchant. Prosperous to be sure, given the quality of his clothing and his horse, but a member of the middle class, not the upper one.

Lynn's experience with so-called gentlemen was limited to her father, her two older brothers, and her husband, but if the four of them were representative of the group, there was little to recommend them. Certainly no gentleman had ever shown her kindness, or gone out of his way to help her. Neither her relatives nor her late husband would have offered to assist a stranger. Most would not help the women they knew, unless there was something in it for them.

But watching him as he efficiently unharnessed the old mare, then brushed and fed her, Lynn was willing to believe that Mr. Winterbrook was different from the gentlemen of her acquaintance. Mostly because the alternative was too horrible to contemplate.

When he finished his self-appointed task, including cleaning the horse's hooves—something, Lynn ruefully acknowledged, she would not have thought to do, nor known how to accomplish if she'd remembered—he picked up the crate from the back of the gig.

"Mr. Winterbrook, you don't have to carry that!"

He smiled down at her. "Yes, ma'am, I do. Unless you tell me closing the door is more difficult than carrying this box."

"No, it closes easily enough."

Side by side they left the stable and walked toward the house. Lynn was proud of her home. After her husband's death, she'd had to sell the house in which they'd lived, and most of their possessions, to pay his debts. Although she'd feared the gambling vowels would consume every penny, there had been just enough money to buy the snug little cottage with its two acres of land. Her only income was her husband's Army pension, and given his disgraceful conduct, she was fortunate to have that.

But as she opened the back door and motioned Mr. Winterbrook inside, Lynn was quite conscious of the fact that her little cottage was probably nothing like his home. She was pleased to note that he scraped his boots carefully before entering. And as soon as he set the box on the kitchen table, he moved to the hearth and added a log to the fire. *Really, he was a most unusual gentleman!*

Before removing his greatcoat, he helped her remove her cloak, then her late husband's uniform coat, which she had worn underneath for warmth.

"Your husband was a soldier?"

"He was." Lynn did not want to discuss Frank with Mr. Winterbrook. Or with anyone.

Something in her voice must have indicated her dislike of the topic, for her guest said, in a neutral tone, "My brother was a major in the Queen's Light Dragoons."

A major in the cavalry! The Winterbrooks must be quite well-to-do. "My husband was a lieutenant in the infantry." Lynn pressed her lips together, determined to say no more about her late, unlamented husband. "Was your brother older or younger than you?"

"I have only one, ma'am. George is four years older." Mr. Winterbrook grinned. "He married a lovely girl last June, and I learned over Christmas that they will present me with a niece or nephew this summer."

"How wonderful for them. And for you." Lynn loved children, but despite her fervent prayers, she had never conceived.

She grabbed the kettle from the hearth and moved to the pump to fill it. As she glanced over her shoulder at her guest, she saw his lips move, then curl into a smile. Cursing her wretched hearing, and her brute of a husband for causing her near deafness, she turned around to face Mr. Winterbrook.

"Forgive me, sir. I could not hear what you said whilst I was pumping the water."

He took the kettle from her, then crossed to the fireplace and hung it from one of the pot hooks. As he stood erect, he smiled again. Lynn's stomach clenched as she realized that he had repeated his statement and was awaiting her response. Unfortunately, he'd had his back to her, and because she had not been able to watch his mouth, she had no idea what he'd said.

With anyone else, she would try to bluff it out—return

the smile and hope it was an appropriate response. That seemed wrong in this case, but she did it anyway, unwilling to confess her hated weakness to a stranger. Even a kind, rather handsome one.

Lynn was well aware that she owed Mr. Winterbrook a debt of gratitude, not only for stopping to help her, but because he had undoubtedly ruined his greatcoat and his boots getting her gig out of the ditch. She had, perhaps, compensated somewhat by offering him a night's shelter, but she knew she was still in his debt.

She would, of course, try to clean his coat and boots when they dried, but she could do nothing until then. Nothing, that is, but feed him. Unfortunately, she had little she could serve with his tea—no scones or macaroons, only bread and butter. Resolving to bake a cake tomorrow if the weather continued inclement and extended his stay, she crossed to the dresser for the teapot and cups. After placing them, and two spoons, on the table, she went to the larder to get the sugar loaf and the cream pitcher.

When she returned, he was standing beside the table. Lynn flushed, realizing she had not even offered him a seat. "Please sit down, Mr. Winterbrook."

He pulled out the chair at the head of the table and seated her before taking the place she had indicated. Lynn seldom had guests, nor was she accustomed to conversing with strangers, but as hostess it was her duty to find a topic of conversation.

The weather would do, she supposed, then remembering something he had said on the road, she asked, "Am I right in thinking you are not from this area, sir?"

"In truth, Mrs. Graves, I have no idea where I am," he confessed, his expression sheepish, "so I cannot accurately answer your question. How far are we from Reading?"

"You are in eastern Berkshire, sir. Reading is five or six miles southeast of Tidmarsh."

"I believe you said earlier that Tidmarsh is about twelve miles from here." It was half statement, half question.

She nodded. "Yes, that is correct."

"I am not the mathematical genius my father and brother are, but I know the Pythagorean theorem. If Tidmarsh is five or six miles northwest of Reading and I live twelve miles north of that city, then it is less than thirteen miles from Tidmarsh to my home in Oxfordshire. Nearly twenty-five miles from here."

A moment later he rose, crossed to the hearth and picked up the kettle, then carried it to the table and began filling the teapot. Lynn stood, too, reaching to take over the task, but he waved her back to her seat. After filling the teapot, he turned toward her expectantly, the kettle still in his hand.

Once again she had no idea what he had said. She felt the color rising to heat her cheeks. When she should have been watching the kettle so that she would know when the water was boiling, she had been watching the movement of his lips to be sure she understood his words. And when she ought to have been looking at him, she had been staring at the table and berating herself for not watching the kettle. She stifled a sigh. "Forgive me, sir. I fear I was woolgathering."

He lifted the kettle. "Should I refill it and put it back on the hob?"

"No." She would need hot water to wash dishes, but not until later. "Thank you."

After moving teapot, cups, and saucers so she could reach them, he walked to the window and looked outside. Lynn cast her gaze heavenward and prayed he was not speaking. Had she realized all the problems inherent in attempting conversation with a stranger, she would have confessed earlier and been done with it.

When she could bear the suspense no longer, she reached for the teapot and poured the beverage into the cups. "The tea is ready, Mr. Winterbrook."

At the sound of her voice, he turned from the window and resumed his seat. To her great relief, his expression was thoughtful, not the annoyance she feared she would see because his statements or questions had been ignored.

"Cream and sugar, sir?"

"A little sugar and just a drop of cream, please."

She prepared his tea, then handed him the cup. "I wish I had scones or cake to offer you, but . . ."

"But you were not expecting any guests today." He had the nicest smile of any man Lynn had ever met.

"No, I was not. But I promise you a hearty stew for supper, with fresh . . . Oh, the bread!" Hoping it was not burnt, she crossed to the wall oven.

"It smells delicious."

"Thank you. I put it in the oven before I left for the squire's, but I completely forgot about it until just now." When she turned back to the table, he was standing beside his chair. Lynn blushed, unaccustomed to such gentlemanly courtesies. "Please sit down and drink your tea."

After one swallow, he set his cup on the table. "The light is fading fast due to the storm. I am going out to settle the horses for the night. Do you have any other animals?"

"Mr. Winterbrook, there is no need for you to care for my animals!"

"I believe we have already had this conversation, ma'am. I do not doubt your ability to care for them, but I will not sit idly while you work. And I am much more effective in a stable than a kitchen." He grinned.

It was impossible to resist that boyish smile. "I have a milk cow and half a dozen chickens, too."

Waiting for him to admit defeat—he had surely never milked a cow—she sipped her tea. And nearly choked when he asked, "Is the barn directly behind the stable?"

"It is."

"Do you have a lantern?"

"Yes." Then, unable to believe this elegantly clad, self-proclaimed gentleman had ever been next or nigh a cow, she challenged, "Have you ever milked a cow, sir?"

"Many times, ma'am." After a moment's pause, he added, "I . . . ah, manage one of the Marquess of Bellingham's estates. I don't believe in asking my workers to do anything that I cannot, so I have performed every farm-related task you can think of—and many that most people never imagine. Milking is a job I do regularly. Every Sunday, to be precise."

Lynn could not have been more surprised if he'd said he could fly. "Why on Sundays?"

"My best milkmaid's father is the leader of an evangelical sect that does not believe in working on the Sabbath. And since I do not believe it is fair to ask the other women to work harder on Sundays, I milk then."

"You are a most unusual man, Mr. Winterbrook."

"Is that a good or bad thing?" he asked, smiling. "My brother has an estate in Dorset, where he breeds and trains horses. I am not a wagering man, but if I were, I would bet that George, too, has performed every task he asks his workers to do."

He stood and reached for his greatcoat. "If you will get the lantern for me, Mrs. Graves, I will go out and settle your animals for the night."

She gave it to him, along with an extra candle and a flint. He put both in his coat pocket, then pulled on his gloves. "Do you have a long rope? Long enough to reach from the stable to the back door?"

"There is rope in the stable. And some in the barn, too, I think, although I doubt any of them are that long."

Her expression must have reflected her puzzlement because he gestured at the window. "The snow is still falling heavily, and the wind seems to be increasing. We may well have a blizzard by morning. Since snowdrifts will make the path look even more unfamiliar than it is, I want to stretch a rope from the cottage to the stable, and another from the stable to the barn, so I can get there and back safely."

"That is an excellent idea!" Lynn reached in the drawer for a sharp knife, which she handed to him. "The door at the back of the stable leads almost straight to the barn. You will probably need to cut one of the ropes to cover that distance. And tie some together to reach from the stable to the house."

He donned his hat, then a moment later removed it. "I would rather not have to chase it around the yard when the wind blows it off."

Lynn smiled at the image his words conjured. "That would be an amusing sight."

Pointing at the puddle of water around her chair, he admonished, "You had best change into dry clothes while I am outside, so you don't catch a chill. I will knock on the door when I return."

"There is no need for that, sir. I will be changed long before you finish." Lynn did not want him standing in the cold if she failed to hear his signal.

His expression was skeptical, but he said nothing more, merely turned toward the door.

"Please be careful, Mr. Winterbrook."

He smiled over his shoulder at her, then opened the door and walked outside. Before he had taken more than three steps, the swirling snow obscured his figure from her view.

Chapter Two

As he mucked out stalls—definitely not one of his favorite occupations—David considered his hostess and the oddities of her character. Knowing that she was the lady he was destined to love for the rest of his life—and given the stories told by every member of three generations of his father's family, he did not question that she was fated to be his one true love—it behooved him to understand her. Or, at least, to make an attempt to do so.

Of course, he had no idea how she felt about him, aside from her very understandable wariness to invite a stranger into her home. Before she'd extended her invitation, she had studied him, taking his measure and judging him according to her criteria, whatever those might be, and she'd made no secret of it. He respected her for that. Had she not been as cautious, and as obviously wary, he probably would not have accepted her offer. He'd been trapped into marriage once by a lady with a secret purpose, and he had no wish to repeat the experience.

But his heart had recognized Mrs. Graves, and that knowledge greatly eased his concern about their possibly compromising situation.

He didn't doubt that he was destined to love her, but that did not necessarily mean that he would find her easy to live with. And despite the family legend, there was no guarantee that she would love, or even like, him.

Apparently, she lived alone, without even a single servant—a very unusual situation for a widow of the upper class. Perhaps it was because she was accustomed to being alone that she fell into abstracted reveries and failed to hear the conversation of those around her, but David believed, although he could not say how or why, that the real reason was more complex. Then, there was the way she stared at him when he talked. And something very subtly different about her voice. But no matter how he rearranged the few, disjointed bits of information he had, they did not fall into place and solve the puzzle of his hostess's behavior.

Eccentricity might well be the explanation. And there were far worse quirks of character a lady—or, indeed, any person, male or female—might possess.

By the time he finished milking the cow, David was cold to his bones. He could not remember a year that had begun with such cold weather. Nor one with a heavy snowfall so early in January. There were five or six inches already on the ground, and the snow was still falling. Perhaps there had been similar occurrences during his boyhood, but not in the five years he had been managing Greendale Manor for his father.

After pulling on his gloves, David picked up the milk pail in one hand, looped a long coil of rope over his shoulder, then grabbed the lantern. He had already stretched a line between the rear door of the stable and the barn, but he still needed to mark the way from the stable to the cottage.

Leaving the barn, he had to set down both bucket and lantern to close the door against the drifting snow. It was useless to wish for a third hand, so he followed the path back to the stable by rubbing his coat sleeve against the cable. After passing through the stable, he again set down his burdens to tie the rope to the stable door. Then, lifting the lantern high, he attempted to retrace his path to the cottage. It was more difficult than he expected; the snow was rapidly filling the boot prints he had left on the outbound journey. When he was about halfway to his destination, they disappeared completely. But a few moments— very long moments—later, a blaze of light appeared, indicating his direction. *Bless you, Mrs. Graves!*

Once he reached the cottage, a new problem reared its ugly head. The stable and barn doors opened outward, so the rope between them was taut when the doors were closed. The cottage's back door, however, swung inward. If he left enough slack in the line so that the door could be opened, then when it was closed, the cable would drag in the snow. And at the rate it was snowing, the rope might well be buried by morning. Before he attempted to find another location to which he could anchor it, he would rid himself of the milk. And ask his hostess to hold the lantern for him.

He knocked on the back door but received no response. Through the kitchen window he could see Mrs. Graves standing at the hearth, but she made no move toward the portal. He rapped again, louder, with the same lack of result. Exasperated, he set down the lantern, opened the door, and stepped inside. The fire flared in a gust of wind; Mrs. Graves started and turned toward him.

"You must be frozen through. Come warm yourself by the fire."

He handed her the pail of milk. "I am not quite finished. I need you to hold the lantern for me, please, so I can attach the rope to the door. Or to something near it."

"Of course." She placed the bucket on the table, then quickly donned her cloak. "Where is the lantern?"

"I had to set it down outside, so I could open the door."

An expression he could not interpret flashed across her features, but she said nothing. After stepping outside, she lifted the lantern high enough to illuminate the doorknob. David placed his hand over hers and raised the light higher, so he could study the door frame, then turned toward the window.

Stepping closer, so she could hear him over the wind's howl, he instructed, "Move closer to the window, please, but do not step off the porch. The snow is quite deep."

"What—"

"I am going to close the shutters, then tie the rope to one of the brackets that holds them open."

She handed him the lantern, then went back into the house, returning a few seconds later with a broom. "There are brackets at the top, too. Willie has to stand on a ladder to reach them, but you may be able to push them off with the broom."

"An excellent suggestion, ma'am!"

But David, although a couple inches taller than average, could not quite reach them, even with the aid of the broom.

After several unsuccessful attempts, Mrs. Graves set down the lantern and darted inside. She returned in less than a minute, carrying one of the kitchen chairs. "If you stand on this, I think you will be able to reach them."

And so it proved. Once the shutters and rope were secured, he carried his makeshift ladder inside while she followed with the lantern and broom.

Fighting the urge to race to the hearth and warm himself, David helped Mrs. Graves remove her cloak before giving in to the impulse.

"We will eat as soon as you are warm, Mr. Winterbrook." She joined him in front of the fire, and after warming her hands, bent over and removed a large pot from the chimney crane and set it on the hearth. The stew bubbling inside smelled delicious. With an ungentlemanly gurgle, David's stomach reminded him that he had not eaten since breakfast, many hours ago. He glanced over his shoulder at his hostess, hoping she had not heard the indelicate sound. If she had, her serene expression gave no indication of it.

She motioned toward the far corner of the kitchen, which now contained a large tub. "I thought you might like a bath before dinner. It will help warm you."

Undoubtedly it would, and it was kind of her to think of it, but David was not at all certain he wanted to bathe in the kitchen. Especially not if she was in it.

"I noticed you did not have a portmanteau. There were a few things of my husband's in a trunk in the attic, so I put them in your room. They will not fit well, but I thought you could wear them while your clothes dry."

"Thank you, ma'am. I appreciate your thoughtfulness."

"Come, I will show you to your room." She crossed to an archway, then led him down a short hall to a room at the end. "I will be in the parlor. When you finish bathing, join me there. Then I will serve dinner."

Lynn lit a fire in the parlor hearth, then crossed to the window and looked out at the falling snow. Due to the quantity that fell, it was clearly visible despite the deepening dusk. This morning, Hatcher, the squire's butler, had predicted several days of wet, heavy snow. The old man's rheumatic joints were generally quite accurate in forecasting the weather, but Lynn hoped that he—and his knees—

were wrong this time. She was more than a bit uneasy about her unexpected guest.

Given the severity of the storm, and his kindness to her, she'd had no choice but to offer him shelter. But extending an invitation was a far cry from extending her trust. That he would have to earn.

Shivering, she walked to the hearth to warm herself. A few minutes later, she sat in a wing chair in front of the fire, her eyes on the flames, but her mind on Mr. Winterbrook. His manners confirmed him to be an inherently courteous gentleman, but his deeds were atypical. Rather, his actions today had been very different from the gentlemen she knew. Neither her husband nor her father and brothers would have performed the menial farm chores Mr. Winterbrook had voluntarily taken on. No matter what the circumstances.

Thus far, her guest's behavior had been impeccable. Exemplary, even. But Frank—and her brothers, too—could be charming on occasion. Her late husband had not shown his cruelty until after they were married. And after her father had refused to give Frank her dowry. Lynn sometimes thought her life would make a fine morality tale for young girls. *The Perils of Eloping with a Man of Whom Your Father Does Not Approve* would be an appropriate title.

Frank's death two years ago had ended his cruelties. Only their results lingered. It was the most obvious of those that concerned her now. If Mr. Winterbrook was going to be stranded here for several days because of the snow, then she would have to confess her near deafness. Not the cause of it—she would never tell anyone that—but the fact of it.

Perhaps she could put it off for a day or two . . .

Lynn started violently when the subject of her thoughts suddenly appeared beside her chair.

"I beg your pardon, Mrs. Graves. I did not mean to startle you."

"'Tis my own fault, Mr. Winterbrook, for woolgathering." She looked away for a moment to gather her composure. "Are you ready for supper, sir?"

"Yes, ma'am. As soon as you tell me where you store the tub, so I can put it away."

"In the larder. Against the wall."

He turned to leave, then glanced back over his shoulder at her. "Thank you very much for thinking of the bath. It did, indeed, warm me. And thank you also for finding me some dry clothes."

Until he spoke, Lynn had not noticed that Mr. Winterbrook was wearing her late husband's pantaloons, shirt, and dressing gown. The pantaloons and dressing gown were several inches too long—and, she guessed, equally too big through the waist and hips—as were the shirtsleeves, which drooped around his wrists. But despite the ill-fitting clothes, her guest was a handsome man, with an inherent elegance nothing could disguise.

She entered the kitchen in time to see Mr. Winterbrook carry the tub, which he had already emptied, into the larder. It surely was not a task he usually performed—as the manager of a marquess's estate, he undoubtedly had several servants—but he did it without complaint. Apparently he was a man who would try his hand at whatever job needed to be done. Lynn greatly appreciated his willingness to help; her husband, father, and brothers would have ignored the tub after stepping out of it. She had waited on the latter three throughout her adolescence, then on Frank for six years, but since his death, she'd reveled in the freedom of doing what she wanted. If she hadn't already sworn not to remarry, the thought of never again being subject to a man's whims was more than enough to convince her to remain unwed.

Taking plates, cups, and silverware from the dresser, she set the table. After filling a small kettle with water and placing it on a pot hook, she reached for the large pot containing the stew. But Mr. Winterbrook was quicker. And had longer arms. He lifted it and, smiling, placed it on the table.

"What else can I do to help, Mrs. Graves?"

"Nothing, sir. Please sit down."

He pulled out her chair and seated her, then took his place to her right. She glanced over at him, wondering if he generally said a prayer before eating. It did not matter, she decided. *She* said one, so his food would be blessed tonight. In fact, since he was so eager to help . . .

"Will you please say the blessing, Mr. Winterbrook?"

Somewhat to her surprise, he complied without demur, thanking God not only for the meal, but for her kindness in inviting him to her home and sharing her food with him. Instead of the embarrassed mumble some of the local men adopted when asked to pray aloud, or the vicar's monotonous, seemingly interminable drone, Mr. Winterbrook spoke to the Almighty in the same rich voice he conducted a conversation. And this time she was close enough to hear every word.

After she served the stew, giving Mr. Winterbrook twice as much as herself, Lynn glanced at the fire to see if the water in the kettle was boiling yet, but it was not. Her guest was probably accustomed to drinking wine with his dinner, but she did not have any. She had sherry to serve when the vicar called, and there was a bit of brandy left in the bottle her father had brought the last time he'd visited, but no wine. And she had no intention of offering Mr. Winterbrook either beverage. She knew all too well that men, even gentlemen, could be brutally cruel when in their cups.

"Have you always lived in this area, Mrs. Graves?"

"I grew up not too far from here, but moved away when I married. I came back two years ago, after my husband's death. Have you always lived in Oxfordshire, sir?"

"No, ma'am. We lived in Dorsetshire—near Weymouth—when I was a babe, and moved to Northumberland when I was four or five."

Had Mr. Winterbrook's father been an estate manager, too? It was too personal a question to ask a stranger. Checking the kettle again, she saw a puff of steam and stood, motioning for her guest to remain seated. "I need to make tea. Please, eat your dinner."

As she filled the teapot, Lynn glanced over her shoulder at him. He had not, however, accepted her invitation; his knife and fork were still on the table beside his plate. Even worse, he was talking! And she had not the slightest idea what he'd said.

She stifled a sigh. If she did not explain her problem, he would think her extremely rude for not responding. Although other people's opinions generally did not concern her, Lynn was rather surprised to realize that she did not want Mr. Winterbrook to think badly of her. Girding herself to confess her hated weakness, she turned toward the dresser. She would tell him of her defect, but she did not want to see the pity on his face when she did.

"You must forgive me, Mr. Winterbrook. I am very hard of hearing due to a . . . an accident several years ago. Unless someone is standing close to me, or facing me when they speak so that I can watch their mouth, conversation is impossible for me."

She started violently when a pair of gentle hands clasped her shoulders and turned her around.

"I shall take care to stomp about"—her guest demonstrated with a grin, lifting his feet high off the floor—"so as not to startle you."

She smiled at his foolishness. "That will not be necessary, sir."

"I think perhaps it will. I do not want you to be uncomfortable in your own home, nor to regret inviting me." His expression shifted from concern to an intense sincerity. "I beg your pardon, Mrs. Graves, for not having realized your difficulty sooner. Do you hear better on one side than the other? That is, will it help if I stand on one side or the other when I talk to you?"

Lynn stared at him, mouth agape. *A very unusual gentleman, indeed!* No man had ever apologized to her. And no one, man or woman, had thought to ask if there was something they could do to help her hear. Emotion clogged her throat, but she managed to say, "A bit better on the right."

He nodded, then cupped his hand beneath her elbow and steered her back to her seat at the head of the table. After resuming his place on her right, he turned his chair slightly so he faced her.

"Mr. Winterbrook, may I ask you to repeat whatever you said before?"

"Of course you may. As often as necessary."

His kindness, and his matter-of-fact acceptance of her deafness, was almost her undoing. Glancing down, she closed her eyes against incipient tears. When she had her emotions under control, she lifted her head—and realized that he had been waiting for her to look at him, as if that were a signal he could begin speaking. Blinking rapidly, she held his gaze and nodded.

"I said nothing profound, ma'am, I merely offered to make the tea."

She nodded, then picked up her fork and began to eat. After several bites, she worked up the courage to make another request. "This afternoon shortly after we arrived, I asked you to repeat something, but I did not hear it the second time, either. Do you remember what you said?"

When he did not immediately reply, she prompted, "It was just after you told me that you learned over Christmas that your brother and sister-in-law will present you with a niece or nephew this summer."

"Ah." A smile replaced the frown he had worn while trying to recall their earlier conversation. "That was not particularly profound, either. I believe I said that it seems fitting that George and Beth—my brother and his wife—provide me with a niece or nephew, since it was because of George's niece, my daughter Isabelle, that he and Beth met."

"So you are a married man with a family."

"I am a widower." It was the set of his mouth, not his tone, that conveyed his dislike for the turn the conversation had taken. Lynn could not help but wonder if his marriage had been unpleasant, too. And why.

Placing her napkin on the table, she rose to pour the tea. But Mr. Winterbrook took on this task as readily as he had assumed all the others this afternoon. After he served them both and resumed eating, Lynn introduced a new—and, she hoped, neutral—topic of conversation. "Tell me about your children."

"I have only one daughter. Isabelle is the light of my life." His smile was testament to the truth of his words.

"How old is she?"

"Four and a half."

Thinking of the children she knew who were that age, Lynn asked, "Does she want to know the how and why of everything?"

"Lord help me, yes," he said, chuckling. "My aunt, who lives with us, claims Isabelle is one big question. Certainly Aunt Caro and I have learned a lot while seeking answers to Isabelle's questions."

"I suppose a four-year-old is too young for a governess."

"I think so. But according to my daughter, it is *almost* too old for a nanny."

"Perhaps you should present her with a governess as a fifth birthday gift."

"Perhaps I should." His sky blue eyes seemed to darken in color when he smiled. "Thank you, Mrs. Graves. That is an excellent suggestion."

"Are your daughter and your aunt expecting you home today?"

David did not particularly want the world to know how and why he had come to be lost in Berkshire, but he saw no reason not to confess his folly to this kind-hearted lady. "They are not expecting me until tomorrow. I have been visiting a friend for the past two days. This morning when I left his home, I was so impatient to return to Isabelle that I sent my coachman and valet on with the carriage and rode cross-country, thinking I would get home more quickly."

"Your coachman might well be stuck somewhere, too."

"Possibly. But"—David grinned—"he, at least, will not be lost."

"Oh, but he might be." Mrs. Graves was an attractive woman with her face in repose, quite lovely when she smiled. "He might have taken a wrong turn. Or the carriage could have slid off the road. Or—"

Laughing at her attempts to cheer him, David held up his hand to halt her conjectures. "No more, please, ma'am. I am rather fond of that carriage."

"Very well, sir." Her smile faded, her expression changing to one of concern. "Will your daughter and your aunt be worried if you don't arrive home tomorrow?"

"Probably not. Unless the coachman makes it through."

"For their sakes, let us hope that he is stuck somewhere, too."

What a remarkably nice lady she was! His late wife would never have worried about two people she had never met. Marie had rarely spared a thought for anyone other than herself. Not even for her husband and daughter.

When they finished eating, he complimented his hostess's cooking. Mrs. Graves merely smiled, then put the leftover stew in the larder and prepared to wash the dishes. "How can I help you, ma'am?"

"You are offering to help wash dishes?" Her look of

surprise was almost comical, eyebrows hovering near her hairline and mouth agape.

"Is there some reason why I shouldn't?"

"Well, no, but . . . Have you ever washed dishes, Mr. Winterbrook?"

"No, I haven't, but I know they should be scrubbed until they are clean. How difficult can it be?"

His response seemed to disconcert her. She sputtered a bit before saying, "If you like, you can keep me company while I wash them."

"Very well, ma'am." It was a good compromise, and he was certainly willing to talk with her while she worked, but neither of them had considered the impossibility of the task she'd set him. Mrs. Graves's back was toward him, and he was either too far away for her to hear his words, or she could not hear them over the splashing water.

Since he could not talk with her, David used the time to study her instead. She was not very tall, perhaps five feet and three inches, and her figure was more rounded than the current fashion, but David thought a curvaceous woman a more pleasant armful than a willowy chit. Not that he had much experience holding either type, except on the dance floor. The blue, woolen round gown she wore was simple in style, unadorned save for a bit of lace at the neck, but it fit her well and the fabric was of good quality. Her hair was a rich, dark brown with auburn highlights and, if the stray wisps around her face were any indication, straight as a stick. Her expressive eyes were a lovely hue that combined blue, green, and brown—hazel was the correct term, he believed—and were framed by a thicket of reddish brown lashes. Most surprising of all, she seemed completely unaware of her beauty.

What kind of accident had caused her hearing problem, he wondered. He had heard of soldiers and sailors temporarily losing their ability to hear after explosions or loud, prolonged cannon barrages. From his friendship with the local doctor, David knew that some diseases caused deafness. But he had never heard of anyone permanently losing their hearing because of an accident. He would have to ask Dr. MacNeill over their next chess game what kind of accidents could cause deafness. And if there were ways to treat such a hearing loss.

Raising a wet hand, Mrs. Graves swiped at a stray lock of hair, then tucked it behind her left ear. The gesture drew David's attention, his gaze locking on the scar just in front of her ear. About an inch and a half long with slightly jagged edges, it was old enough to have faded from red to white, but not pale enough to be the result of a childhood injury. *Was the scar, or whatever had caused it, the reason for her hearing problem?* David thought it might well be. *But what kind of accident could have resulted in such a singular, oddly placed injury?*

He returned rather abruptly to the present when his hostess turned to him and smiled, drying her hands on a towel. "Do you play chess or cards, Mr. Winterbrook?"

He rose to his feet. "A bit of both, ma'am. Would you rather play chess or cards?"

"That depends on what card game you have in mind. My favorite games are whist, cribbage, and piquet, although I prefer whist with four players."

"I like it better with four players myself. I don't often play piquet, so I probably cannot give you a good game. That narrows our choices to cribbage and chess. Which would you prefer?"

She peeked up at him through her lashes. "Are you a very good chess player?"

"Tolerable, I suppose. I play every week or so with the local doctor and win about as often as I lose, but I don't fare as well against my father or my brother. They say I don't plan my moves far enough in advance."

"I have been told the same. Shall we play a game? If my skill is too inferior to provide a challenge for you, we can switch to cribbage."

Why did she assume she was the poorer player? "It is just as likely that you are the better player, Mrs. Graves."

She laughed, the sound more bitter than mirthful. "I doubt it, sir."

"Why? There is no rule that says men are better chess players than women. You must know a number of men whose intelligence is no match for your own."

The idea seemed to surprise her, as if she had never considered it before, but after a moment she said, "I have sometimes thought that, but it could not have been true. They had been to university."

"I am not speaking of education, but of natural intelligence." *Who had belittled her, that she had such a poor opinion of herself? Her husband? Her father? Both of them?* Although many men believed women were inferior, intellectually and in most every other way, David did not. There were far too many stupid men in the world, and too many intelligent women, for him to accept such a gross generality.

"Hmm . . . I will have to think about that a bit."

"We can discuss it more tomorrow if you like." David smiled, hoping to lighten the mood—and to ease the frown creasing her forehead. "Now, do you still wish to play a game of chess?"

"Yes, please."

He offered his arm to escort her to the parlor. While she set up the board, he built up the fire, then studied the room. Like the bedchambers, the parlor was rather sparsely furnished. The basic furnishings were there, well-made pieces, too, by the look of them, but little more. All the rooms were scrupulously clean, but something was missing. Unable to identify exactly what that something was, he put the thought aside for later consideration.

After repositioning the two wing chairs to face the small table in front of the hearth, he took his seat across from his opponent. With all his heart, David hoped that he and Mrs. Graves would be equally matched, or nearly so, in skill. The lady did not realize her own worth, and a win would help to bolster her self-esteem.

An hour and a half later, they had battled to a draw. And it had, indeed, been a battle. David leaned against the back of his chair in mock exhaustion. "I have never worked so hard for a draw in my entire life."

A flush of color turned his companion's cheeks rosy, but she smiled with pleasure. "I am delighted to know you had to work for it, sir."

"With whom do you usually play, ma'am?"

"With my father, although not very often. We are . . . not close."

Geographically distant or emotionally? It was too personal a question to ask, so he picked up a handful of chessmen and put them back in their box. "I consider myself fortunate that you don't play more frequently. If you did, you would have trounced me in short order."

"I think not, sir, but you are kind to say so. Would you like a cup of tea?"

"If you are going to make a pot, I will share it with you, but you need not make it on my account."

"I usually have a cup of chamomile tea before retiring."

David did not like chamomile tea, or any herbal infusion, but he would not insult his hostess by retracting his acceptance. "Chamomile is fine."

After putting the chessmen and the board in a cabinet of the sideboard, she headed for the kitchen to boil water for their tea. David banked the fire and set the fire screen in place. Then, as he did every night at home, he checked that the windows were firmly shut and the front door was locked. Assured that they were safe and snug, despite the snow that still fell, he joined Mrs. Graves in the kitchen.

It wasn't until much later, when he was lying in bed, that David realized what the elusive "something" missing from the cottage's rooms was. There were no portraits or paintings, no bibelots or objets d'art. What, he wondered, had brought the lovely, well-bred Mrs. Graves to such a simple place? After an afternoon and evening in her company, David was quite certain a cottage was not the lady's proper milieu.

Chapter Three

*D*avid awoke before dawn, chilled to his bones. The fire in the grate was little more than embers, and since there were no servants—at least, none who lived in the cottage—he knew he would have to leave his cozy nest of blankets and add a log or two to the fire. Getting cold in order to get warmer was completely illogical, but there was no help for it. Resigned, he sat up, reached for the late Lieutenant Graves's dressing gown, which was draped across the foot of the bed, and shrugged it on. He raced to the hearth, used the bellows to breathe life into the glowing embers, then added two logs and darted back under the covers, dressing gown and all.

Ten minutes later, when the room began to warm, David was still awake. Wide awake. As manager of one of his father's largest estates, he habitually rose early, as all farmers did, although rarely before dawn. But there was little point in lying abed alone, so he got up. After donning Graves's pantaloons and one of his shirts, both much too large as well as several inches too long, David walked quietly down the hall to the kitchen to heat water with which to wash and to shave. Although he was grateful there had been a razor, a strop, and a bit of shaving soap among the items Mrs. Graves had given him last night, he could not help but wonder why she had kept them. And why she still had some of her late husband's clothes.

As he added wood to the kitchen fire, David wondered if his hostess had tenants who provided it, and how often they did so. The snow was still falling heavily, the drifts near the stable about knee height. Since the storm had sent the boy who cared for the horses home early yesterday, the lad probably would not come today. David resolved to feed Mrs. Graves's animals after he washed and shaved.

What else could he do for his hostess? If she had eggs and either ham or bacon, he could make breakfast. That was the extent of his culinary ability, but Mrs. Graves might welcome a respite from cooking. Of course, she also might think him a presumptuous, encroaching upstart, but if she did, he doubted she would say so. His presence here was evidence of the lady's kind heart.

Checking the larder, he found food, but not very much of it. How often, he wondered, did the squire's servants bring Mrs. Graves supplies from Tidmarsh? An even more pressing question was: Could she afford to feed a guest for several days? David was determined to get answers to his questions, which meant he and his hostess were going to have to discuss her circumstances in rather more detail than either of them would find comfortable. He would not allow her to suffer in any way because of his presence. Even if he had to ask impolite questions to ensure that she did not.

When he returned to the cottage after caring for the animals—and just walking to and from the stable was a task in itself—David carried a pail of milk and had six eggs in the pocket of his greatcoat. The hens had taken exception to his large, unfamiliar hands, but despite their harried pecking, he felt triumphant, since he now had the ingredients to cook breakfast for his hostess. Unfortunately, he had neglected to inform her of his intentions. When he opened the back door, she was mixing batter for oat cakes or bannocks, and a griddle was heating on the hob.

She looked up at him and smiled. Just like yesterday, the first sight of her face sent a shiver snaking down his spine. "Good morning, Mr. Winterbrook. It was very kind of you to feed the horses."

He returned her greeting, then asked, "Should I put the milk and eggs in the larder?"

A strange expression crossed her face. "Yes, please."

"Mrs. Graves, have I displeased you in some way by milking the cow and gathering the eggs?"

"No, sir, not at all." Despite her words, David knew his actions had unsettled her, although he did not understand why.

After placing the items where she indicated, he removed his gloves, hat, and greatcoat, then crossed to the pump to wash his hands.

"Oh, your poor hands! What happened?" She hurried to his side and took his hands in her smaller ones, examining the cuts and gouges.

"I am fine. Your hens took exception to me gathering their eggs."

"You are not fine!" She glanced up at him, her beautiful hazel eyes troubled, then tugged him toward the table. "Sit down. I am going to get the medicine chest, then I will treat your injuries."

David did not feel any treatment was required, but he wouldn't argue with her. Not about this. If she wanted to wrap his hands in bandages, he would let her. He only hoped that, in the future, she would be as agreeable to his requests.

Stretching his legs toward the fire, he wished he'd had an opportunity to change into dry clothes before she'd begun her ministrations. Graves's too large pantaloons were rather uncomfortable when dry, damnably so when soaking wet.

Mrs. Graves returned, carrying a large box. Out of habit, David stood and reached to take it from her, but subsided back into his chair when she scowled. After filling a basin with water from the kettle hanging over the fire, she added a bit of cold water to it, then dumped a fair portion of the contents of a small bottle from the chest into the mixture and stirred it with a wooden spoon.

"Soak your hands in the basin," she instructed, then crossed to the hearth and spooned batter onto the griddle.

"Yes, ma'am." David slid his hands into the basin, then had to grit his teeth to keep from jerking them out of the stinging liquid. *Lud, the cure was worse than the injury!*

"Are you making oat cakes?" he asked, then realized she could not hear him, nor see his face.

Yet again he wondered what had caused her hearing loss. Although he knew she was not completely deaf, he was amazed by her ability to understand a conversation by hearing part of it and discerning the rest from the movements of the speaker's lips. *How long had it taken her to learn to do that?* Years, probably, but he would not distress her by asking. Yesterday he had realized there were two topics she discussed only when absolutely unavoidable: her marriage and her hearing difficulty. *Could there be some relation between the two? Was it possible . . .*

The thought splintered when she lifted his hands out of the basin. After gently drying them with a soft towel, she sprinkled them with powder from a tiny green jar and reached for a length of rolled cloth.

David lifted a hand to touch her chin, to elevate her gaze to his face—and was shocked nearly speechless when she cringed and jerked away.

"Mrs. Graves, I beg your pardon. I did not mean to startle you." It was far from an eloquent apology, but it was heartfelt. And the best he could do at the moment as he grappled with her reaction. "I only wanted you to look at me, so I could ask you a question."

"It is I who owe you an apology, sir. In the corner of my eye, I saw your fist and I . . . I don't know what came over me."

Revelation hit with the force of a battering ram. If the late Lieutenant Graves had appeared at that moment, David would have beaten him to a bloody pulp. With the very fist his hand had *not* formed when he'd lifted it toward Mrs. Graves. He was not a violent man, but the thought of Graves striking his wife—with his damned fists!—was more than enough to make David want to pummel the brute. Repeatedly, as he had obviously done to his wife, and so thoroughly that the dastard begged for mercy.

Since Graves's death put him beyond David's reach, he sought to calm his hostess. Later, he would attempt to convince her, with words and deeds, that most men would never dream of hurting a woman.

"Well," he said, mustering a smile, "now that I have your attention, ma'am, may I ask my question?"

"Yes, of course." Her voice betrayed her agitation, and she did not meet his gaze.

"Is it really necessary to bandage my hands?"

The pungent smell of burning oats assailed David's nostrils. Mrs. Graves's, too, obviously; she jumped up and ran toward the hearth. "Be careful," he shouted, following her.

She stopped and glanced back at him. "What?"

"Be careful you don't burn your hands."

He picked up a thick, quilted cloth, then reached past her, removed the griddle from the hob, and set it on the hearth. Straightening, he turned toward her. "When it cools, you can start anew."

She looked at him, staring as if he'd suddenly grown another head. "You are quite unlike any gentleman I have ever met."

"Am I?" He cupped a hand under her elbow and led her back to the table. "I can't imagine why. My behavior is no different than that of my friends, or the male members of my family."

"That is difficult to credit."

"Is it? What have I done that is different than, say, your father would do?" David wanted to ask about her husband but had substituted "father" at the last second. Questions about her spouse would have to wait until he knew her better. And until she trusted him more.

"If my father had deigned to enter the kitchen, he would have yelled at me for ruining breakfast."

"But it was my fault that you forgot about the oat cakes."

"Neither my father nor my brothers would give a moment's thought to who was at fault."

David could not imagine any of the men in his family behaving with such a lack of consideration. "One of the first things I learned as a child was to take responsibility for my actions. Good or bad."

"I was taught that, too, as were my brothers, but"—she shrugged—"they either forgot those lessons or have chosen to ignore them."

"I have not," he averred. Then, obliquely returning to their previous discussion, "If I am standing or sitting near you, do you need to watch my face when I talk?"

"Not necessarily, though I generally do. I guess it has become a habit. But when you are nearby, I can hear you fairly well without watching. At least," she amended, with a wobbly, rather rueful smile, "I think I do. You are the best judge of that."

He smiled to reassure her. "Our conversations have not been a series of non sequiturs, if that is your concern."

Then, more seriously, because he wanted to understand her problem, "Are some people's voices harder to hear than others?"

"Yes. Women are much more difficult to hear. And men with very deep voices."

"So high pitches and very low ones cause the most problems?" For the first time, David was grateful for his light tenor voice. He wondered if Mrs. Graves would have difficulty hearing his father's and brother's baritones, which he'd always secretly envied. Or Isabelle's childish treble.

"I have never thought of it quite like that, but those are the worst for me. It is also very difficult to distinguish one voice when several people are talking at once."

"If you do not mind, ma'am, I would like to move around the room and talk to you, so I have a better idea of how close I need to be for you to hear me. Would you just sit there for a few minutes and not watch me, please?"

Mrs. Graves looked down at the floor and folded her hands in her lap, allowing him to conduct his little experiment. Some of the results surprised him; others confirmed what he already suspected. She heard nothing from the left unless the speaker was mere inches away. On the right, however, she could hear him from about two feet away, a few inches farther if he was in front of her. That, he suspected, was not a function of her hearing, but awareness of his presence and increased concentration.

Such asymmetrical damage must have resulted from a very unusual accident. Given this morning's revelations, David could not help but wonder if Graves's fists had played any part in the incident that caused his wife's hearing loss.

Kneeling in front of her chair—he wanted to see her face and those remarkable hazel eyes—David covered Mrs. Graves's hands with his. "Thank you for indulging me, ma'am. I now have a much better idea of how close I must stand for you to hear me when I speak."

"It is I who must thank you, Mr. Winterbrook. No one has ever made the slightest effort to help me hear." After a moment she added, "Well, except for shouting."

"If I may say so, ma'am, your friends and family do not deserve you."

Blushing a bit, she shook her head. "Don't judge my

family too harshly. I did not have this problem until after I left home."

David was not surprised by that revelation. Although well aware that he might be leaping to conclusions, he felt certain Mrs. Graves's late husband was at least partially responsible for her problem. As well as for her seemingly straitened circumstances.

"One other thing, if I may, ma'am." Mentally, David added, *so I don't scare you as I did earlier*. "If I need to get your attention, may I have your permission to touch your arm? Or your hand? I know it is a presumptuous familiarity for a stranger, but—"

"You may, Mr. Winterbrook. I feel certain you would never take undue liberties."

Given his feelings when he first saw Mrs. Graves, and again at his first sight of her this morning, David hoped that in the future he would be permitted a great number of liberties—all those due a husband. But he could not tell her that lest she think him a madman. "If ever I do, ma'am, you must slap me. As hard as you can."

"I could never do that!"

"Yes, you could. And you should do it, if a man—any man—ever does something you dislike." Hoping to remove the haunted look from her eyes, he quipped, "According to my aunts, a good, sound slap rattles a man's brains back into proper working order."

"But then he would hit me, and men hit much harder than women do."

Raw fury propelled David to his feet. "I have never struck a woman in my life. Regardless of the provocation." He strode toward the hearth, trying to bring his emotions under control. "There is no reason—"

"Mr. Winterbrook, if you are speaking, I cannot hear you."

He exhaled heavily in an attempt to expel his anger, then walked to the table and sat down. "I have never in my life struck a woman."

"I heard that, but I could not hear the rest."

"There is no reason for a man to strike a woman. *Ever*. Any man that does is beneath contempt." His feelings about the late Lieutenant Graves colored the tone of David's last statement rather more than he would have liked, but Mrs. Graves seemed much more interested in what he said than in how he said it.

"I know that it happens," he continued more mildly, "that there are men who beat their wives. And their children. Just as there are boys at schools all over the country who pick on younger children. Those schoolboys—and men who strike women and children—are bullies, ma'am. They prey on people weaker than they are. But they never hit people who could, and would, fight back."

"Really? Only on the weaker?"

"Physically weaker, I should have said." After a moment he added, "Bullies are often quite stupid. That isn't always the case, but in my experience, it is true more often than not."

"Have you encountered many bullies, sir?"

"Quite a few at school, but not many since then."

Her gaze swept him from head to toe. "It is hard to believe you had any problems at school."

"I was rather small for my age until I was fourteen or fifteen." To lighten the conversation, he jested, "And I am still the runt of the family."

She smiled slightly and shook her head. "I think you are bamming me, sir."

"Indeed I am not. I am five feet and ten inches tall in my stocking feet. My father is two inches over six feet, my brother four inches over."

A sudden shiver racked David's frame. "If you don't mind, ma'am, I am going to change into dry clothes. Then I will help you prepare breakfast."

"You need not help, sir. You earned your breakfast by caring for my animals this morning. Now it is time for me to do something for you."

"Let me set the table, at least. I don't like to sit idly." He rose to his feet, then pushed the chair beneath the table. "Well, not unless I am reading the newspaper. Or a book."

"Very well, sir. You may set the table when you return."

Shaking her head in bemusement, Lynn watched Mr. Winterbrook stride from the kitchen. *What an unusual gentleman!* Yet, according to him, he was not. It did seem strange that the four members of the breed she had encountered were atypical, but then again, perhaps not. Fate had never looked kindly upon Madeline Patterson Graves. Her mother had died when Lynn was born. Her father had married again a few years later, but her stepmother was not at all maternal, nor did she like children. When her father refused to give Frank her dowry, the charming officer who had courted her changed into a cruel, hateful man overly fond of wine, women, and cards.

But that was all in the past. Now the only gentleman with whom she need concern herself was Mr. Winterbrook, and thus far, he had been kind, helpful, courteous, and considerate. Oh, she had been a bit annoyed when he'd asked to conduct his "experiment," but once she understood the reason behind his request, she could not help but be pleased by his thoughtfulness. It was, she believed, an indication of the esteem in which he held her.

She crossed to the hearth and picked up the griddle, then carried it to the sink. After scraping off the burnt oat cakes, she put it back on the hob. The grease in the skillet was sizzling, so she slid in four pieces of bacon. Since Mr. Winterbrook had worked like a farmhand this morning and would probably have an appetite to match, she got two eggs from the larder. She would cook them when the bacon was done.

When the griddle was hot, she turned, reaching for the bowl of batter, and espied her guest leaning against the door frame, once again dressed in his own clothes, but with his boots dangling from one hand. "Do not stand in the doorway, sir. Come in and sit down. Your breakfast will be ready in just a few minutes."

"I was afraid I would startle you if I came in without you realizing it, but I couldn't stomp my feet because I need to dry my boots."

"You need not stomp around my home, Mr. Winterbrook."

"How else can I warn you of my presence? I do not want you to feel uncomfortable, wondering if I am suddenly going to appear. Nor do I want you to regret having invited me to shelter from the storm here." He crossed the room and set his boots at the far end of the hearth, where they would not be in her way.

"You can say something to me when you enter a room. If I do not hear you, step closer and speak again."

"But—"

"An occasional startlement will not overtax my nerves. I am neither feeble nor fragile." She spooned batter onto the griddle, then turned the bacon. "As for regrets, I have none. Thus far, you have been an exemplary guest."

"I hope you will continue to think so, ma'am. Now"— he smiled and reached for the plates on the dresser—"I had best . . ."

Lynn flipped over the oat cakes, then turned toward him. She had not heard the last part of his statement and wanted to watch his mouth when he repeated it. "You had best what?"

He glanced over his shoulder as he set the plates on the table. Then, his expression chagrined, he moved several steps closer and looked directly at her. "I had best set the table before I fall from your good graces."

"It would take a great deal more than not setting the table for you to fall from grace. Especially since you have already done so much for me this morning." Smiling her thanks, she turned back to the hearth. She did not want to burn his breakfast again.

While she finished preparing breakfast, Mr. Winterbrook set the table, made the tea, then served it. Lynn was surprised when he prepared hers with lots of cream but only a little sugar, just the way she liked it. On the rare occasions Frank had deigned to prepare her tea, he'd had to ask each time how she drank it. That Mr. Winterbrook knew after having tea with her twice was further proof that he was a very unusual gentleman. But unusual in the nicest possible way.

After seating her, Mr. Winterbrook took the chair to her right. "Would you like me to say the blessing again, Mrs. Graves?"

"Yes, please."

As he had last night, Mr. Winterbrook gave a thorough, thoughtful, but not overlong prayer of thanks. Lynn wondered if he usually said a blessing before meals, but it was too personal a question to ask someone she had known less than a day.

That she had known him only for about eighteen hours was difficult to believe. Even harder to credit was that his presence in her home did not make her uncomfortable. Oh, she had been quite apprehensive yesterday afternoon, but his kindness and consideration had done much to ease her wariness. As had his shock this morning when she'd inadvertently alluded to Frank hitting her. Mr. Winterbrook's sincerity when he vowed that he had never hit a woman, and his disgust of men who did, were also apparent. And vastly reassuring.

"Does it often snow in this part of the country, Mrs. Graves?"

Lynn ate a bite of oat cake. "I have lived in this area for most of my life, so I have little basis for comparison. But the vicar, who is of a rather scientific bent, has kept daily records of the weather in the various parishes he has served, and he says this area has colder temperatures and more snow than Twyford or Maidenhead. He believes it is because we are in a dell."

"So the lower elevation results in colder temperatures and more snow." After several seconds spent pondering the vicar's theory, Mr. Winterbrook nodded. "That seems like a reasonable, and logical, explanation. What amazes me is that it is still snowing as hard, and accumulating as fast, as it was yesterday."

"How deep is the snow? It is difficult to judge its depth from inside."

"About ten inches, but much deeper where it has drifted. In front of the stable, the snow was almost to the top of my boots."

"Your poor boots. They will be ruined, if they aren't already." Much as she wished to replace them, Lynn could not afford to do so. "You must regret that you stopped to help me yesterday."

Mr. Winterbrook's dazzling smile brightened the kitchen. And Lynn's heart. "I do not regret it at all, Mrs. Graves."

That was mere politeness. At least, the words were. That brilliant smile was more than just a courteous response. "It is very kind of you to say so, sir, but I know you would prefer to be home with your daughter."

"Yes." His nod acknowledged the truth of her statement. "But we both know I could not have traveled another twenty-five miles yesterday. You did not think I could safely ride the five miles to the squire's house. And you were right. If I had attempted to continue my journey, I would have been forced to stop somewhere between here and . . . what is the name of the village near the squire's home?"

"Little Twigham."

"If I must be stranded somewhere between here and Little Twigham, I am glad it is here"—he smiled, his sky blue eyes twinkling—"with a kind-hearted lady who serves delicious meals, puts up with my foibles, and is smart enough to test my mettle at chess."

Lynn laughed, as he had undoubtedly intended, but her heart glowed at the compliment. "Foibles, Mr. Winterbrook? What would those be?"

Hearing the slightly teasing note that had entered her voice, Lynn's breath caught. *Dear God, was I flirting?* She pushed away from the table and, almost blindly, crossed to the sink, gripping the edge so hard her knuckles turned white. She, who for years had been extremely uncomfortable—and sometimes jumpier than a hare—in the presence of any man other than her father and brothers, had been flirting with Mr. David Winterbrook, whom she had known for less than twenty-four hours!

How could this happen? What did it mean? With trembling hands, she picked up a pitcher of water and poured some into a glass, spilling more than flowed into the glass. And her effort was for naught. Even though she used both hands to raise the glass to her lips, they shook so hard that the liquid came nowhere near her mouth.

"Mrs. Graves?"

At the sound of his voice, Lynn started and dropped the glass, which dumped a fair portion of its contents down the front of her gown, then shattered when it hit the floor. Completely overset, she burst into tears and ran from the room, unable to deal with the shambles of her life or the mess she had made in the kitchen.

Chapter Four

*D*avid had watched with mounting concern as his hostess suddenly paled, then shoved away from the table. Fearing she had taken ill, he wanted to help her, but was not at all certain she would welcome his assistance. When tremors racked her frame so violently that she could not drink the water she'd just poured, he approached her.

"Mrs. Graves?"

Much to his dismay, his gently spoken query startled her. She cried out and dropped the glass, spilling water down the front of her gown. The glass shattered when it hit the flagstone floor. Mrs. Graves stared at the puddle at her feet for a second, then burst into tears and ran from the room.

Alarmed, he followed her, reaching the hallway in time to glimpse the hem of her gown—brownish red today but as simple and unadorned as the blue one she'd worn last night—as it trailed the lady into her bedchamber. The door closed rather forcefully behind her.

Truly worried now, he covered the distance in three quick strides and knocked on her door. When he received no response, he rapped again, harder, and called her name. With no way to determine if she was ignoring him or if she could not hear him over her sobs, David resorted to his usual method for figuring out a woman's perplexing behavior: he imagined one of his aunts acting the same way and how she would want him to respond.

The only problem was that it was impossible to envision his unflappable Aunt Tilly, known to the rest of the world as Lady Matilda Elliott, bursting into tears and running from a room. Tilly had followed the drum with her soldier husband and, after his death, had returned home to Belling-

ham Castle, where she served as her brother's hostess and
chatelaine and oversaw the estate during his absences. Tilly
was the rock of David's childhood. She'd come back to
England when he was seven, and because his mother had
died the year before, Tilly had bandaged scraped knees,
provided hugs and bedtime stories, found solutions to his
boyhood problems, and dispensed advice and lectures when
needed. He had never seen her cry, although occasional
red-rimmed eyes gave testament to the fact that she did,
never seen her flustered. The image of Aunt Tilly running
from a room in tears just would not form in David's mind.

Aunt Caroline, formally known as Lady Richard Winterbrook, was more emotional. Although far from a watering pot, she had cried when Isabelle was kidnapped last
year, and shed a few tears—which, she had assured them
all, were "happy tears"—at George's wedding. Caro was
more easily rattled than Tilly, but neither was the sort of
woman to suddenly burst into tears and flee as if the
Hounds of Hell were nipping at her heels. In the seven
months that she had lived with him and Isabelle at Greendale Manor, David had, on a couple of occasions, seen Caro
upset. She always retired to her room, reappearing thirty
minutes to an hour later with suspiciously red eyes but with
her composure restored.

"Very well, Mrs. Graves," David announced to the
wooden panel that separated them, "you have thirty minutes." Had he not been so worried that she was ill—she had
blanched nearly as white as his cravat before she jumped up
from the table—he would have given her an hour, but if
she was sick, he wanted to know sooner rather than later.
Given the weather, fetching a doctor or surgeon from
Tidmarsh was impossible, but if necessary, he could walk
the two miles to the nearest house and ask for help.

He pulled out his watch to mark the time, then turned
toward the kitchen. Halfway to his destination, he halted
in mid-step. If he had to summon assistance, Mrs. Graves
would be here all alone. There was no one to send on the
errand, no one who could sit with her while he performed
that duty.

Suddenly, Aunt Tilly's voice sounded in his head, the oft-
repeated words echoing from his boyhood to the present.
Don't borrow trouble. Deal with one problem at a time.

"Yes, Aunt Tilly," he muttered as he walked to the kitchen. Tidying up and washing the dishes was not the task he had intended to perform for his hostess after breakfast, but it would occupy his time. And keep him inside so he could hear her if she cried out in pain.

By the time the kitchen was restored to its usual, pristine state, David was no closer to figuring out what had caused Mrs. Graves's distress, and very worried about her health. Their conversation had been unexceptional: the weather, the depth of the snow, and his pleasure at being stranded here with a hostess who prepared delicious meals and was his match at chess. She had said something after that, but since he tended to watch her face when she spoke, just as she did his, he remembered only her sudden pallor, not the words she had spoken.

He dried the last plate and placed it on the dresser. Rolling down his shirtsleeves, he glanced at the clock. Forty-five minutes had passed since Mrs. Graves's precipitous departure. As he buttoned the right cuff—always so much more difficult than the left one—he turned toward the table, where his coat was draped over the back of what he thought of as "his" chair. Movement at the edge of his vision brought his head up. Mrs. Graves stood in the doorway, wearing a different gown—a green one—and a bemused expression. A bit of color had returned to her cheeks, and there was a tinge of pink around her nose and eyes.

"Mrs. Graves!" He closed the distance between them with one long, quick stride, then gently took her arm and led her to the table. "Are you feeling better, ma'am?"

Lynn sank into the chair Mr. Winterbrook pulled out and looked around the kitchen, wondering from whence he had summoned the faeries to clean it.

Then she looked—really looked—at her guest, who had moved to the other end of the table to make a pot of tea. He was in his shirtsleeves, and the cuff on the right sleeve was either unbuttoned or missing its button; it flopped around his wrist whenever he moved his arm. His navy superfine coat was neatly hung over the back of the chair to the right of hers. When he crossed to the pump to refill the kettle, she suddenly realized that it was he, not faeries, who had cleared the table, washed the dishes, and cleaned the water and broken glass from the floor. The idea of a man cleaning anything save a rifle or pistol was still astonishing, but delightfully so. She appreciated his cosseting—and she would enjoy every moment of it.

As he worked the pump, the cuff of his right sleeve slid all the way to his elbow, revealing a lean but muscled forearm dusted with light brown hair. With a bit of a start, she realized that lean but muscled described all of him, not just his arm. His waistcoat, light blue with thin red stripes, accented a torso that tapered from his shoulders—broad but not brawny—to a slim waist. His hips and legs, well defined by cream cord riding breeches that fit like a second skin, were also slender but well muscled. Watching as he carried the kettle back to the fireplace and bent to hang it on a pot hook, she felt a little frisson of . . . something. Before she could put a name to it, he was seated beside her, studying her rather intently.

"Are you feeling better, ma'am? Do you need me to fetch a doctor?"

"A doctor?" *He'd thought she was ill?* "No. I am not ill, Mr. Winterbrook."

After several more seconds of his scrutiny, she dropped her gaze, feeling slightly uncomfortable. A moment later, he touched her hand fleetingly. "I apologize for staring, ma'am, but just before you left the table earlier, your face suddenly lost all color. I feared you had taken sick."

"No. I was merely . . . overset."

"I beg your pardon, Mrs. Graves, if something I said upset you. I assure you that was not my intent."

At his obvious distress, which rang in his voice as clearly as church bells on a Sunday morning, Lynn raised her eyes to his face. She gathered her courage, then, with a great deal of trepidation, confessed, "It was not your words, sir, but my own."

"Yours?" He frowned as if perplexed. "I have reviewed our conversation. Several times. I do not know what you said just before you left the table—I was watching your face and the sight of you blanching is clear in my mind, although your words are not—but, to me, our discussion seemed unexceptional."

Thank God! "It was just foolishness, sir." Lynn knew it

for a feeble excuse even as she uttered it, but she hoped he would accept it.

He did. He didn't like it—at least that was her interpretation of the thinning of his lips—but he did not question her further. Instead, he reached for the teapot, poured two cups of tea, then prepared hers just as she liked it before passing the cup and saucer to her.

With the movement, his right cuff again slid nearly to his elbow. Blushing, he scrambled to his feet and grabbed his coat from the back of the chair. "I beg your pardon, Mrs. Graves. I forgot I had taken off my coat." Turning his back, he wrestled with his right cuff. After a moment, he said something she couldn't quite hear and pulled on his coat.

When he resumed his seat, he tucked something into the pocket of his waistcoat. Lynn lifted her teacup to her lips to hide a smile. His cuff had not been missing its button before, but it was now.

Apparently her effort was not quite successful, for he asked, "What amuses you, ma'am? That I stand before you in my stocking feet and apologize for not wearing my coat?" A rather sheepish smile blossomed on his face. "I confess, I quite forgot that my feet are equally ill clad."

"I hadn't noticed you were not wearing your boots, sir." A glance at the hearth confirmed they were still drying there. "I smiled because I wondered earlier if your cuff button was missing. Now I know that it is, but that it wasn't before. I will sew it back on for you after you drink your tea."

"I . . . um . . . thank you, ma'am. It is very kind of you to offer."

Lynn shook her head. "'Tis a simple task, not nearly as arduous as cleaning this kitchen. Thank you very much for doing that. I beg your pardon for running off before."

"I could say that cleaning the kitchen was naught compared to all that you have done for me, but if I did, we might well spend the rest of the morning thanking each other."

His boyish grin was contagious. Lynn laughed; she could easily imagine them doing just that. But her smile faded when he said, "Instead, I would like to ask you a question."

"What is your question, sir?" She prayed it would be one she was prepared to answer.

"When I was outside this morning, I looked for a wood-pile so that I could bring more logs inside, but I didn't find one. Is there someone who provides you with wood? Are they likely to bring more soon, or do I need to chop some?"

Lynn looked at the elegantly clad man beside her. It was difficult to envision him chopping wood, but she had not been able to imagine him milking a cow, either, and he had already done that several times. "The woodpile is behind the barn. Willie, the boy who takes care of the horses, chops it for me, but he will not return until the snow stops. Since he carries wood into the house for me every morning, I cannot say how much is there."

"I didn't look behind the barn. Beside it, but not behind it."

"I don't know where the ax is, but there is one somewhere."

"It is in the barn, ma'am, hanging on the wall to the left of the door."

Mr. Winterbrook added cream and sugar to his tea, stirring far more than was necessary. Lynn braced herself for another query—one she probably would not like.

"Another question if I may, ma'am?"

"You may ask, sir."

Chuckling, he lifted his eyes from his cup and met hers. "But you may not answer, eh?"

"That will depend upon the question." She smiled slightly to take the sting out of her words.

"Fair enough." He lifted his teacup and drank half the contents before posing his query. "Yesterday, you mentioned that the squire had bought food for you in Tidmarsh. How often does he do so?"

"His *housekeeper* picks up things for me every week when she goes shopping, but anything she buys for me is charged to my account, not the squire's."

Mr. Winterbrook's eyebrows rose slightly, as if he did not understand her rather fierce assertion of her independence. "I did not mean to imply otherwise, ma'am." After a moment he asked, "Must you to go the squire's home to pick up the purchases made on your behalf?"

Lynn was not certain what he was asking. Or why. "I have always done so, but if for some reason I could not, I daresay his housekeeper would instruct a footman or groom to deliver it."

"Do you send a list to the squire's housekeeper every week or does she get the same things for you each time?"

"Is there something in particular you want, Mr. Winterbrook? Some purpose to your questions?" Lynn's tone was rather more testy than she would have liked, but where and when and how she obtained food was not his concern.

His expression contrite, he explained, "I was trying, in my rather ham-fisted way, to determine if you are likely to suffer a shortage of food as a result of my presence. Since that does not appear to be the case, I shall cease plaguing you and bring in some wood." He stood and crossed to the hearth to don his boots.

Regretting both her hasty words and the tone in which she had spoken them, she quickly rose, positioning herself between him and the door. When he stomped into the second boot and turned toward the door, Lynn spoke quickly but from the heart. "Mr. Winterbrook, I beg your pardon for my imprudent words. I did not realize there was a reason for your questions. Nor that your concern was for me, not yourself. I daresay I should have, but—"

Realizing she had strayed from the subject, she waved a hand in the air as if she could wipe her words off a slate in his mind. "I truly am sorry for my pettishness. And for my tears and abrupt departure earlier."

His smile was nothing like the brilliant one he'd given her at breakfast, but it signaled his relief that they were back on good terms and could be comfortable with each other again. "Apology accepted, ma'am. I am sorry that my questions upset you." After a rather tense second or two of silence, he laughed, but it was a more brittle sound than usual. "It is a good thing I didn't choose a career in the diplomatic corps."

Tilting her head slightly to one side, Lynn studied him. "I think you would be an asset to the corps. You are kind, courteous, intelligent, and very tactful." *Rather handsome, too. And a bit of a charmer.*

"I hope you will still think so tonight. I will probably have other questions."

It sounded as if he had more now, but chose not to ask them. After a moment's hesitation, he did venture an additional one. "Mrs. Graves, what was it you started to say before? Something about realizing—or, rather, not realizing—that my concern was for you."

Lynn looked down at the floor. *Why couldn't he have forgotten that?* "I was going to say that I am not accustomed to people worrying about me, but that is not an excuse for my unkindness to you."

"Your unkindness—and that is far too harsh a word—has been forgiven and forgotten." He touched her arm fleetingly, drawing her eyes back to his face. "If I may say so, ma'am, you are very young to have been alone so long."

"I am five-and-twenty, sir, and have been a widow for almost two years." Left unspoken was the fact that for years before his death, Frank's concern for her was limited to keeping her out of sight of his cronies and his men when she was bruised and battered. She arched an eyebrow, inviting him to provide the same information.

"I am six-and-twenty and have been a widower for four years."

She opened her mouth to ask a question, but decided it would be best not to inquire further, lest he did the same.

"Go on, ma'am. Ask your question."

Despite the invitation, Lynn would pose no more queries. But she had to say something, so she reworded what she'd thought better of asking. "How sad that your wife died so soon after your daughter's birth."

She watched the play of emotions across his countenance, unable to interpret them. After several moments he sighed, then said, "Four months later. But it is much more complicated than that. Let me bring in some wood, then I will explain."

As he donned his outer garments and walked out the door, his shoulders seemed bowed under a great weight. Suddenly, Lynn was not at all certain she wanted to hear what he would say.

Trudging through the still-falling snow to the barn, David hoped he would not come to regret the decision he'd just made. He hoped that if he told Mrs. Graves about his mockery of a marriage, she would be more inclined to speak about hers. In any relationship, someone had to take the first step, to show their trust in the other. In theirs, whatever it was to be, he was willing to make the initial move.

Even though he feared that she might think him a fool.

When he carried the first load of logs into the kitchen, she was measuring flour into a large bowl. Something for their luncheon, perhaps, since neither had eaten more than a few bites at breakfast. He stacked the wood in the box beside the hearth, then went back outside for more.

An hour later, the wood boxes in all four rooms of the cottage were full, and there was a stack of logs just outside the back door. Whatever Mrs. Graves had been mixing earlier was in the bread oven, its mouth-watering scent permeating the kitchen—and setting his stomach arumble the moment he walked in the door.

"Hmmm. What is that delicious smell, ma'am?"

"Either roast or cake, depending on which smell you mean."

"Both, ma'am." He smiled, then reached up to unwind the muffler she had insisted he wear around his neck.

"Before you take off your coat, Mr. Winterbrook, could we step outside, please?"

"Of course. But if there is something you need, let me bring it in for you. The snow is quite deep."

"I just wondered if it is possible to open the shutters without disturbing your rope. It is rather dark in here with them closed, and I don't like not being able to look outside. Even if my view is restricted by the falling snow."

"Let me see what I can do." He started for the door, then turned back and grabbed a chair to stand on to reach the brackets at the top of the shutters.

Much as he wanted to do so, David was not certain it was possible to fulfill her request. At least, not completely. He could, and did, open the left shutter, delighting in the smile she gave him when he clambered up on the chair to fasten the panel in place. The right one, however, presented more of a problem. The rope was too thick, and the brackets too tight, for the lower one to both hold the shutter open and secure the cord. Using just the upper fastening would serve for the nonce, provided the wind did not increase. But if he checked several times a day that the weight of the unsupported panel was not twisting the hinges, and that it was not banging itself to splinters against the house, a single bracket might be enough. He would have to remember to close the shutters tonight, in case the wind rose while he was asleep.

Pleased with his solution, temporary though it might prove to be, he carried the chair back inside—and was greeted with a beaming smile.

"Thank you, Mr. Winterbrook, that is such an improvement. You are a very resourceful man."

Shrugging off his greatcoat, he hung it on a peg near the door. "It isn't a permanent solution, ma'am. If it gets windy, I will have to close the right shutter. Er, the left one from this perspective. Or if the shutter twists the hinges." He crossed to the pump to wash his hands.

"Oh, your poor hands! What have you done to them now?"

"I just scraped my knuckles against the house."

She grasped his hands, turning them this way and that. "They are *bleeding*."

"Just a bit." *Lud, she was as fussy as a mother hen with one chick.*

"Sit down," she ordered, leading him to the table.

All too soon, his hands were back in the same stinging liquid she'd concocted this morning. But this time he did not escape the bandages.

Foolish man! Did he think her wish to see outside so important that he would scrape his knuckles raw to ensure she could? Lynn fumed as she bandaged Mr. Winterbrook's left hand. She did not like the dark; it brought back too many unpleasant memories of her marriage—or, more precisely, of the things her husband had done in the darkness of the night. But knowing that Frank was dead and that she need no longer fear nightfall, she could endure the lack of light in her kitchen until the snowstorm passed.

In her annoyance at her guest for his blithe dismissal of his injuries, she tied off the bandage with rather more force than necessary. When he winced, she was stricken with remorse for her thoughtlessness. "I am sorry, sir. I did not—"

"There is no need for you to apologize, ma'am. I am well aware that any pangs I suffer are due to my clumsiness."

"But if I had not asked—" She ceased speaking when

Mr. Winterbrook slid his bandaged hand from between hers and placed it atop them.

"If you had not asked me to open the shutters, it is quite possible I would have scraped my knuckles doing something else."

He was either a saint among gentlemen or Frank had been a devil. Or, perhaps, both were true. "But—" The gentle squeeze he gave her hand halted the flow of her words.

"Did I not sit in this same spot this morning with my hands in that basin?"

"Yes."

"My earlier injuries were not due to anything you asked, were they?"

"No," she conceded, reaching for another roll of linen.

"If you bandage both my hands, ma'am, I will not be able to eat. And given the delicious smells wafting around your kitchen, I do not want to miss luncheon." His blue eyes twinkled with good humor.

"Let me see your right hand again, please."

He held it out for her inspection. She clasped it in hers, turning it so she could examine all his fingers. "It is not as badly scraped as the left . . ." She bit her lip, uncertain what would be best.

"Just apply the salve. It will be fine."

She opened her mouth to voice her doubt, but he reassured her before she could. "If it needs a bandage, or even looks like it might need one, I will tell you."

"Very well, sir. I will trust you to keep your promise."

"You can, Mrs. Graves. You can trust me to keep any promises I make."

Lynn was astonished to realize that she did believe David Winterbrook would keep his word. She was not certain how or why she knew that he would, but she hadn't the slightest doubt. And if she trusted him to that extent in less than a day, was it possible that, in the future, she might come to trust him completely?

Chapter Five

As he'd carried in wood, and later, while soaking his hands and having them bandaged, David had considered what, and how much, to tell Mrs. Graves about his marriage. He had to say enough so that she would understand why he was discussing it, and to show that he trusted her, but he hoped he would not have to reveal every ignoble detail.

Only two other people knew the truth of it: his father and his brother. Marie's sister, Lady Arabella Smalley, was aware of certain aspects of it, as were David's aunts, but he had never discussed his mockery of a marriage with anyone save his father and George. And there was a vast difference between what a man might say to his two closest male relatives and what he could tell a lady he had known for only a day. Even if that lady was fated to be the love of his life.

Thus, as his hostess put her salves and potions back in the medicine chest, then stored it away—in the larder this time, presumably so it would be close at hand during his stay—David set the table and braced himself to divulge his tale. And prayed that Mrs. Graves would not take him in disgust when she heard the sordid story.

After seating his hostess, who said the blessing for this meal, David took a quick bite of the delicious food. "Mrs. Graves, I told you earlier that my marriage and my wife's death—"

"Eat while the food is hot. Afterward you can tell me whatever you want."

Feeling like a man reprieved from the gallows just before

the trapdoor opened, David picked up his fork and resumed eating. But, like the condemned man, he was not certain whether to celebrate or bemoan the delay.

When the meal was over, the dishes washed, and the kitchen tidy, Mrs. Graves checked the cake baking in the bread oven, then led him to the parlor. After seating her and starting a fire in the hearth, David sat in the wing chair to his hostess's right and directed his gaze toward the flames. The distance between their chairs was near the limit of her ability to hear, so he would have to speak clearly. He knew he did not want—and perhaps would not be able—to repeat portions of his story.

"Like many young men, after I finished university I went to London to enjoy the Season. But unlike most, I was . . . rather naive. I did not realize it, of course. I thought myself quite worldly, up to every rig and row in Town. 'Twas amazing how much I learned in those few months."

"How old were you?" Mrs. Graves lifted knitting needles and a ball of yarn from her workbasket.

"One-and-twenty. By my twenty-second birthday—early May—I felt much older. And infinitely wiser. But the lessons I learned were hard ones, and often cruelly taught."

Hearing the bitterness that had crept into his voice, he paused, then resumed his tale in a more neutral tone. "Lady Marie Smalley was one of the most popular young ladies making her come-out that year. She had quite a large court of admirers, of which I was one. She never did anything to indicate she favored me—or any of her other suitors—over another, but neither did she discourage my interest."

"Were your father and brother in London, too?"

"George was in the Peninsula. My father was in Town, and he attended a number of social events, but his reasons for going were different than mine. He was there to discuss government business with his cronies, not to dance and enjoy himself. Before the Season started, he warned me of the blunders young men often make when they first come to Town, and how best to avoid them. The mistake I made was not because I did not heed his words, but because I was . . . too trusting."

David glanced at Mrs. Graves, who nodded for him to

continue. "One evening at a ball, a footman handed me a note purportedly from my brother. It looked enough like George's hand that I didn't question its authenticity, even though his last letter, which we'd received only a few days earlier, had clearly been sent from the Peninsula."

"His letters must have taken weeks to arrive."

"Yes, they did. I feared he had been sent home because he was injured, so I hurried to meet him in the library as the note requested.

"George was not there, of course. But Lady Marie was, although I did not realize it until after I'd entered the room to wait for my brother. It was obvious she had been crying, and she practically threw herself into my arms. A few moments later when her older sister and several other people arrived, it appeared as if we were embracing."

"Oh dear."

"My reaction was a bit stronger, ma'am," he drawled. "Especially when Marie claimed I had . . . um, taken liberties with her person. But as you might expect, my protests were ignored. The argument became rather heated, and drew quite a crowd. If Marie's reputation was only slightly blemished when her sister arrived, it was in tatters by the end. Mostly because of her lies, and her sister's gross exaggerations.

"Knowing I was innocent, I ought to have stood firm in my resolve not to marry her, but I feared my honor would be questioned. I made an offer in form to satisfy the conventions, fully expecting Marie to refuse—"

"But she did not." It was more statement than question.

"You are quite right, Mrs. Graves. Marie accepted the instant the words were out of my mouth. My family urged us to wait until the end of the Season to marry. They thought, no doubt correctly, that a quick wedding would be perceived as an implicit admission of guilt. Marie's family—well, her sister—insisted that we marry immediately by special license. Three days later, we did."

David returned his gaze to the fire. The rest of the story was even more sordid, and he did not think he could look Mrs. Graves in the eye while telling it. "On our wedding night, my bride informed me there was no need to consummate the marriage because she was already with child."

Mrs. Graves gasped, but he did not give her a chance to

comment, fearing he would lose the thread of his tale—or his nerve. "Four months later, Isabelle was born. Although she is not of my blood, by law and in my heart, she is my daughter.

"I don't know who her father is," he barreled on. "Marie would never say, and now I am glad that she did not."

The quiet clicking of the knitting needles and the crackling of the fire formed a peaceful counterpoint to his disreputable story. "Marie rejected us both. Once I had given her my name, she wanted nothing to do with me. And she ignored Isabelle completely—never held her, fed her, or bathed her. A month after the birth, Marie eloped with a lover."

A second gasp and a shocked exclamation punctuated his statement.

"Three months later, she and her lover were killed in a carriage accident," he concluded. "I did not mourn her. Neither publicly nor privately. I had no stomach for such hypocrisy. She had never been a wife to me, and by the time she died, proceedings for a divorce were well under way—she'd already been summoned to appear in Ecclesiastical Court."

Feeling unaccountably weary, he leaned against the back of his chair, turning his head toward his hostess. "The tragedy of my marriage was not that Marie died four months after Isabelle was born, but that we wed at all. Even so, I cannot regret it, since I have a lovely, loving daughter who has brought joy to my life, and given purpose to my days, ever since her birth."

"Your daughter is very fortunate to have such a loving father."

"I suppose she is. If Marie had chosen to marry another, he might not have accepted Isabelle."

"I always wanted a child, but was never so blessed. Strange, isn't it, that some women do not appreciate the gifts they are given—and, in essence, throw them away— while others yearn in vain for those same gifts."

"It is not just women who don't always cherish what they have."

"You are right, of course." Mrs. Graves stopped knitting, her knuckles white on the needles. "I am glad for Isabelle's sake that your wife left the babe with you, but I do not understand how she could. Even if she was not maternal, didn't her lover want his child?"

"I do not believe the man with whom she eloped fathered Isabelle."

"She had more than one lover?" This in an incredulous tone that was an equal blend of shock and astonishment.

"I think so, although I do not know for certain. When she was in a temper, Marie would say—scream—horrible things, things she knew would hurt the person with whom she was quarreling, but she never revealed the name of the man who fathered Isabelle. I could never quite decide if she was protecting him, or if she'd had several lovers and did not know which one had gotten her with child."

Mrs. Graves gaped at him. Then her lips moved, but no sound issued forth.

Damnation! "I beg your pardon, ma'am, if I have shocked you, or offended you, with my plain speaking."

"It is not your plain speaking I find shocking, sir, but your wife's lack of morals."

"It shocked me, too," he said dryly. "Marie never disclosed the name of Isabelle's father, but she made no secret of the identity of the man with whom she eloped."

"Hmm. That does make it seem as if it were a different man." She pursed her lips. "Why did she not wed Isabelle's father?"

"I asked her once, and she said he would not marry her."

"Why didn't she compromise him into marriage instead of you?"

"Perhaps he was already married. Or maybe he was a bachelor but knew there was a possibility he wasn't the child's father."

"Why did she choose you to be her husband?"

Damn! David rose, covering the distance to the hearth in one long stride, then poked needlessly at the blazing logs. "I asked that, too. She picked me because she thought I would be a complaisant husband."

"Because she thought what?"

Knowing he'd flushed with mortification, he could not face Mrs. Graves. Instead of turning so she could watch his lips, he spoke a bit louder. "Because she thought I would be a complaisant husband."

"I daresay you would have been a very good husband—

and much better than she deserved—had she allowed you to be. And if she had not lied to you.''

Surprised by her perspicacity, he turned. "Yes, I might well have been. I would like to think so, at least."

"I am certain of it." She smiled, and David felt warmed to the depths of his soul.

"Thank you, Mrs. Graves." He returned to his seat, turning his chair toward her. "Might I ask your first name, ma'am? It is a bit disconcerting to realize that I have confided my deepest, darkest secrets to a lady I could not properly introduce were I called upon to do so."

She laughed, then said, "My given name is Madeline."

"Do your friends and family call you Maddie?"

"My family does"—her lips thinned—"and my husband did. I prefer Lynn."

"Thank you, Mrs. Graves. My given name is David."

"Yes, I know." Her smile returned, more of a grin this time. "Your introduction yesterday was all that was proper."

He had introduced himself by name, but not by his courtesy title. He never did. Upon hearing his name, most people knew he was Lord David. But apparently this kindhearted lady had spent little time among the *ton*. She might even be rather distressed to know that the guest who had been mucking out her horse's stall and milking her cow was a peer's son.

"Now that we have taken care of the niceties, ma'am, I would like to thank you for listening to my tale. And for my daughter's sake, I would ask that you not reveal to anyone what I told you today."

"I shan't tell a soul, Mr. Winterbrook. For Isabelle's sake, and for yours. I know it was not easy for you to talk about your marriage. I suspect you have told very few people."

"Only my father and my brother know the truth of it. My aunts know parts of the tale, as does Marie's sister."

Her beautiful eyes—they looked green this afternoon, almost the same color as her gown—widened in surprise. "I am honored to be included in such a select group. And I promise that I will tell no one."

Her mouth twisted almost into a grimace. "If you do not believe a woman's word is as good as a man's—"

David made no attempt to control his astonishment. "Why wouldn't I accept your promise?"

"Some men do not believe women capable of keeping their word."

"Some men are fools," he said flatly. Then, in a more moderate tone, "I have known a few women whose promises could not be believed. Marie, for one. But I could name an equal or larger number of men whose word is lightly, even carelessly, given. I do not doubt that you will honor your promise, Mrs. Graves."

"Thank you, sir." She smiled, clearly pleased.

"Was—" David broke off, shaking his head at his folly. He could not ask her that. Not yet.

Lynn took a deep breath and released it slowly, hoping that Mr. Winterbrook was as trustworthy, and as honorable, as he seemed. The fact that he trusted her enough to confide in her, and asked nothing in return save that she not breech his confidence, helped her come to a decision. Given that she had not trusted a man—any man—for more than eight years, it was surprising, and rather alarming, to feel that she could trust this man she had known for only a day. Especially since she could not cite a specific reason why she believed she could.

"Ask your question, sir. Since my earlier query forced you to tell me something you would not have chosen to reveal, I cannot quibble about a question from you."

"You did not force me to do anything, ma'am. Had I wished, I could have allowed you to believe that Marie's death was a tragedy for Isabelle and me."

"I would question why you didn't do just that, except I think your sense of honor would not permit it."

"Exactly so," he confirmed.

"What did you wish to ask me, sir?"

"I only wondered if your husband was the type of man who did not believe a woman's word was as good as a man's."

"Yes, he was. Probably, in large part, because he believed women were inferior creatures. He regularly broke promises to me."

"You think he broke his promises to you because he believed you less worthy than a man?"

Lynn did not know if the incredulity in Mr. Winterbrook's voice meant he thought her foolish beyond permission for believing such a thing, or if it indicated that his opinion was far different from Frank's. "Yes, sir, I do. I think he used that belief to justify breaking promises to me. As if a promise made to a mere woman was not as important as one made to a man."

He muttered something she could not hear.

"Would you repeat that please?"

Smiling a bit ruefully, he shook his head. "Best not. I was . . . ah, questioning your husband's intelligence."

"I questioned it sometimes myself."

"As his wife, that was your right. Some might even say your duty. I, however, ought not to have disparaged a man I never met."

Such a fine sense of honor! And of right and wrong.

Mr. Winterbrook shifted in his chair as if uncomfortable with his lapse, then rose and crossed to the window. Pushing the draperies to the side, he looked out. After several seconds, he turned to face her. "It is still snowing as hard as yesterday!"

Lynn could not hear the words; she had to interpret the movement of his lips. Since he stood in front of the window, blocking what little light the storm had not obscured, it was a more difficult task than usual.

"Are you worried that your daughter and your aunt will fret when you don't arrive home today?"

"No. Well, yes, that is a concern, but it isn't what is troubling me the most. Given the severity of this storm, it must be snowing at Greendale, too, so they will know why I have been delayed."

Lynn sighed. She had not understood half of his statement. "Mr. Winterbrook, may I trouble you to return to your chair? You are standing in the shadows, and I cannot see your face very well."

His chagrined expression was very clear as he made his way toward her. "I beg your pardon, Mrs. Graves. I was not thinking. Rather, I was thinking of myself, not you. And I tend to pace when I am trying to work something out in my mind."

"You may pace with my blessing, sir, provided you do so in front of the hearth. From there I can hear your words."

He smiled—a lovely, sweet smile—then bowed. "You are

a most gracious hostess." After resuming his seat, he repeated what he'd said.

"Would you like to talk about whatever is troubling you? It is said that sharing a burden makes it seem lighter."

"I would, yes." He looked down for a moment, as if gathering his thoughts, then locked his gaze with hers and asked, "Do you regret having invited me here? You initially intended only to offer me a cup of tea and to clean my greatcoat."

"I do not regret my invitation. Nor do I regret that the storm's severity extended, and will continue to extend, your stay. Your life is more important than any momentary qualms I might have had."

"So you did have some misgivings?"

"Of course. Any woman would. I daresay you probably would, too, if circumstances required you to offer shelter to a stranger. But your kindness and consideration soon laid my fears to rest."

"I don't recall doing anything special, but I am glad whatever I did or said eased your mind."

Lynn almost smiled at his lack of awareness. It was because his kindness and courtesy were, for him, normal behavior that she no longer feared him. He would no more harm her than . . . than . . . She could not think of an appropriate comparison, but he was more likely to sprout wings and fly home than to hurt her. Nor would he abuse her hospitality by making improper advances. He belonged to a far different—and vastly superior—category of gentlemen than Frank and her brothers.

"I cannot help but wonder what you are thinking, ma'am. The smile you are wearing is not one I have seen before." Her guest's droll tone penetrated her reverie.

Lynn hesitated; weighing her words before she spoke was a habit of long-standing. But there was nothing to be lost by revealing her thoughts, and perhaps something to be gained. He might be as curious about her as she was about him. "I was thinking that you are a different type of gentleman than I have encountered heretofore. Much nicer and kinder."

He bowed from his seat. "I thank you for the compliment, ma'am."

"And I am thinking I had best check to see if that cake

has finished baking." She made quick work of the last five stitches in the row she was knitting, then placed needles and yarn in her workbasket.

"Should you need someone to taste the cake, I would be happy to volunteer."

"Sacrificing yourself for the good of all, are you?" Laughing, Lynn stood.

Mr. Winterbrook rose in one lithe motion, and, chuckling, offered his arm to escort her to the kitchen. "Nothing so noble, ma'am. More like fortifying myself to go outside."

"Then you most certainly shall have a piece, and some tea, before you do."

When they reached the kitchen, Lynn crossed to the pump to wash her hands, looking out the window as she dried them. It seemed early in the afternoon to milk the cow and feed the animals, but the sky was so overcast that it was impossible to judge time from the sun's position. As she turned to face her guest, she glanced at the clock on top of the dresser. "Did you intend to go outside soon, sir? The cake will take an hour or so to cool."

He pulled out his watch and checked the time. "I will wait until about four o'clock."

She walked to the fireplace, pulled open the door of the bread oven, and pressed lightly on the top of the cake with her fingertip. When it sprang back instantly, leaving no mark, she knew it was done. Grasping the pan with a quilted cloth, she removed the cake from the oven, then turned and set it on the table.

Mr. Winterbrook inhaled deeply. "Hmmm, it smells wonderful."

"I hope the taste will match the aroma." After closing the oven's door, she lifted the lid of the pot in which she was cooking a beef roast for dinner and stirred the contents. Since she refused to spend hours turning a spit, and since Willie could never be persuaded to take on the task, Lynn had discovered that the same cut of meat could be cooked in a pot with potatoes and vegetables over a very low fire all day. It wasn't really a roast, she supposed, but it tasted just as good. Replacing the lid, she turned to face her suddenly silent guest.

He stood near the head of the table with his eyes closed and his head tipped backward. *What is he doing?*

After a moment, he opened his eyes. "I will have to spend more time in kitchens. I had no idea such wonderful scents were an everyday occurrence."

"Please sit down, Mr. Winterbrook." Lynn felt like a very poor hostess for not having invited him to do so earlier. She ought to have realized by now that he would never sit while she was standing. "I think we need to make an agreement."

"What kind of agreement, ma'am?"

"That when we are in the kitchen, there is no disrespect or discourtesy intended if you do not rise every time I stand. I will not think you ill-mannered, nor will you fall in my esteem, if you remain seated."

When he did not immediately agree, she recalled the candor he had demonstrated during their conversation in the parlor and felt entitled to display some of her own. "It is a bit disconcerting to turn around and find you standing, and because I am not accustomed to having such a well-mannered gentleman around, I often forget to tell you to stay seated."

"In that case, I agree, although I cannot promise that I will always remember. After all these years, it is a deeply ingrained habit—something I do without conscious thought."

"I understand, sir. I only ask that you try."

He smiled. "That I can certainly promise."

"Please sit down, sir." She waved a hand toward the table and its four chairs.

Sit, sit, sit! David wanted to pace. He was like to go mad from inactivity, or from being stuck indoors most of the day. "I would much prefer that you give me something to do, ma'am. I am not accustomed to such enforced idleness."

He pulled out the chair at the head of the table for her, then took his place on her right. Belatedly realizing that she might interpret his last remark as a complaint, or due to some failure on her part, he added, "Not that I am not enjoying your company. I do enjoy it. But I spend most of my days working around the estate, and I fear lack of activity is beginning to adversely affect my disposition."

"Not noticeably so, sir." She cocked her head to one side. "I thought estate managers just assigned tasks to the tenants and estate workers and"—she waved a hand in the air as if trying to conjure up another responsibility—"and kept ledgers."

"Perhaps that is all that some of them do. But I—"

"I know you said that you don't ask your laborers to do any job that you can't do, but I didn't realize that you worked with them."

He smiled, pleased that she remembered. "I don't always, of course. It depends upon the job. There are some I go to great lengths to avoid."

"Oh? And what would those be?"

David's smile widened at the almost teasing tone in her voice. Yesterday he would not have thought her capable of it. And perhaps she wouldn't have been then.

"I try to avoid clearing out blocked drainage ditches—it is wet, filthy work. And I would not want to muck out all the stalls in Greendale's stables, although I don't mind doing the two here." *Nice save, Winterbrook. You almost put your foot in your mouth.* "I am always tired of harvesting well before the last crops are brought in, but I join the workers every day." He dropped his voice to a conspiratorial whisper. "Since my second year there, I have been careful to secure a place on the wagons, piling the crop, instead of swinging a scythe in the field."

"Why didn't you do that the first two years?"

"The first year, I was so damned angry at Marie—" He broke off, appalled that he'd used such profanity in the presence of a lady. Especially this lady. "I beg your pardon, Mrs. Graves. I ought not—"

"Apology accepted, sir. I imagine that is an accurate description of your mood at the time. Please continue. The first year, you were so very angry at your wife . . ."

"I was so angry at Marie that swinging a scythe or hoe was an excellent way to work off my fury. Much better to vent my ire on shocks of grain or the dirt of the potato and turnip fields than on the people around me. By the end of the day, I was too exhausted to do more than soak my aching muscles in a hot bath and climb into bed."

"A very sensible solution, but one that most men would not consider." Mrs. Graves must have heard the note of bitterness that had crept into her voice; she closed her eyes and paused for a moment. When she resumed speaking, her tone was as even as usual. "I have always found churning butter to be an excellent means of venting wrath. Cleaning the house works well, too."

David chuckled, but he could not help but wonder how often she'd cleaned her house from top to bottom during her marriage.

"And the second year you were at Greendale?"

"With the first crop we harvested the second year, I learned what grueling labor it was. Without anger to sustain me in the fields—I had been a widower for seven or eight months by then—the exhaustion and sore muscles were not at all appealing. Especially since I was almost too tired in the evening to play with Isabelle."

"So you found a position on the wagon when it was time to harvest the next crop?" It was half statement, half question, but Mrs. Graves smiled as if she were certain of his answer.

"Indeed I did," he confirmed, returning her smile.

"You must be heartily sick of my tales, ma'am. I hope I haven't bored you unforgivably."

"Not at all, sir."

"I am said to be an excellent listener and confidant, too, and would be honored if, someday, you would allow me to return the kindness."

Her beautiful eyes—which had danced when she'd laughed in the parlor and, more recently, had brightened when she'd smiled—dimmed a bit. *David Winterbrook, you are an addlepated idiot!* Her expression was not as shuttered as yesterday when he'd innocently asked if her husband had been a soldier, but even so, David was certain there would be no more confidences exchanged today. *Damn, damn, damn!*

Chapter Six

*L*ynn's first inclination was to run from the room when Mr. Winterbrook offered himself as a listener and confidant. He was neither presumptuous nor encroaching—it was clearly an invitation to confide if she wished, not a demand that she must—but even so, the thought of telling anyone the secrets she had guarded for so many years was enough to cause a sudden and alarming bout of shuddering.

Mr. Winterbrook slid from his chair and knelt beside her. "Mrs. Graves, are you ill?"

With her teeth clenched against the tremors that racked her frame, she was unable to respond. He clasped her hands between his own, much warmer ones. "Lord, your hands are as cold as ice!"

Jerking to his feet, he strode to the other end of the table, grabbed a chair, and set it in front of the hearth. As he turned back toward her, he reached out and shoved the kettle of water toward the heart of the fire. A moment later, he was bending over her, his sky blue eyes nearly obscured by his concerned frown. Without warning, he scooped her up in his arms, then carried her to the chair by the fire and, very gently, set her down.

He whirled toward the door, plucked his greatcoat off the peg from which it hung, and wrapped it around her, back to front, tucking the placket between her spine and the spindles of the chair. The buttons, although not large, felt like boulders digging into her back, but the garment's welcome warmth made the discomfort bearable.

"Mrs. Graves?"

Hearing the worry in his voice, she looked up at him, but she still was unable to respond. He stood for a moment, wearing an expression akin to that of a lost child, then ran from the room and down the hall. Less than a minute later he returned, carrying all the blankets from his bed and her late husband's dressing gown.

At the sight of the latter garment, Lynn's tremors, which had begun to ease, suddenly increased. When Mr. Winterbrook bent over to wrap the heavy red-and-gold brocade garment around her, she managed to hiss, "No."

Surprised, either by the word or her vehemence, he pulled back, a question in his eyes.

"Not . . . *that*," she forced out between shudders. "Blankets . . . but . . . not . . . that."

Comprehension dawned in his eyes, and he threw the dressing gown behind her. Then, giving her time to refuse each one, he wrapped the blankets around her, tucking the ends behind her with the same care a mother—or a father—would use to tuck a child in bed.

His forehead still creased with worry, he crouched beside her. "What else can I do?"

Before she could unclench her jaw enough to respond, the water in the kettle began to boil. Mr. Winterbrook surged to his feet and crossed to the dresser to get the teapot, two cups, and a spoon. Measuring tea into the pot, he reached bare-handed for the kettle. His expression never changed as he poured water over the tea leaves; Lynn could not decide if he did not notice the heat of the kettle's handle or if the bandage on his hand absorbed most of it.

He reached over to set the kettle on the hearth, but immediately lifted it again and checked the amount of liquid remaining inside. After bending down to peer into her face, he carried the kettle to the pump and refilled it, then hung it from the pot hook farthest from the heart of the fire. His task completed, he turned his scrutiny on her, absentmindedly rubbing his bandaged left palm against the leg of his breeches.

He knelt beside her chair, then raised his hand toward her, but before it had traversed half of the eight or ten inches between them, he returned it to his side. Catching her gaze, he said, "I need to touch your face to determine if you have a fever."

If a more caring, considerate man had ever been born in England, he had undoubtedly been canonized. Still shivering violently despite the blankets, Lynn nodded to indicate she understood his intent—and to grant permission. He rested his palm on her forehead for several seconds, then stroked the back of his fingers against her cheek. That tender touch set off a new, but very different, bout of tremors. Darting a glance at him to see if he was similarly afflicted, Lynn did not quite know what to think when she saw him staring bemusedly at his hand.

He sat back on his heels, his expression rather sheepish. "I am not sure whether you have a fever or not. Sometimes with Isabelle, the only way I can tell if she is feverish is to kiss her forehead."

"My . . . nurse . . . used . . . to . . . do . . . that."

"So did mine, and my mother, too."

He rose to his feet with one lithe movement, then stepped behind her. Lynn could neither hear nor see what he was doing, but when he reappeared beside her a minute or so later, he carried a cup of tea. Sans saucer. This, then, was medicinal tea, not a social occasion.

Wrapped in blankets as she was, Lynn could not free her hands to hold the cup. Not that she would be able to keep it steady enough to drink from if her hands were free. Apparently Mr. Winterbrook had already reached the same conclusion. Kneeling beside her, he raised the cup and warned, "It is sweeter than you usually drink it."

Lynn nodded to indicate she understood, then pursed her lips so she could sip the beverage. Instead of bringing the cup to her mouth, he said, "I am not accustomed to feeding anyone but myself. I want the tea to go inside you, not on the blankets beneath your chin, but with you shaking like a leaf in a high wind, I am not confident of the outcome. May I put my left hand on the back of your head to support it?" He raised the appendage in question into view, but well away from her face.

His kindness and consideration brought tears to her eyes. Blinking them back, she nodded and even managed to reply. "Yes."

Lynn could not recall any man ever touching her with gentleness. Perhaps her father had when she was a babe, but she did not remember. He had never been cruel to her, just . . . aloof. And rather indifferent. But Mr. Winterbrook's hand somehow managed to be both gentle and strongly supporting, as impossibly contradictory as that seemed.

Several seconds passed—no doubt to allow her to grow accustomed to his touch—before he lifted the cup. "Shall we test my skill, Mrs. Graves?" The tone of his voice was wry, as was the smile quirking his lips.

"Yes."

Lynn drank eagerly. Had he not restricted her to small sips, she would have consumed the entire cup at once. Feeling a bit like a nestling raising its open beak toward its mother, she requested, "More, please."

Smiling, he rose to his feet in one swift, graceful movement—even though she watched, she did not know how he accomplished it—and vanished out of sight. "Bring yours, too." Her voice, although not quite normal, was not as halting as before. The tremors were easing a bit as she got warmer.

But this was more than just a sudden case of the shudders. The thought of confiding her deepest secrets might have been the cause of her initial, violent trembling, but its continuation, and the chills, must have a different source. Perhaps, after getting so wet and cold the day her gig went off the road—*was that yesterday or the day before?*—she now had the ague. But Mr. Winterbrook had gotten even wetter and colder than she—

Her guest hove into view and bent over to place a cup of tea on the floor, then vanished again. *What was he doing?* A few moments later he reappeared with another cup and knelt at her side.

"Are you ready for more tea, ma'am?"

"Yes, please, but surely you need not kneel to help me drink it."

"I am loath to change a successful method for one that may not work as well. Besides"—he smiled, his blue eyes dancing with mirth—"I thought ladies liked to bring gentlemen to their knees."

His foolish banter brought a smile to her face. A wistful one, no doubt, for no man had ever been so enamored of her. "I have heard that, too, but this is not the same thing."

He held up his hand—his bandaged left hand—and as he positioned it to support her head, Lynn was glad she had not put her question into words when he hadn't carried both cups of tea at the same time. He would have thought her quite a fool, since she had insisted on wrapping his hand this morning, and she did not want him to think she was stupid. It had been one of Frank's favorite descriptors, and the phrase "stupid woman" had nearly always presaged a slap. Or worse.

Recalling a conversation they'd had early this morning, Lynn asked, "How do schoolboys deal with bullies?"

The abrupt change of topic must have seemed like a non sequitur, but Mr. Winterbrook accepted it with scarce more than a blink. "At Eton, if a boy from an upper form picked on a younger lad, members of the older boy's form would often hear of it and put a stop to it—usually by threatening the older boy with the same treatment he was doling out."

"How did the members of the older boy's form learn about the bully?"

"Many students had an older brother or cousin in an upper form, so word of such infamous behavior was easily spread."

"Was your brother at Eton when you were?"

"He was the first year I was there. An older cousin was . . . two forms ahead of me, I believe. And his brother started the year after I did."

"Ah, so at first you were protected, then you were the protector." Lynn could see him in the latter role more easily than the former.

"Yes." He lifted her cup. "Would you like more tea, ma'am?"

"Yes, please." When her thirst was sated, she continued the conversation. "Did bullies ever pick on a boy in the same form?"

"They did. Invariably on smaller boys, particularly those who excelled at their studies. In such a case, a group of boys would get together and challenge the bully."

"They would fight him?"

"Sometimes, yes. But frequently the challenge would be a sporting one—boxing or fencing or rowing or swimming."

Lynn did not understand how that would help, but since it was not a viable solution for a woman, she chose not to pursue it. "The boys who were bullies, did they change their ways? Or are they still the same as adults?"

He shrugged. "Some changed, others did not. Probably because they had no wish to change."

It was the answer she expected, but disappointing all the same. "Please, sir, sit down—in a chair—and drink your tea."

"I am fine here, ma'am. And"—he drained his cup, then set it on the floor with an elaborate flourish—"I have finished. It is you who have not drunk all of yours."

He raised her cup, but Lynn began shivering again. "Wait." The spasms were not as violent as they had been earlier, but they were too strong to attempt to drink.

Apparently the blankets concealed her tremors from his gaze. "What is it, ma'am?"

"I fear . . . I have . . . the ague."

"May I touch your face again, Mrs. Graves, to check for fever?"

"Yes."

If a man could determine such a thing solely by the force of his will, Mr. Winterbrook would surely succeed, so intent was his frowning concentration. And when he stroked the backs of his fingers down her cheek, Lynn again felt that strange but pleasant quiver in her stomach. *What was that? And what caused it?* She had an even more inexplicable urge to rub her cheek against his fingers.

But determination was not sufficient.

"I cannot say for certain, ma'am." Her guest sank back on his heels, looking thoroughly disgusted with himself for failing.

She studied his downcast face. "Go ahead, sir."

He glanced up, one sandy eyebrow rising inquiringly.

Flustered, Lynn averted her gaze. "Pretend I am your daughter."

"An impossibility, I fear," he said, chuckling, "but I am willing to use the same method. *If* you are certain you are willing to allow a stranger to take such a liberty."

"Yes, sir, I believe I am. You do not seem like a stranger." And he hadn't, she realized, since last night.

"Nor do you, Mrs. Graves."

Still watching her face, he rose to his knees. Slowly—or so it seemed to her—he lifted his hands to her shoulders. For several seconds he did not move, and she rather thought he was giving her time to change her mind.

Lynn had no intention of doing that. Only to herself would she admit that she was as interested in seeing what he did, and how he behaved, as she was in learning if she had a fever.

He leaned forward slightly, then bent his head and gently pressed his lips to the center of her forehead. It was the touch of a moment, as soft as the brush of a butterfly's wing. A second later, he repeated the action, this time on her right temple. The fluttering in her stomach returned, feeling rather like dozens of butterflies had suddenly found themselves there and burst into flight. Her heart was similarly affected. Or afflicted. If she'd ever known that a kiss could be so pleasant, Frank's had driven the knowledge from her mind. Now she would never forget. Indeed, she would probably remember this one until her dying day— and it had not even been a real kiss!

If ever Mr. Winterbrook truly kissed her, she might well swoon.

Chapter Seven

*H*e was sunk. Going down for the third time with no rope in sight to pull him back. Not that he would grab it if there were.

As slowly as he had advanced toward Mrs. Graves, David moved away and removed his hands from her shoulders, hoping she would not realize that his heart was pounding like a drum. The words he needed to say clogged his throat, and he felt a flush of color rising to his cheeks.

She raised her eyes to his, then quickly looked away, blushing prettily. He exhaled a breath he had not realized he was holding, then coughed to clear his throat. "I believe you have a touch of fever, ma'am, as well as the chills." He had felt her shivers when his hands were on her shoulders. "Are you still cold?"

"Yes, but not as cold as before."

Picking up his cup, he rose to his feet. With assumed nonchalance, he walked behind his hostess and placed it on the table, then added another log to the fire. *Zounds!* Kissing Lynn Graves on the forehead had affected him as profoundly as anything he had ever experienced. The ground had rocked beneath him with more force than an earthquake. He had felt that little kiss in every fiber of his being, from his brain box to his toes, which, he would swear, had curled in delighted pleasure. And those appendages had not been the only parts of him to rise.

He dare not contemplate how a real kiss might affect him. At least, not until he was alone in his bedchamber.

When his composure was restored, David set the poker aside and turned to his hostess. "More tea, ma'am?" He knelt beside her, but she shook her head and huddled deeper into the blankets.

What, other than tea, would warm her? Soup was hot and would also provide nourishment, but Mrs. Graves had not made any. Brandy would do the trick, too, but he had seen no wine or spirits in her home.

"What can I do, ma'am?"

"Do?" She looked at him as if she did not understand his question.

"What can I do to help you?"

"Nothing."

Not certain whether she meant there was nothing he could do, or if she merely wanted him to leave her alone, he tried a different approach. "If your father or brothers had a fever, what would you do to make them feel better?"

"Feed them soup or broth, and give them infusions of willow bark to bring down the fever."

"And if you didn't have any soup or broth?"

"I would make some."

She undoubtedly would, but he did not have the slightest idea how to make either. "To make an infusion, you brew the leaves like tea, do you not?"

"That is correct."

"Would you prepare a pot of willow bark in the morning and serve it throughout the day?"

Mrs. Graves considered the matter for several moments before replying. "Probably not. If only one or two people were sick, I would brew a cup when it was needed."

"How often should it be taken? And when you brewed it, how much willow bark would you use?"

"Are you interested in herbs and their curative abilities, sir?" The look she shot him was brimming with curiosity.

"No more than anyone else, I suppose. I am, however, very interested in doing whatever I can to help you feel better."

"Oh!" Obviously disconcerted by his reply, she shook her head, then smiled ruefully. "I daresay you must think me quite the ninny for not realizing why you were asking such questions."

"Not at all, ma'am. But I do want to know how to prepare the willow bark—and anything else that might help. Soup, too."

"Thank you, Mr. Winterbrook. I appreciate your kindness, and your willingness to take care of me, but I do not believe it will be necessary. I am not so sick that I cannot cook for you."

"I sincerely hope you will not become ill—more ill than you are at this moment—but I will feel much better if I know what to do should that happen."

"You are a very nice man, David Winterbrook."

He did not know if it was her words or her smile that gladdened his heart. From what she had said—and had not said—he did not think that many males of her acquaintance had ever received such a tribute from her. Possibly no man ever had. "Thank you, Mrs. Graves. May I say that you are one of the kindest and loveliest ladies I have ever met."

She blushed at the compliment, then graciously thanked him.

After several seconds of silence, he prompted, "Will you please tell me how to prepare a willow bark infusion? And how to make soup?"

"Very well, sir. But if you want instructions for the role of nurse and cook, you'd best get a sheet or two of paper from the escritoire in the parlor."

By the time he had covered two sheets—front and back—with detailed instructions, Mrs. Graves's voice was hoarse. And she was again shivering uncontrollably.

"I am going to brew some willow bark for you, ma'am. While I do, please tell me what you have prepared for dinner, as well as what else must be done."

"Everything is cooking in the large pot on the left side of the fire. All you need to do is stir it occasionally. It should be ready in"—she glanced at the clock on top of the dresser—"about an hour."

"What is the doctor's name and where does he live?"

"I don't need a doctor," she insisted. "And you cannot ride all the way to Tidmarsh, even if it has stopped snowing."

A glance out the window confirmed that the snow was still falling as heavily as ever. After more than twenty-four hours, the clouds ought to have been empty of flakes. Obviously, they were not.

While waiting for the water to boil, he strode from the kitchen and down the hallway to Mrs. Graves's bedchamber. He started a fire in the hearth, then looked around the tidy room, which was furnished in cream and blue. Whether she wished it or not, she was going to lie in bed while he fed the animals and milked the cow. He feared that, in his absence, her shivers might become so violent that she would fall off the chair and injure herself.

After preparing the willow bark, David crouched beside his hostess and held the cup as she drank. "Mrs. Graves, I lit the fire in your chamber. Would you like to lie down while I am in the barn? I will bring you a tray when dinner is ready."

Anticipating her retort, he added with perfect sincerity, "It would give me great pleasure to serve you in this small way."

In her face, her eyes, he watched the battle her spirit—and her need to be independent—waged with her weary, tremor-racked body. Saw, too, her stricken expression the instant she acknowledged her physical limitations. With all his heart, David wished he could change the past, so that she did not feel the need to prove she could stand alone. But no wizard has the power to rewrite history. Even if such a thing were possible, David was not a sorcerer. He was merely a man falling fathoms deep in love with this generous, kind-hearted, and sometimes prickly lady who had never been loved and cherished as she deserved. But he could—and if she let him, he would—change Mrs. Graves's present and her future.

"Yes, I would," she conceded reluctantly and, he thought, with some embarrassment.

"Hold the blankets close, ma'am, and lean forward a bit. I will carry you, so you don't get chilled again."

She opened her mouth to protest, but something—perhaps his words or her exhaustion—kept her silent. Her eyes closed for a moment. When she opened them, she caught his gaze, then scrutinized his face, as if judging his sincerity. Or his intentions.

Still and silent as a statue, he waited for her decision. She was analyzing more than his ability to carry her. This was nothing less—and possibly a great deal more—than a judgment of whether or not she could trust him. Given the glimpses she'd allowed him into her past, it was a momentous decision. And, perhaps, a leap of faith.

When she nodded and whispered "thank you," David knew he had been given a precious, and priceless, gift. And he vowed that she would never regret bestowing it. Placing an arm behind her back and the other under her knees, he lifted her, holding her close to his chest—and his heart— as he stood and carried her to her chamber.

He laid her gently on the bed, then straightened the blankets covering her. "Would you like me to remove your shoes?"

Again she swallowed the protest that was almost instinctive, and halted her move to sit up and do it herself. "Yes, please."

He flipped up the bottom edge of the blankets, and her gown, just far enough to expose the ribbons around her ankles, then bent to his task. Her feet were small and slender, her ankles, trim. Despite her heavy woolen stockings, the sight was surprisingly erotic, perhaps because it was not one he expected to see. At least, not until after they were married. Assuming, of course, that she felt the same way about him as he did about her.

Keeping his movements slow and gentle, he untied and unwrapped the ribbons, slipped off her shoes, then folded down her gown and the blankets, tucking the latter under her feet to keep them warm. After a moment's hesitation, he sat on the edge of the bed. "Is there anything else I can do to make you comfortable, ma'am? Shall I bring your nightrail and dressing gown? You might want to put them on while I am outside."

He thought she blushed, but he had closed the draperies when he'd lit the fire, which provided insufficient illumination for him to be certain. Again she studied his face, but this time her answer came much more quickly. "Yes, please. They are hanging in the armoire."

Indeed they were, from pegs right in front so he did not have to search for them. The nightrail was of heavy flannel, decidedly worn but undoubtedly warm; the dressing gown, a rather coarse wool. Cream and blue, respectively, although that was undoubtedly coincidence. Marie might have chosen her nightclothes to match the colors of the room, but Mrs. Graves would not. Not that Marie would ever have worn such serviceable, unfashionable garments, even in the solitude of her bedchamber. Lynn Graves would look far more enticing in the lacy silks his late wife had favored than she ever had, but—

Lord help him! David felt the sudden heat suffusing his face. As he draped the garments across the foot of the bed, he prayed that the light was too dim for Mrs. Graves to see his heightened color. Or that, if she could see it, she would think he was blushing in embarrassment.

To give himself time for the telltale flush to fade, he crossed to the hearth, poked at the fire, then added another log. Walking back to the bed, he again perched on the edge. "Is there anything else I can get for you, ma'am?"

A lock of hair had fallen across her cheek, and she twisted her head to the side, attempting to dislodge it. After another equally unsuccessful effort, he guessed that she was reluctant to move her hand from beneath the cozy confines of the blankets and asked, "May I?"

"Yes, please. It is . . . annoying."

"Hold your head still for a moment." He lifted his right hand and, keeping it fully in her vision, slowly moved it toward her face. Brushing his fingers against her cheek in a gesture he would admit, if only to himself, was fully intended as a caress, he tucked the strand of hair behind her ear. Then he trailed the backs of his fingers down her cheek and caught her gaze. "Better?"

"Yes. Thank you."

"Hmm." Deliberately frowning a bit, he cupped her jaw in his palm. "You feel a bit warm."

"Do I?"

He rubbed his thumb against her cheek. "Yes, I think so." There was no question about it; her fever had definitely risen.

Continuing the caress, he slowly leaned forward and kissed her forehead again. "Rest well, ma'am." With one final brush of his thumb, he rose and left the room, leaving the door slightly ajar so that he could hear her if she called him.

As he walked down the hall to his room, David realized that his machinations to accustom Mrs. Graves to his touch, and to kiss her again, had distracted him somewhat. His greatcoat was still wrapped around her, underneath the blankets. But he was loath to disturb her, especially since he might surprise her in the act of donning her nightrail and dressing gown. He could, he supposed, wear Graves's uniform jacket. It would not be as warm, but it was better than nothing.

Changing into the man's shirt and pantaloons, which he preferred to wear while doing chores, thus saving his own clothes for the time he spent with the late lieutenant's wife, David realized there was something else he needed to discuss with her. Something in addition to her finances, a topic he had yet to broach. This new, more imperative subject might remove the need to discuss her straitened circumstances, but it was an even more delicate matter. Not being one to rush his fences, he decided to ponder the best approach to this sensitive, possibly knotty discussion while he tended the animals.

It was a decision he would come to regret.

Chapter Eight

Lying in bed, once again warm but otherwise feeling quite wretched, Lynn allowed her thoughts to drift. *Mr. Winterbrook was a most unusual gentleman.* Never in her life had a man demonstrated such concern for her, or treated her with such kindness. *And his kisses!* It was rather alarming that the brush of his lips on her forehead could make her feel so much. So alive. When he'd rubbed his thumb against her cheek, tingles of . . . something had raced from her head to her toes and back again. Although it was, in a way, frightening to experience wellsprings of emotion from what most women would consider unexceptional gestures, Lynn had no wish to call a halt to the simple, innocent pleasures. Kisses and caresses would not be part of her future. Nor had there been many in her past. But she could, and would, enjoy the present ones.

She knew she could trust David Winterbrook. She knew it as surely as she knew her own name. And she was glad, very glad, she had invited him to her home.

Because she could trust him, Lynn sat up and reached for her nightrail and dressing gown. A man whose honor compelled him to marry a woman who deliberately compromised him because he might have contributed in some small way to her tarnished reputation, and whose principles constrained him from consummating his marriage to that woman because she carried another man's child, was not a threat to a hard-of-hearing widow with few social graces who could, at best, be described as unexceptional. Even if that widow was wearing her nightclothes. And very unattractive ones, at that.

All her clothes dated from her marriage, and had been

chosen to make her as inconspicuous as possible. She certainly had not wanted to draw Frank's notice, nor had she wanted him to find her attractive. Thus, all her gowns were made of sturdy fabrics in dark colors. The necklines were high, and most had long sleeves. When he'd complained that she looked like a governess, she had smiled inwardly since that was her intent.

Now, though, she could not help but wish she had at least one attractive, rather stylish gown. But despite her governess-y attire, Mr. Winterbrook seemed attracted—

"You are building castles in the air, old girl." Lynn wobbled across the room to the armoire and hung her gown and petticoat on their pegs. "Just because you are attracted to him—as any woman of sense between six and sixty would be—does not mean he finds you equally entrancing."

He has been very attentive, though, argued a little voice in her head.

Abandoning the idea of serving that attentive gentleman his dinner—her legs seemed to have turned to jelly—Lynn returned to bed and burrowed under the blankets. Mr. Winterbrook was an intelligent man, willing to take on any task. He was certainly capable of serving himself a meal, even if he had never done so before.

When Frank died, she swore never to remarry, but despite her vow, she could not help but wonder how different her life might have been if she had met a gentleman like Mr. Winterbrook eight years ago. She drifted off to sleep imagining the delights of being courted by a man as kind, considerate, and respectful as he.

Returning to the cottage after settling the animals for the night, David noticed that the right shutter on the kitchen window was banging against the house due to the increasingly gusting wind. He berated himself for not having checked it during the afternoon as he had intended, but fortunately, the wooden panel was not significantly damaged. He closed both shutters, latching them into place, and entered the kitchen's welcome warmth. After washing and changing back into his own clothes, he checked on Mrs. Graves, who was sound asleep. He thought she was beneath the quilt rather than on top of it, but with all the blankets covering her, he could not be certain. Not without peeking under the blankets, which he refused to do. He wondered if she had donned her nightrail—she would be more comfortable in it than in her gown—but she was huddled so completely under the covers that he could see only her head.

He ate dinner, but although the food was as delicious as at every other meal she had prepared for him, it was not as enjoyable without her company and conversation. David was not a particularly social creature: he attended most of the dinners and parties that made up the social whirl in Oxfordshire because it was expected of him, but he much preferred to spend his evenings at home, with Isabelle and Aunt Caro. Or, when his friend's schedule permitted, with Dr. MacNeill.

The past day and a half spent almost entirely in Mrs. Graves's company was a new experience for David. A very pleasant one. The contrasts between the months of his marriage and his time in this cottage were as vast, and as diverse, as the differences between chalk and cheese. Until his aunt had come to live with Isabelle and him seven months ago, he had never experienced the simple joys of a quiet evening spent in a lady's company. And wasn't that a pathetic thing for a man of six-and-twenty to admit?

When he finished eating, he checked again on Mrs. Graves, but she was still asleep. He put the uneaten food in the larder, then washed and dried the dishes. Try as he might, he could not recall any of the other tasks his hostess performed in the evening. After looking in again on her—she appeared to be sleeping deeply—he heated water for a bath. It was undoubtedly the shortest, quickest one of his life; he did not want to be caught in her kitchen naked as the day he was born if she suddenly awoke. Fortunately for them both, he completed his ablutions without interruption. After donning Graves's dressing gown, David also dunked his linen in the soapy water, rinsed them under the pump, and hung the garments near the fire to dry. His shirt and cravat would undoubtedly be a mass of wrinkles, but at least they would be clean. Or, rather, cleaner.

Walking past Mrs. Graves's chamber on his way back to his room, David peeked inside and noticed a change: she had thrown off the blankets. At some point, she had pulled back the sheet and quilt and crawled beneath them, and she'd changed into her nightrail and dressing gown, but her hair remained in a knot at the back of her head. Knowing it was important to keep her warm, he tiptoed in and recovered her, tucking everything save his greatcoat tightly around her, then placing that garment on top.

He brushed his fingers against her cheek, which was much warmer than before. Although he wanted to give her more willow bark, he was loath to awaken her. The oft-repeated words of his good friend, Dr. MacNeill, echoed in his mind. *Sleep is a great healer, and one of the best medicines a physician can prescribe.* David decided to wait an hour or so, to see if Mrs. Graves roused of her own accord. But he was determined that she would have another dose of the fever medicine this evening. Even if he had to disturb her slumber to administer it.

He wandered about the cottage looking for some task—any task—to occupy his hands. And his thoughts. Although he found no chores, David discovered something almost as good: a novel which his brother, his sister-in-law, and his father praised highly—*Pride and Prejudice* by A Lady. He would read later this evening; now he needed a less sedentary activity, so he decided to try his hand at making broth. By testing his culinary skills tonight, he could make another pot tomorrow morning if the first was inedible. With his hostess's instructions in hand, David headed for the kitchen.

Lynn woke with a start at the sound of a man's voice calling her name. Before she was even fully awake, she realized there was no need for alarm: it was not her late husband's shout, but Mr. Winterbrook's kinder, gentler tones. She inhaled deeply, then slowly released her breath, trying to calm her racing heart.

"Mrs. Graves."

Why was he in her bedchamber? Suddenly apprehensive, she twisted onto her back. The abrupt movement raised a protest from every joint in her body, and she barely restrained a groan.

"Madeline, please wake up."

"I am awake." Opening her eyes, she saw him standing beside her bed, balancing a large, slightly tarnished, silver tea tray between his hands and wearing a worried frown.

The juxtaposition of her late husband's dressing gown and an expression of concern was so incongruous that it took Lynn several seconds to understand why. When Mr. Winterbrook wore the garment, the dragon pattern of the brocade was not menacing, as it had been when Frank wore it. Nor had her husband ever directed such a caring look at her.

"Why are you in my bedroom, sir?"

Mr. Winterbrook carefully placed the tray on the small table beside her bed. "I am here to give you another dose of willow bark."

"Willow bark?" Lynn raised her arm and touched the back of her wrist to her forehead. She did, indeed, have a fever. "How long have I been ill?"

"Since this afternoon. You suddenly started shivering uncontrollably, and later told me that you thought you had the ague."

"I remember now." She struggled to sit up—a difficult task when weighted down by a large pile of blankets and quilts. "What time is it?"

"Almost nine o'clock. You slept for about five hours." He leaned over and piled pillows behind her. "Are you hungry?"

"No, just thirsty. But you must be famished."

"Not at all. I ate dinner while you were sleeping." With a smile that seemed a bit sad, he added, "It was as delicious as everything else you have prepared, but less enjoyable without your company."

Lynn was glad he turned to pick up something from the tray, so he did not see her blushing. "You are very kind to say so, Mr. Winterbrook."

"A simple statement of fact, ma'am." He handed her a cup. "Drink the willow bark. When you finish that, I have a pot of chamomile tea for you. And a piece of your wonderful cake."

Lynn smiled. "I am glad you like the cake. Did you have some before you went out to the stables?"

"No, I forgot about it then because I was worried about you, but I had a piece when I finished my dinner."

"Please sit down," she invited, forgetting that there was no chair in the room. "Is it still snowing?"

"It is." He sat at the foot of the bed and leaned back

against the bedpost. "At four o'clock, the snow was more than a foot deep, and the drifts were well above my knees. It seemed colder, too, but I could be mistaken about that."

"I am sorry, sir. You need to sit a bit closer or speak a little louder."

"My apologies, ma'am." He did not move, but repeated his statement so she could hear it.

Lynn sipped the fever remedy. "How could you mistake whether or not it was colder?"

"I was not wearing my greatcoat, so it might have seemed colder than it really was."

"You should not have gone outdoors without your coat!" she scolded. "You will get sick."

"I wore a coat," he reassured, his calm voice soothing her fears. "Your husband's uniform jacket."

"Why did you wear it instead of your greatcoat? Because it was shorter?" Certainly the jacket was too short to drag in the dirty straw in the stable and barn as his greatcoat must.

"Not for that reason, although that was an unexpected benefit. With your permission, I would like to continue wearing it when I do chores outside."

"Of course you may wear it, sir. You are doing me a great favor—" She broke off when he shook his head, then she raised an eyebrow in inquiry.

"It is you who have done me a great favor, Mrs. Graves, by offering me shelter from the storm. Tending your animals is the least I can do to show my gratitude for your kindness."

"But you did the first favor by getting my gig out of the ditch." She drank the last of the willow bark and set the cup aside. "I daresay we could spend the rest of the evening thanking each other, but in the end, both of us would still feel we owed a debt to the other."

He inclined his head, acknowledging the truth of her statement. "Undoubtedly so, ma'am." He stood, crossed the few feet to the nightstand, and picked up the teapot. "May I serve you tea and cake, ma'am?"

"Yes, please." It was such a novelty to be waited on. Especially by a gentleman.

After preparing her tea and handing her the cup, as well as a plate bearing a slice of cake with a fork perched precariously on the rim, Mr. Winterbrook poured a cup for himself, then returned to his seat at the foot of her bed.

Lynn tilted her head, watching him as he sipped the herbal brew. "Last night I had the impression that you are not terribly fond of chamomile tea."

He glanced up, clearly startled by her observation. "I prefer India or China tea, but yours is much better than the chamomile tea I have been served in the past."

"Thank you." The compliment pleased her as much as his earlier ones had. Several minutes passed in silence as they drank their tea and she ate a few bites of the cake. It was not, however, an uncomfortable silence, and Lynn marveled that she could feel so at ease in a man's company. Especially since he was in her bedchamber!

A wistful expression settled on his countenance. Certain she knew what prompted it, she ventured, "You must regret your impulse to eschew the comfort of your carriage on Monday and ride cross-country."

"Not at all, ma'am." He smiled again, but there was no sadness this time. "Had I ridden in the carriage, I would not have met you. And that would be most regrettable."

"Gallant nonsense, but nonsense all the same." Even so, it warmed her heart.

"You think I offer Spanish coin? I assure you, Mrs. Graves, I do not."

"Spanish coin?" The phrase was not one Lynn knew.

"False flattery."

Was it false flattery? Perhaps, although Mr. Winterbrook did not seem the type of man to utter meaningless compliments. He had been very honest in his dealings with her—excruciatingly so—and had revealed far more of his history than one would expect from a chance-met stranger. Indeed, he had told her secrets he had carefully guarded from all the world save his father and brother.

No, his words were not Spanish coin. He meant what he said, although she could not fathom why he was so pleased to have made her acquaintance. Certainly she was glad to have met him. Not only because she was happy to learn that there were gentlemen worthy of the name in the world, but also because he was a very nice, very likeable man. He accepted her defects, treated her with great courtesy and consideration, and seemed to enjoy her company. Mr. Winterbrook was the first man ever to respect and admire her as a person—an equal. She would very much have regretted missing that!

If I had met David Winterbrook eight years ago, I would have known how a true gentleman treats a lady, and I would not have fallen for Frank's practiced, and very superficial, charm. Unfortunately, fate had not been kind enough to reverse the order of her acquaintance with the two men, but Lynn had learnt from her mistakes.

What would it be like to be married to a man like David Winterbrook? A gentleman who treated a lady with courtesy and respect. A kind, considerate, gentle man who lifted his hands only to perform a task or to assist a lady, and who was more likely to cut off his arm than to strike a woman or child. It would, she was certain, be quite wonderful. Mr. Winterbrook's wife, for surely he would remarry, would be a very fortunate woman. Unless . . .

Although she found it difficult to believe that Mr. Winterbrook's behavior in his lady's bedchamber would be vastly different than in her own kitchen or parlor, Lynn's experience as a wife had taught her that only the couple involved knew for certain what happened in their marriage bed. A servant might suspect that all was not well—that was, she believed, why Frank had fired their first housekeeper and thereafter limited their servants to his batman and a cook-housekeeper who came in for the day—but only she and her husband knew what she'd endured when their bedroom door was closed.

Despite the evidence they saw, neither servant ever spoke against her husband. Perhaps because he paid their wages. Or maybe they had never looked beyond his surface charm and bonhomie. His cronies and superior officers hadn't either; at least, not until just before his death. Even her family had given no credence to her reports. Her brothers had not believed her when she'd appealed to them for aid, and her father had told her she'd made her bed and must lie in it.

Given such callous disregard, it was little wonder she was so wary of men. All but this one . . .

Watching the parade of emotions cross Lynn Graves's face—wonder, fear, disgust or dismay, amazement—David was glad he had lit the candles on the mantel and the one on the nightstand, so he could see her clearly. "A penny for your thoughts, ma'am."

She blushed. "You would be paying far too much. I doubt they are worth a farthing."

"I believe I can stand the nonsense." He made a great show of searching his pockets, which drew a smile from her. "I seem to have left my purse in the pocket of my coat. Is my credit good with you, ma'am, or shall you demand immediate payment?" His tone was teasing, but the question—at least the first part of it—was serious.

"Your credit is excellent, sir."

"Thank you." He bowed as best he could from his seated position. "In that case, ma'am, I again offer a penny—to be paid tomorrow morning—for your thoughts."

Color again flushed her cheeks, and she averted her gaze. "Actually, sir, I was thinking how different my life might have been if I'd met you eight years ago. If I had made your acquaintance before I met Frank Graves, I would have known how a true gentleman behaves, and I would not have been taken in by his specious charm and cozening ways."

"Eight years ago, I was"—he calculated quickly—"eighteen and still at Oxford. If I had met you then, *I* would not have fallen prey to Marie's false smiles and manipulations."

Mrs. Graves's beautiful eyes—they looked blue now, in this room and by the candles' light—darted back to his face, studying his features as if she questioned his sincerity. "I cannot believe, sir, that a squire's daughter with few social graces could alter your perceptions of a high-born lady."

Should I tell her why meeting her first would have changed what happened with Marie? Or is it too soon to declare myself? Several moments' thought, and his hostess's continued scrutiny, convinced David that she was not yet ready to hear—or, more precisely, to believe—that he loved her. "You may not be an earl's daughter, Madeline Graves, but you have more grace and kindness and compassion in your little finger than Lady Marie Smalley had in her entire body. She was not a lady at heart, despite the courtesy title she bore so proudly. You are."

"Th-thank you." She seemed flustered by the compliment. It was rather maladroit to praise her in comparison with a woman he had despised, but that did not affect the truth of his statement.

Bravely, he forged on, hoping he could say what he wanted—needed—to say with more eloquence. "I cannot change your past, Mrs. Graves, nor you mine, but if we choose, we can affect each other's futures."

"What do you mean, sir?" David did not know whether her frown was one of puzzlement or wariness. There had been a distinct trace of the latter in her voice.

"Simply that, now that we have met, we can decide to pursue the acquaintance or not. I would like to think we could be friends."

Realizing that his words might be misconstrued, he added, "I do not mean 'friends' in any of its euphemistic forms, but in the truest sense of the word."

He smiled and spread his arms wide. "Why, we might even come to love each other and decide to marry." *There, I have introduced the subject.*

The sound she muffled behind her hands might have been laughter or a snort. "I think it highly unlikely that you will succumb to my nonexistent charms, sir. A man who has his pick of Society's beauties would not choose to marry an impoverished, hard-of-hearing widow."

"Although I dislike to contradict a lady, my honor requires it in this instance. Your charms are legion, ma'am." The rest was trickier ground, no doubt full of treacherous bogs for a man groping his way in the dark. "In my father's family, there is a tradition—which holds true for every member of the family for at least the last three generations—of marrying for love. Obviously, my first marriage was not a love match, but I am determined that my second shall be. The social position and financial status of the lady who captures my heart will not be a factor."

"Isn't there a saying that it is as easy to fall in love with a wealthy, beautiful woman as a poor, ugly one?"

"There may be, but I have not heard it. I don't believe love is that fickle. Nor does such cynicism bode well for marital happiness."

He arched a brow. "As for your claim that a man would prefer a Society beauty over a hard-of-hearing widow, again I must disagree. You are the only lady I know who fits that description, and I fall a little more in love with you every hour I spend in your company. I was never in love with Marie, who was an acclaimed Beauty, and I liked her less the more I knew her."

Change the subject before you scare her. Although he had told himself, only a few minutes ago, that Lynn was not ready to hear—or to believe—that he loved her, her disparaging remarks had compelled a declaration of sorts. Not the one he'd intended, nor the discussion he'd debated about while tending the animals, but his words would, he hoped, provide food for her thoughts. Fortunately, her countenance revealed neither alarm nor disbelief. Nor anything else, come to that. If his declaration had drawn a reaction from her, there was no sign of it in her expression. *Change the subject. Give her time to ponder what you said.*

"Do you have any more of your late husband's clothing, ma'am?"

"I . . . uh . . . I don't believe so, Mr. Winterbrook, although there may be another shirt. I will look in the morning."

"If you tell me where to search, I can look for it myself."

"Up in the attic, in the trunk on the back wall."

"How do I get into the attic?" He had not seen a staircase in the cottage.

"The door across from your room gives access to the attic stairs."

"I will look tomorrow morning." He stood, then placed his cup and saucer on the tray. "More tea, ma'am?"

"No, thank you."

He crossed to the hearth and added another log to the fire. "I tried my hand at making broth earlier tonight. Would you like to have it for breakfast, or would you prefer tea and toast? Or eggs and ham? I am sorry I cannot offer you a more varied menu."

She did not respond to his questions, but even after he glanced over his shoulder at her, it took him several seconds to realize that he was too far away for her to have heard him. Returning to his seat at the foot of her bed, he repeated his queries.

"I hope to fix breakfast for you tomorrow, sir."

That statement garnered her the same look he would

give one of Isabelle's more foolish claims. "As much as I would enjoy that, I know that fevers usually last for several days."

Mrs. Graves sighed, probably in resignation, although weariness might have been the cause. "I suppose they do. In that case, I would like tea and toast and some of your broth."

As soon as she set her teacup on the tray, he rose. "Is there anything I can get for you before I leave? Your hairbrush, perhaps?"

She raised a hand to her hair. "Yes, please. And that little dish on the dressing table for my hairpins."

After giving her both items, he crossed to the hearth and snuffed the candles on the mantel. Then he picked up the tray and, resisting the urge to kiss her, took his leave. "Sleep well, ma'am. If you feel unwell during the night, or if you need something, call me. I will leave your door and mine ajar an inch or two so that I can hear you."

"I am sure that won't be necessary, Mr. Winterbrook, but thank you."

When he reached the portal, he turned back. "Sweet dreams, Mrs. Graves." *Dream of me.*

Chapter Nine

*L*ynn stared at her bedroom door, thinking about the man who had just left the room. And about the things he'd said. Although she had no reason to doubt his veracity, some of his statements were difficult to credit. Oh, she could believe he wanted to be her friend—in the true sense of the word—but she did not know any woman who claimed friendship with a man.

The idea that they might come to care for each other was not preposterous. She already cared about David Winterbrook far more than she would have thought possible. And a bit more than was comfortable. But that they might come to love each other and marry? Absurd! If they did, indeed, pursue the acquaintance, she might well come to love him, but Lynn did not believe he would ever feel the same about her.

Picking up her hairbrush, she began her nightly one hundred strokes and pondered the things he had said.

Your charms are legion, ma'am. With a less than delicate snort, she now answered, "Of course. Any man would be charmed by a plump, graceless widow who can barely hear." He would, no doubt, counter that she was neither plump nor graceless, and that she heard just fine, but Lynn knew that few people, if any, would agree with him. Especially since she herself did not.

You have more grace and kindness and compassion in your little finger than Lady Marie Smalley had in her entire body. Grace again. Perhaps she was not as lacking in that trait as she had heretofore thought. Lynn believed she was kind and compassionate—more so than some people, probably not as much as others—but why did Mr. Winterbrook think she possessed those qualities in such abundance? She had done nothing extraordinary; she had merely invited him to tea so that she could clean his greatcoat.

She was not a lady at heart . . . you are. A lady at heart. Lynn liked the sound of that; the eloquent phrase suggested an elegance of manners for which she had always striven. But surely such behavior was not that unusual. All she did was treat people the way she wanted them to treat her. Then again, if it were the norm, the vicar would not preach so many sermons on the Golden Rule, would he?

I fall a little more in love with you every hour I spend in your company. Ah, this was the statement Lynn most wanted to believe and found hardest to credit. Only to herself she would admit that she was falling in love with him. But what did David Winterbrook see in her that caused him to experience that profound emotion?

It was an unanswerable question, at least for the nonce. Having long since lost count, Lynn set the brush on the nightstand and quickly braided her hair. Since it was impossible to make sense of nonsense—and that was, or so it seemed, an accurate description of her thoughts—she pushed away from the headboard and snuggled under the covers, settling herself for sleep. Perhaps tomorrow things would seem clearer.

Instead of enlightenment, the morning brought a raging fever. Throughout the day on Wednesday, Lynn was able to suggest remedies with which David could dose her, and tell him how to prepare them, but by Thursday morning, as her fever continued to rise, most of her words were delirious mutterings.

David was so engrossed in battling Lynn's fever that he was not even aware it had stopped snowing until Thursday evening when he went out to feed the animals and milk the cow. The snow was far too deep to travel anywhere, but even if it weren't, he could not leave Mrs. Graves while she was so ill. Hoping for several days of warmer weather so that the accumulated snow would melt, he was quite dismayed on Friday morning to discover that it had turned bitterly cold. But not as upset as he would have been had he been staying at an inn, or at the home of someone he did not like. In truth, as eager as he was to return home and see his daughter, he was equally loath to leave Madeline Graves.

Thursday night, David carried one of the wing chairs from the parlor to his hostess's bedchamber, so he could sit, and perhaps doze, in between bouts of bathing her hands and face—and, though he would never admit it to her, her body—with cold water to bring down her fever. And between attempts, generally unsuccessful, to rouse her so he could dose her with willow bark. Waking a fever patient was difficult enough; rousing a nearly deaf one was damned near impossible.

He learnt a great deal of her history that night while she was in the throes of delirium. His suspicions that Graves had abused her, physically and emotionally, had been correct. But what David heard Friday afternoon was even more appalling. He felt sick just thinking of the depravities and degradations she had endured. Given her experiences, it was a wonder she ever let a man get close enough that she could hear his conversation. And even more surprising that she'd invited him to her home.

By Friday evening, David was light-headed from fatigue. He dipped a cloth in a basin of melting snow, then bent over his patient and bathed her face and hands. "You need to throw off this fever, ma'am, ere I develop a permanent stoop. Every time I straighten, I feel like an old man with a severe case of the rheumatics."

Mrs. Graves was too deep in delirium to respond, but even so, he spoke to her. Dr. MacNeill believed that sometimes seemingly unconscious patients heard what was said around them, even though they could not respond. Since the physician was rarely wrong, David conversed with his patient. Besides, talking to her seemed natural. And it made him feel better.

He dropped the cloth into the basin and moved the candle on the nightstand closer. Sitting on the edge of the bed—*Lord, it felt good to sit down!*—he lifted her left arm onto his thigh and frowned at the tiny buttons on her cuff. "Why three buttons, ma'am? Surely one is sufficient." Grumbling softly, he added, "If there was only one, it could be larger." Yesterday afternoon, he had left the buttons unfastened, but even in her feverish state, Mrs. Graves had attempted to fasten them. She'd pulled off two and become so upset that he'd had to find another nightrail—with buttons intact—for her to wear. And to help her don it.

Fortunately, she had not realized who was tending her then. Half the time she did not, but when she did, the knowledge did not distress her. On the contrary, she apologized for being such a burden. *As if she could ever be that!*

Having emerged victorious in the battle of the buttons, David dipped the cloth in the icy water, then wiped it up and down her arm. "You told me on Wednesday that bathing a patient with cold water would bring down a fever. But my fingers are nigh frozen, and your fever isn't noticeably lower."

He fastened the cuff, but with only the lowest button. Then, too tired to walk around the bed, he leaned over and gently grasped her right arm, laying it across her body so he could reach the buttons on her sleeve. "You need to fight this fever, Lynn. To shake it off, or throw it off, or however people rid themselves of one. I am honored that you allow me to take care of you, and a bit awed by your trust, especially since I am a stranger, and a man. But I want you well. I need to know that you are happy in my company, and if you will allow me to care for you when you are healthy."

He finished bathing her right arm. "Only one button, ma'am, until your fever breaks. If you want them all buttoned, you must get well and fasten them yourself."

Dropping the cloth into the basin, he stood. After a quick glance at her face, he reached for the edge of the blankets, lifting them from the side and uncovering one leg. He raised the hem of her nightrail, then reached for the cloth and stroked it up her leg to her knee. "You don't realize the intimacy involved in tending someone as sick as you are. I know you would object were you able to do so." After repeating the motion several times, he covered her and walked around the bed to bathe her other leg.

When he finished, he crossed to the fireplace to warm his hands. And cool his loins. He was ashamed of his body's reaction, but the depth of his remorse did not affect his arousal.

Silently reciting the multiplication tables—backward—he returned to the bed. Sitting on the edge, he looked at the woman lying there. The lady he loved, and whom he would love until the day he died. He wanted to protect her, to ensure that she would never suffer again as she had in the past, yet he'd never felt more helpless or ineffective in his life.

He dipped the cloth in the icy water and again bathed her face and neck. "Five days, Lynn. On Monday morning, I did not even know you existed, but now I cannot imagine my life without you in it."

Taking a deep breath, he dropped the cloth in the basin, pulled the covers down to her waist, and set to work on the line of buttons down the front of her nightrail. To distract himself, he continued his conversation with her, wondering if she was aware he was speaking. Or that anyone was talking to her.

"There is much we need to discuss, ma'am. On Tuesday evening, I told you something of my feelings, but I do not know yours. I regret now that I did not say more. We ought to have discussed the damage to your reputation should my stay here become known. And my wish to marry you, whether or not it does."

With his eyes firmly fixed on her face, he lifted one side of her nightrail and bathed her chest. "At the time, I thought it best just to hint at my feelings, and not to speak of anything more than friendship between us in the future. I thought you needed to know me better before I proposed. To discover for yourself that I am not at all like your late husband, so you would not be afraid to accept my offer. Now I regret that I did not say more."

Dampening the cloth, he switched hands. *A chest. It is just her chest. Not so very different from mine.* He shook his head and chuckled softly. No matter how hard he tried—and he'd been trying very hard for two days—he could not convince himself of that. He could *feel* significant differences. But until she gave him the right to do so, he refused to look.

"Please get well, Lynn. I miss your smiles, rare as they are, and your conversation. And, of course, your cooking."

He tossed the cloth in the basin, then turned his attention, and his gaze, to her buttons. "I want to show you a different side of men, and of life. To teach you about love and families. And I want you to teach me how to be a good husband."

Throughout the night, he continued his ministrations. And the conversation. His voice grew hoarse, and only God knew if the words made any sense, but David did not stop.

Midnight came and went, and time seemed to slow, each hour longer than the last. Perhaps fatigue altered his perceptions, or fear of the cause of Lynn's increasing restlessness. His words became prayers, his actions more frantic.

Around four o'clock, Lynn began shivering. David raced to add a log to the fire, then exchanged the basin of melting snow for one of warm water. It took several minutes for his exhausted mind to realize that her fever had finally broken—and that she was gazing up at him, her beautiful eyes once more clear and coherent.

"Thank God." David hugged her, then kissed her cheek. "How do you feel, sweetheart?"

Lynn considered her reply as he piled pillows behind her with one hand, then eased her back against them. "Tired. And sore all over."

Keeping one arm around her, he stretched out beside her, but on top of the blankets, propping his head on the hand of his bent right arm. "You have been very, very ill with a fever for the past three days."

"If I have been sick, then why do you look so tired and pale?"

He lifted his arm from around her waist and stroked the backs of his fingers against her cheek. "Because I have been taking care of you and haven't slept much the past three nights."

The dark circles under his eyes led her to believe he'd slept very little, if at all. "Then I shall take care of you now, and tell you to go to sleep."

"Yes, ma'am," he said obediently. Smiling, he bent and kissed her cheek, this time near the corner of her mouth. Then he wrapped his arm around her waist again, laid his head on the pillow beside hers, and, between one breath and the next, fell asleep. Just before he did, he said, quite clearly, "I love you, Madeline Graves."

It was a long time before Lynn slept. When she did, her dreams were a mix of old nightmares and bright, new hopes.

Chapter Ten

*D*avid awoke with a start, his heart pounding like a drum setting the pace for a military double-time march. Not certain what had disturbed his slumber, he glanced around and was astounded to find himself in—or, more precisely, on—Madeline Graves's bed. She was lying beside him, sleeping soundly, and when he rubbed the backs of his fingers against her cheek, he was relieved to note that her fever was on the wane. A rhythmic banging brought David to his feet; the sound of muffled voices drew him out of the bedroom and into the hallway. The chill air there swept the cobwebs of sleep from his brain, and when the banging resumed, he realized someone was knocking on the front door.

Striding toward the portal, he attempted to tidy his appearance, but quickly abandoned the impossible task. An unshaven man in his stocking feet is not very presentable, wrinkled shirt or not. Wondering at the identity—and discretion—of the person who would, in a moment, discover his presence in the cottage, David unbolted the door.

"Who the hell are you?" The man standing outside, his arm raised to knock again, was heavily bundled against the cold and appeared to be in his mid or late fifties. Behind him were two younger men, their garments equally heavy but of lesser quality, each carrying a large box. A sleigh, drawn by a team of plow horses, was parked in front of the cottage, a groom or coachman standing at the leaders' heads.

David stood foursquare in the doorway, blocking the entrance. Folly perhaps, since the older man, who was about his height, outweighed him by three or four stone, but he would do his best to guard the portal. "I am Lord David Winterbrook," he replied, deliberately using—and slightly emphasizing—his title. "Who are you?"

"Henry Patterson."

Patterson. Wasn't that the squire's name? David thought so, but he was not certain. If, however, Patterson was the squire, he was not one of Lynn's suitors. The man was at least thirty years older than she was.

"Where is Madeline? And what are you doing here?" The man's curt tone demanded answers.

David rued his decision to postpone discussing with Lynn the fact that her reputation would be ruined if his stay at the cottage became known. He had wanted time to consider how best to convince her that he wanted to marry her, damaged reputation or not, but after she became ill, he'd had no opportunity to bring up the subject. Now he—and she—were out of time.

His presence in her home, unchaperoned, had been discovered, her reputation compromised.

Although he hated to do so without having first discussed the matter with Lynn, David bowed to the inevitable. "I am Mrs. Graves's fiancé. I was stranded here—"

"Maddie isn't promised to anyone."

Who was this man? Why did he call Lynn by the nickname she disliked? And why was he so certain that she was not engaged? David did not know the answer to any of those questions, so he merely repeated, "I am Mrs. Graves's fiancé. I was stranded here by the blizzard. Fortuitously, as it happens—she has been ill."

"She is sick? I want to see her," the man on the doorstep all but demanded.

David stood his ground. "Sir, I don't know who you are—"

"I am her father, damn it!" the older man bellowed, slamming his fist against the door.

Stunned, David stepped back and allowed Patterson to enter. Regaining his wits in time to prevent the man from charging farther into the house, David motioned toward the parlor and said, in a tone that brooked no possibility of refusal, "Please sit down, sir. Lynn is sleeping now, and there are several things you and I need to discuss before you see her."

Patterson frowned but grunted. Ever the optimist, David took that as acceptance of his dictum. Without argument, Lynn's father removed his hat and gloves, then turned his attention to the rest of his outerwear.

Much as he wanted to bar the door—with Patterson and his men on the other side—David was too kind-hearted to make anyone stand outside on such a bitterly cold day. "Come inside before you freeze. You can wait in the kitchen."

The servants accepted his invitation with far more grace than their master.

After directing the footmen and the coachman to the kitchen, David rubbed his hands over his face as he considered what he needed to say and how best to express it. Then, figuratively girding his loins, he entered the parlor.

Patterson was sitting on the sofa. It was, perhaps, a tactical error on the older man's part, and David did not hesitate to use it against him. He strode to the center of the room, prepared to test the adage that the best defense is a good offense.

"What kind of father allows his daughter to live in such straitened circumstances as this"—David gestured around the room—"without a single servant and with barely enough food to sustain her?"

"She—"

"What kind of father allows his daughter to marry a man like Frank Graves?"

"She chose—"

"What kind of man ignores a woman's—his daughter's!— pleas for help when her husband beats her?"

A pained expression crossed Patterson's face, and he slumped against the sofa cushions. "I warned her against marrying Graves. I feared the man was a fortune hunter. As it turned out, I was right."

The older man was silent for several minutes, the look in his eyes that of a man gazing into the past and not liking what he saw. "I was angry at Maddie for defying me, so I refused to give Graves her dowry. Not until after his death did I realize what a terrible decision that was. And that she suffered because of it."

In her delirium, Lynn had told a very different story. David believed her; it was impossible not to, given what she'd endured. Determined to probe deeply enough to find out why her father's memory of the occasion diverged so drastically from hers, he said, baldly, "Lynn came to you years before Graves died and told you that he beat her, but you ignored her claims. And her pleas for help."

"I thought it was just a lover's quarrel—"

"Your daughter came to you battered and bloody, and you thought it was a lover's quarrel?" David could not keep the incredulity from his voice, which rose in astonishment. And in anger.

"She wasn't bloody," Patterson blustered. "And before that day, she'd given no indication that she was unhappy in her marriage. Quite the contrary. So it was difficult to believe her tale."

"Her bruises and broken arm and ribs were not evidence enough for you?" Hearing the sneer in his voice, David dragged in a deep breath, hoping to regain control of his fleeting temper.

"You don't understand—"

"No, I certainly do not," he snapped. "If anyone harmed—"

"Now, see here, young man." The testy tone made it clear that the older man's ire was increasing rapidly. "Raising a child is not as easy as you might think. Until you have one, you can't know the difficulties a parent faces."

"I have a daughter, and I am well aware that a father's duties are not always easy. That, however, is not the point. The question is why you failed to assist your daughter, not just in freeing her from an abusive husband, but now?"

"I am here, aren't I?" Patterson shouted. "I fought my way through the snow to bring her food."

"Yes, you are here now, but where were you the past three days when she was out of her head with fever? Where were you Monday when her gig went off the road and into a ditch?"

Lynn woke to the sound of men's voices raised in anger. She could not distinguish the words, only the tone. And the volume, which had to be considerable if she could hear it when she was in another room. Despite the fact she'd never heard him speak in tones of anger or impatience, she recognized one of the voices as David Winterbrook's, but she heard the other only as a deep bass rumble. The realization that there was another voice roused her to complete wakefulness far more quickly than usual. Sliding to the edge of the bed, she stuffed her feet into her slippers and, with one hand on the bedpost, stood. Although she felt as weak as a newborn kitten, her legs seemed steady enough. She was not dressed to receive guests, but since she hadn't expected visitors, nor did she want them, they would have to take her as they found her. She was not at all certain that she had enough energy to dress, make her way to the kitchen or parlor, and confront the intruder who had provoked David's ire. Thus, she made do with tightening the sash of her dressing gown and smoothing her hair back from her face as she crossed to the door of her bedchamber.

When she reached the open doors of the parlor, Lynn was shocked nearly speechless to witness mild-mannered David Winterbrook excoriating her father for his treatment of her. Or, rather, for her parent's seeming unconcern for her health and welfare. Even more astonishing than her father's presence in her home—*why is he here?*—was that he seemed to accept the scold as his due.

She must have made some sound because David broke off abruptly and hurried to her side. "Lynn, what is wrong?"

"Nothing." She smiled up at him, hoping to ease the concerned frown from his brow. "I heard angry voices, so I came to see who was here and what was amiss."

"You should be in bed." He wrapped his arm around her shoulders and escorted her to the wing chair in front of the hearth. After seating her, he knelt and set the logs on the grate ablaze, then came to stand beside her. "You must not overtax your strength. You have been very sick for the past three days."

Although she wondered what had triggered the men's dispute, and how it could have begun so quickly after her father's arrival that David had no opportunity to light a fire, she would save those questions until later. Instead, she smiled at him, then turned to the squire and said, "Father, this is an unexpected surprise. Why are you here? And how on earth did you get here through the snow?"

"I am here because I was worried about you, Maddie.

And because my housekeeper feared you might not have enough food for next week. I got through because the coachman hitched a team of plow horses to that old sleigh in the carriage house, and every footman, groom, tenant, and gardener helped to clear a path from the Grange to your cottage."

Her father's deep voice made it very difficult for Lynn to hear his words, despite the fact that when she was growing up, his voice had seemed louder than most. And the problem was compounded by his singular ability to speak with barely any movement of his lips. She understood his first two statements, but missed most of the rest. Later, she would have to ask David what the squire had said.

She got her answer much sooner than she expected. As if his legs had suddenly given out, David sat on the arm of her chair and, in tones of the deepest astonishment, inquired, "You had your servants and tenants clear the snow from five or six miles of the road?"

The squire crossed his arms over his chest and nodded. "Yes, I did. If I had not, I couldn't have gotten here, and I needed to assure myself that Maddie was safe and well. And that she had enough food to last until the roads are clear enough for travel."

Touched by her father's concern—which was far greater than he had ever demonstrated, or even alluded to, in the past—Lynn stood and reached across the table between their seats to clasp his hand. "Thank you, Father."

He squeezed her hand, then released it. "You are quite welcome, Maddie girl. There are two boxes of food in the kitchen. If you run out, send word to the Grange."

Bemused, she sank back into her chair. While she was still seeking a response, David asked, "How deep is the snow on the road east of the Grange?"

Deep. Please, Lord, let it be deep. I don't want him to leave yet.

Startled by the implications behind such a wish, she glanced up at David—and breathed a sigh of relief at the squire's answer. "It appears to be deeper east of the Grange than on this side. There hasn't been a carriage, or even a rider, on the road since . . . since Monday afternoon, shortly after Maddie left."

He pinned David with a steely gaze. "How long have you been here, young man?"

"He has a name, Father," Lynn chided, hoping to divert her parent's attention. "Did you not introduce yourself?"

Chuckling softly, David smiled down at her. "It was not a formal introduction, but we did exchange names."

"Aye, we did," the squire confirmed, "but I have forgotten his."

With a dismayed tsk at her father's ill-mannered response, Lynn gestured to her guest. "Father, this is David Winterbrook." Then she glanced up at David and pointed to her parent. "This forgetful gentleman is my father, Squire Henry Patterson."

Her father's response sounded like a grunt, but David politely acknowledged the introduction. "I am pleased to meet you, sir."

"If you are promised to my daughter, Winterbrook, why haven't I met you before today?"

Thinking she misunderstood her father's words, she looked at David for clarification. He smiled and took her hand. "Lynn has not yet accepted my proposal, sir. Since she is of age, she does not need your permission to marry, although I am certain she would like your blessing."

Lynn stifled a gasp, but just barely. She did not recall hearing such an offer, only his comment, several days ago, that in time they might come to love each other and marry. *Had he since proposed?* She remembered little of the past few days, so it was possible he had. But it was very difficult to believe she could have forgotten such a momentous event. Being courted by David Winterbrook was the secret wish of her recent dreams.

It was also utterly impossible.

Chapter Eleven

While Lynn was still seeking her voice, her father's coachman came into the room. "I beg pardon for interruptin', but we need to leave, sir. The wind has picked up and is blowin' snow everywhere. And the horses have been standing overlong."

The squire skewed David with a testy look in which annoyance seemed to be the predominant factor. "Get your things, Winterbrook. I cannot wait all day for you."

"With all due respect, sir, if you are leaving, then I am not. Someone must stay here to take care of your daughter. As well as of her animals."

"Maddie is quite capable of taking care of herself. She has been doing so for the past two years. And she has a lad to tend the animals."

"Sir, your daughter has the ague. She has been out of her head with fever for the past two days, and she is still far from well. Someone has to cook her meals and dose her with willow bark. And someone has to feed her animals, milk her cow, and muck out stalls because her stable boy hasn't been here since Monday morning."

David crossed his arms over his chest and challenged the squire. "If you won't remain here to care for your daughter until she is well, and do all the chores, I will."

Knowing that her father had never attempted to cook anything, and probably had never milked a cow or mucked out a stall, Lynn was not surprised that he did not take up the gauntlet. But instead of directly declining David's challenge, her father threw a different gauntlet at her. "Well, daughter, shall I take Winterbrook with me and send a cook and a maid to care for you, and one of my grooms to do the chores? Or shall I leave *your fiancé* here?"

It was quite clear from her father's tone that he expected a betrothal announcement if she chose to have David stay. But Lynn had no intention—and no wish—to force him into marriage, so she sought a compromise that would placate her father for the nonce. "Since it is quite likely the weather will prevent your servants from coming, and since Mr. Winterbrook has already been exposed to my illness, it is probably best that he stay."

Her father glared at David and muttered something she could not hear. Then he bid her good-bye and departed.

Lynn sighed wearily. She was relieved to know she had regained enough self-confidence that she could stand up to her father, but the effort had exhausted her.

After barring the door behind the squire and his servants, David returned to the parlor. *When had she begun thinking of him as David?* "You should rest, Lynn. Even if you don't feel sleepy, you have been very ill." His concern, which was apparent on his face, in his eyes, and in his voice, warmed her heart. "Or, since you are out of bed, would you like to have breakfast in the kitchen?"

"I am tired, and I will go back to bed soon, but I would like to have breakfast first."

He offered his arm to escort—and, did he but know it, support—her. "I hope you are in the mood for bacon and eggs. That is about the extent of my culinary talent."

"I have no doubt that you are as skilled at making breakfast as at everything else you do."

"Thank you, ma'am. That is a very fine compliment. I hope you will not be disappointed—" He stopped abruptly, his expression stricken. "Good God!"

"What is wrong?"

"I am an idiot."

"No, you are not."

"Aye, I am." His tone was rife with disgust. "I just spent several minutes explaining to your father that someone has to be here to care for your animals, but in all that time, it did not occur to me that I haven't fed them or mucked out the stalls this morning."

Surprised—he usually finished those chores before she awoke—she looked up at him. Although he had slept for several hours, his fatigue was apparent in the dark shadows that lingered like bruises beneath his eyes. "You are not an idiot, David Winterbrook. You are exhausted."

He ducked his head like a bashful schoolboy and confessed, "If your father hadn't knocked on the door, I might still be sleeping."

"I regret being the cause of your lack of sleep, but I thank you most sincerely for taking care of me when I was ill."

A slight frown creasing his brow, he led her to the kitchen and seated her. "Lynn, there is much we need to discuss."

"Yes, there is," she agreed, her tone void of inflection. She could not help but wonder if he had, in fact, proposed or if his honor had compelled him to declare himself her fiancé so that her reputation would not be ruined.

To satisfy his honor, David had sacrificed himself to save a lady's reputation once before. Was he again doing so?

As he pumped water to fill the kettle, David darted a glance at the clock. His frown deepened, causing Lynn to look at the clock, too. It was almost half past ten. After hanging the kettle over the fire, he gathered teapot, cups, saucers, and spoons from the dresser and placed them on the table within her reach. "Can you wait twenty or thirty minutes for breakfast? So that I can milk the poor cow and feed the horses?"

"Of course I can." Lynn wanted—needed—to think, and to recall as much of the past three days as she could, before they discussed his role, imaginary or not, as her fiancé. As well as the reasons for it.

He crouched in front of her and took her hands in his. "And, so that you do not overtax your strength, will you agree to do nothing more strenuous than drink tea while I am outside?"

"I will do nothing more than drink tea and"—she inclined her head toward the two boxes on the table—"inventory the food my father brought."

"You are the best judge of your abilities," he conceded, concern still furrowing his brow.

She was, of course, although neither Frank nor her father and brothers would ever have admitted a woman might be more knowledgeable about anything than they were. But

David Winterbrook did realize it. And admitted it. "I promise to be careful. And not to over do."

His frown eased, and a smile flashed across his face as he stood. "I cannot ask for more than that."

David wished he were better prepared for the coming . . . discussion. As he'd changed into Graves's clothes, then hurried through the barn and stable chores, he prayed that it would be a discussion, not an argument or a confrontation. He'd replayed Lynn's words, both to him and to her father, half a dozen times, but he still had no idea what she was thinking. Or feeling. Now, as he washed and dressed in his own clothes, he reviewed her words again.

Unfortunately, it did not help a bit.

God, he was tired. Here he was, about to engage in the most important discussion of his life, and he could hardly string two thoughts together. Eloquence was beyond him. He devoutly hoped that coherence was not.

Looping his limp, wrinkled cravat around his neck, he stepped in front of the pier glass. "Bloody hell."

He looked like a demmed ruffian. Or a sandy-haired gypsy. He pulled off his shirt and stropped the razor. Although his hand was less steady than usual, he managed to shave without cutting himself. Dressed again, with the bedraggled cravat tied in what was supposed to be a Mathematical, although the knot bore little resemblance to the fashionable style favored by the men in his family, he sent a prayer winging heavenward. Then, with feigned nonchalance, he shrugged on his coat and sauntered down the hall.

It was time to put his luck—and his love—to the test.

David Winterbrook entered the kitchen wearing a smile, his boots, and his coat—all of which had been missing during her father's visit. Lynn wondered if he'd felt at a disadvantage because of their absence. In her nightrail and dressing gown, she certainly had. Surprisingly, though, her earlier discomfiture was gone.

"I am sorry to keep you waiting for your breakfast, ma'am."

She returned his smile. "There is no reason for you to apologize. Especially since the delay was the result of yet another service you performed for me. Indeed, it is I who must beg your pardon since my father's shockingly early call interrupted your much-needed rest."

"I shall do well enough. Provided"—he flashed a grin over his shoulder as he strode toward the larder—"you do not wish to engage in a philosophical debate."

"Fear not, sir. I am feeling decidedly dull-witted this morning."

Dropping the things he carried on the table, he hurried to her side. "You have taken a turn for the worse?"

"No. I—" He brushed the back of his fingers down her cheek, scrambling her wits even further. "I feel much the same as I did earlier."

"You seem a bit flushed."

"Embarrassment, perhaps. My father was rather rude."

"Maybe so, but I cannot—will not—fault him for his concern."

Before she could respond, he stepped away and began preparing breakfast. Lynn chose to postpone their discussion until she had his full attention. Instead, she took pleasure in watching his graceful yet efficient movements. Although he was not as muscular as Frank, she had no doubt that David Winterbrook was a skilled athlete. A fencer, perhaps, as well as an excellent rider and a skilled whip. He was probably a wonderful dancer, too.

The meal seemed no different than those they had shared earlier in the week, except that she was far more aware of him than before. Aware of him not as a guest, but as a man. A rather handsome man, at that.

Before she was quite ready, the meal was over, the dishes were soaking in the sink, and David resumed his seat beside her, his expression serious and, at the same time, a bit wary. A tingle of unease shivered up Lynn's spine.

He angled his chair so that he faced her. "I don't know how much of the past few days you remember, Lynn, but—" Clearly chagrined, he interrupted himself. "I beg your pardon. Although you have not given me leave to do so, I called you by name when you were feverish. You responded more readily to Lynn than to Mrs. Graves," he explained.

"My informality is *not* a sign of disrespect. I hold you in the highest regard. Given all that has occurred, it seems a bit ludicrous to return to more formal address, but if that is what is you would prefer—"

Delighted to know he so esteemed her, she answered readily, "You have my permission to call me by name, if you wish."

"Thank you, Lynn." His beaming smile, as well as his words, made it quite clear that he was delighted by this unanticipated sign of her favor. "It would please me greatly if you would call me David."

Never having called any man except her husband and brothers by name, Lynn was not at all certain that she was daring enough to address him by his Christian name. Instead of parroting his thanks, she nodded her acquiescence.

Disappointment flashed across his features. His unexpected vulnerability—so similar in some respects to her own—touched her heart. "I daresay it will take me a few days to become accustomed to addressing you so informally. I hope that you will forgive my occasional blunders, David."

"Of course I will." They smiled at each other in perfect accord.

He looked down for a moment, as if gathering his thoughts. "Do you remember the conversation we had Tuesday evening?"

"In truth, I don't know what day this is. Tuesday was the day after you arrived, was it not?"

"Today is Saturday. And I did, indeed, arrive on Monday."

To give herself time to think, Lynn reached for the teapot and refilled their cups. *Is he referring to the conversation we had after I fell sick? The one in my bedchamber about . . .*

"We discussed friendship, and the fact that I fall more in love with you every hour I spend in your company."

Whoever said men are more reluctant to speak of their feelings than women had not met David Winterbrook! He had bravely, and boldly, introduced a subject that she would have mentioned as obliquely as possible. "Yes, I remember. At least, I remember that part of the conversation."

"And do you remember me telling you that I love you?"

"Not then. But . . . but you told me last night." She remembered his declaration, and the feelings—both good and ill—it had evoked.

He rubbed his hands over his face, then raked them back through his hair. "I did not tell you on Tuesday, although I knew it—"

"Why did you not tell me then?"

He held her gaze, although she sensed that he would prefer to look away. "Because I feared you would not believe me. That you would dismiss my words as nonsense."

He was undoubtedly correct, but the answer still stung. "I . . . I—" She toyed with her teaspoon, seeking a response.

"Lynn"—he clasped her hand between his—"perhaps I was wrong to believe you would react that way, but even if my assumption was erroneous, my feelings are true. I love you. And I am in love with you, more so every day. Will you do me the very great honor of becoming my wife?"

Panic assailed her, nearly overwhelming her. She retained enough sense, and sufficient manners, to reply, "No. I am sorry, but I cannot."

Then, like the terrified coward she was, she bolted from the room.

Chapter Twelve

*D*ismayed, David watched the woman he loved flee as if chased by the Hounds of Hell. *Did my marriage proposal scare her? Or the questions begging answers in light of her refusal?* Thinking back over their conversation, he realized that although he'd bared his heart, she had not even hinted at her feelings. If, indeed, she felt anything at all.

Much as he wanted to follow Lynn, to ask all the questions for which his heart demanded answers, he knew such an action would be foolish in the extreme. No doubt his proposal had surprised her. Given her history, it was possible it had also alarmed—perhaps even frightened—her. She would reappear when she was ready to discuss it. And not a moment before.

Too upset to sit still, he paced around the kitchen as he analyzed the situation.

His declaration, he realized now, had been too precipitous. He had not explained why her father thought they were betrothed. Nor did she know that David regretted embarking on that course without her agreement. Now she probably thought he was as big a bully as Frank Graves, albeit in a different way.

David Winterbrook, you are an idiot! A bacon-brained, beef-witted fool. You know what she has suffered, yet you did nothing to ease her fears. Nothing to reassure her that you would never, could never mistreat her as her late husband had. Now you must find a way out of the hole—this very deep abyss—you dug, then fell into, even though your eyes were wide open.

When his circuitous perambulations took him past the

sink, the dishes soaking there caught his eye. Lynn's retreat temporarily prevented him from telling her what was in his heart. But if it was true that actions spoke louder than words, mayhap he could show her instead.

Fool, fool, fool! Lynn collapsed on her bed and succumbed to a rather prolonged bout of tears. But afterward she still felt like the veriest goosecap.

Dipping a cloth in the basin of water on the nightstand, she pressed it against her red-rimmed, aching eyes. Exhausted, she laid back against the pillows and wondered what had possessed her to act so . . . so stupidly missish. David Winterbrook, the kindest, most gentle of men, had told her he loved her and asked her to marry him. As if that were not astonishing enough, she had . . . In truth, she was not exactly certain what she'd done, other than rudely refuse and then bolt as if he'd assaulted her.

At the very least, she owed him a handsome apology, and an explanation for her behavior.

But how can a person explain something she does not understand?

Shivering, she slid under the blankets and curled into a ball. She ought to have added a log to the fire, which was little more than embers now, but she was not certain her legs would support her if she attempted to walk across the room. Instead of composing her apology or pondering her answers to the questions David was sure to ask, Lynn considered the impossible, but suddenly quite appealing, future that beckoned in the wake of his proposal.

If he offered for her again, would she be strong enough to refuse as she must?

When Lynn awoke several hours later, a fire blazed in the hearth and a pot of tea sat on a silver tray on the nightstand. A tray that a few days ago had been tarnished but now shone brightly, reflecting the leaping flames. *Surely David hadn't polished the silver!*

Since she was no longer feverish, perhaps she should be shocked that he had entered her bedchamber while she slept. Instead of indignation, she felt gratitude that, even angry with her as he must be, David would care for her, and see to her comfort.

She pushed herself into a sitting position and leaned back against the headboard, considering the man who had nursed her through a fever, and who had taken her father to task. The man who had asked her to marry him.

Gripped by the sudden fear that she was alone in the cottage, she attempted to stand, but her knees buckled before she took a step. "David!"

The panic in her voice brought him on the run. "What is wrong?"

Relief rushed through her at the sight of him, turning her bones to jelly, and she fell back against the pillows. "Nothing now. I . . . I feared you had left."

His left eyebrow arched upward, but when he spoke, his tone was even. "What strange notions you have of my character."

"I think you are an extremely kind, very honorable gentleman. But"—she averted her gaze—"I wouldn't have blamed you if you had abandoned me."

"Lynn." It was half sigh, half admonishment. "There are several things—rather important things—we need to discuss. Do you feel well enough for such a discussion?"

She met his gaze and, with more confidence than she felt, replied, "Yes, I think so."

"I am not going to eat you, you know." He grinned as he moved the wing chair closer to her bed, so that she would be able to hear him. "I only want to clear up some misconceptions—or, rather, what I think might be misconceptions—and to be certain that we understand each other."

Once he was satisfied with the position of the chair, he slumped into it, quite obviously weary. But after a moment, as if remembering his manners, he straightened. "I am not certain how—or where—to begin."

Lynn clenched her hands tightly together. "I will start. David, I beg your pardon for my unforgivable rudeness earlier. I . . . There is no excuse for such . . . such—"

"Do not distress yourself, my dear. I accept your apology."

"Why should I not suffer some distress? I caused you a great deal, I believe."

"A bit perhaps," he said after a moment. "But only because you were upset."

"That is no excuse!"

He smiled slightly as if amused by her indignant rejection of his attempt to exonerate her. "Not an excuse, but a reason for it. Lynn, I offer you my deepest apology for anything I said this morning that upset you."

Absently, he rubbed his hand along the arm of the chair. Before she could decide if he was distracted or if he was gathering his thoughts, he spoke again. "More importantly, we need to determine why we were upset."

She nodded in agreement, although she had not the slightest idea how they could determine such a thing. Or things.

"I don't really know how best to do that, except to talk honestly about everything that happened this morning, and how we felt about each event."

"That seems logical." Difficult—at least for her—but logical.

"Would you like to begin or shall I?"

Lynn did not want to speak first, but David very likely felt the same. "Was my father's arrival the start of everything?"

"More or less."

It was not a very helpful answer. Frustrated and uncertain, she glanced away and spied the teapot on the nightstand. "Before we begin, may I pour you a cup of tea?"

After serving them both, she felt calm enough to ask, "If we start our discussion with my father's arrival, will we eventually cover everything that . . . bothered you?"

His brow furrowed as he considered her question. "Yes, I believe so. Other, related events occurred before he arrived, but they can be woven into the discussion when necessary."

Lynn nodded. Much of her explanation would involve past incidents, but she could tell him about them by describing their effect on her behavior this morning. "In that case, perhaps you should begin by telling me what happened when my father arrived. Including," she appended with delicate yet pointed emphasis, "whatever was said or done that led him to believe that you are my fiancé."

David resisted the urge to squirm in his seat and, instead,

sipped his tea as he gathered his thoughts. Then, after a deep breath and a quick prayer, he began. "I awoke to the sound of banging, but it took me some time, perhaps as long as half a minute, to realize that someone was knocking on the door. When I opened it, your father—although I did not know then that he was your father—demanded to know who I was. I told him my name. And, fearing that gossip about my presence here would ruin your reputation, I told him I was your fiancé."

Locking his gaze with Lynn's, he reached over and took her hand in his. "I shouldn't have made that declaration without your permission. I knew it then, just as I know it now, but there wasn't time to ask. I had to decide quickly, and I made my choice based on my feelings for you. On what I hope our future will be."

Her lack of response made him feel like he was teetering on the edge of a cliff, but he plunged forward. If he crashed on the rocks below, it wouldn't be because he had not tried to achieve his goal. "The night you got sick, I told you that I am in love with you, and hinted that I want to marry you. You said this morning that I told you again last night."

He waited, wanting Lynn to acknowledge or deny his statement. His incorrect paraphrase of her words was deliberate, uttered in the hope that she would say something. Anything. Finally, she did.

"Last night you said 'I love you.' But you didn't say you wanted to marry me."

"I may not have mentioned it last night—I was so tired, I don't remember exactly what I said—but we did speak of marriage earlier this week."

"Only as something that might happen in the future!"

Smiling at her naïveté, he moved to sit on the edge of the bed. "Sweetheart, no man mentions marriage to a lady unless he is seriously considering it."

She studied his face, feature by feature, but said nothing.

"Since we have previously spoken of marriage, you know that my proposal this morning was not made to satisfy the proprieties, but because I love you." He lifted her hand to his lips and brushed a kiss over her knuckles.

"Now that you know my feelings, and my hopes, perhaps you will tell me yours."

Confusion swirled in her beautiful eyes, which were more blue than brown this afternoon. "David." Just one word, but it was rife with uncertainty.

"What, sweetheart?" He twined his fingers with hers. "If you cannot tell me your feelings—"

"I don't know what I feel. Except bewildered." After a moment's pause, she added softly, "And frightened."

"Frightened of me?" Incredulity made his voice half an octave higher than usual.

She shook her head. "No. Not of you. Of . . . this situation."

"Of having me in your home?"

Another shake, this one accompanied by a small, slightly wobbly smile. "Of course not."

Now *he* was confused. "What frightens you then?"

She shrugged, then her forehead wrinkled into a frown as she sought the answer to his question. He waited, motionless, and eventually was rewarded with a response. "Just thinking about marriage."

That did not bode well for his plans. He mentally debated the advantages and disadvantages of probing further and decided to proceed. Cautiously. "From the things you have said—and from what was left unsaid—I know that your marriage was not a happy one. Your husband abused you, didn't he? With his words and his fists."

She ducked her head and covered her face with her hands, but not before he saw the tears brimming in her eyes. When the first sob escaped, he slid his hands very slowly up her arms to her shoulders, then down her back, pulling her into a loose embrace and guiding her head to rest on his shoulder.

"Shhh. Everything is fine. . . . You are safe now, Lynn. . . . He cannot hurt you anymore."

Stroking his hand along her spine, he repeated the phrases over and over. When he kissed the top of her head, he realized that his words and actions were almost identical to those he used to comfort Isabelle after a bad dream. But Lynn's nightmare had lasted for years. For the first time, David wondered if her wounds were too deep for him to heal. Before his thoughts wandered too far down that depressing path, she stirred and mumbled something against his waistcoat.

Mortified and embarrassed, Lynn wanted, more than anything, to hide. To hide from the shame of her past. To hide from the too perceptive eyes of the man who held and comforted her. That, however, was not possible. Nor, when she considered it, was she certain she really wanted to flee from this kind, caring, gentle man.

She had never been more confused, or more terrified, in her life.

Not terrified of David, but of the things he made her feel.

He stroked the back of his fingers down her cheek, setting off those strange but pleasant shivers inside her. Then, with a gentle finger under her chin, he tilted her face up to his and kissed her lightly, and far too fleetingly, on the forehead. "I am sorry that you had to endure such suffering when you were married to Graves. And I can understand your wariness to risk your heart—and yourself—again. I hope you know that I will never hurt you. At least," he amended, ever honest, "I would never deliberately do or say anything to hurt you."

Lynn's honor compelled her to match his honesty with her own. Or, at least, to try. She raised a hand—*when had she looped her arms around his waist?*—to cup his jaw. "I know you would not, David. In my mind, I know. But my heart is not as certain."

Hearing the words caused her to question the truth of her statement. "Or perhaps it is my heart that is certain and my mind that doubts." Still unsure which version was correct, she shrugged.

Although she longed to tuck her head back into the comfortable, and comforting, niche where his shoulder met his neck, she would give her explanation with the same honesty and directness he had granted her. "You are a very kind, gentle, and caring man, David Winterbrook. And I am falling—have fallen—in love with you." She stroked his cheek with her thumb, then withdrew her hand.

Quiet joy lit his sky blue eyes. She allowed herself a few moments to bask in the soft blue glow, then ducked her head. "But after Frank died, I swore I would not marry again. That I would never allow another man to control my life."

She heard him swallow hard, then take a deep breath. "Was that one vow or two?"

"What?" The question was so unexpected, and so puzzling, that her eyes slewed back to his face.

"Did you make two separate vows or just one? That is, did you vow never to remarry and also swear never to allow another man to control your life? Or did you vow never to marry a man who wanted to control your life?"

"I don't recall." Nor did she see the difference. "Why do you ask?"

"Because, my darling, if you made a single vow—not to wed a man who would control your life—you can marry me without foreswearing yourself. I do not want to control your life, I only want to share it."

"Ah." She swallowed, but could not dislodge the lump in her throat.

"Does that make a difference?" The hopeful lilt of his voice, and the look in his eyes, were impossible to ignore.

"Yes, it does." Whether it made enough of a difference was a question she could not yet answer. "David, you are the only man I have ever met whom I would even consider as a husband. But," she closed her eyes and tucked her head into that comforting spot beneath his jaw before confessing, "I do not know if I can be any man's wife."

"I don't understand." His hands cupped her shoulders. Knowing he meant to draw her away from his chest so that he could see her, but well aware that she could not face him and explain—if, indeed, she could find the courage to bare her soul and attempt an explanation—she wrapped her arms around his waist and shook her head.

His chest rose and fell in a deep sigh. He slid his hands from her shoulders; one rose to cup the back of her head, the other caressed the length of her spine. Several seconds elapsed before he said, in a level voice without the slightest inflection, "You love me—or have fallen in love with me—and I am the only man you could consider as a husband, but you do not know if you can be my wife."

"It sounds contradictory, doesn't it, but it really is not. I will try to explain, but—"

"Please try." He kissed the top of her head. "I want to understand."

"As you have guessed, my marriage was not a happy one. Frank was a cruel and angry man, and I was the—or, at least, one of—the targets of his anger.

"After my father refused to give Frank my dowry, I never received a compliment, or any words of praise, from him unless there were others nearby to hear. It was as if there were two sides to his character. The public one was pleasant and genial, but when no one else was around, he was . . . very different."

"Cruel and vindictive?"

"Yes." She drew in a shuddering breath. "Cutting remarks were commonplace, and I heard many of them every day. But when he drank too much, he used his fists to . . . to punctuate his cruel words."

"Ah, Lynn—"

She pushed back from David's chest to look up at him. "Please do not interrupt. I don't know if I can tell this at all, but my best chance of succeeding is if I do it quickly."

"I will try to remain silent." He pulled her close again, his hand still soothing up and down her spine.

She snuggled against him, reveling in his warmth and gentle strength as she sought words to complete her explanation. "Even worse than the beatings, although they were often a part of it, was . . ." Squeezing her eyes shut, she took a deep, and hopefully fortifying, breath. "Was what he did in our marriage bed. He . . . he took pleasure in humiliating and degrading me." She swallowed the bile that rose in her throat. "I do not know if I will ever again be able to trust a man sufficiently to . . . to permit physical intimacy."

David had to exert considerable effort to hide his reaction to Lynn's disclosure. Disgust and anger at Graves warred with pity for her plight. Their plight now. After a momentary hesitation, his hand continued caressing her spine. Now that he knew the problem, he needed to find a solution. Quickly. "I understand now why you refused me this morning, sweetheart."

He pressed a kiss against her hair, since that was the only part of her he could reach. "But given our position at the moment, I believe you already trust me to a fair degree."

"Yes, I do, but—"

"There is a big difference between allowing a man to hold and comfort you and the intimacies of marriage, but we have made a good start, I think."

"Yes, we have."

"Lynn, will you look at me, please?" He stroked the backs of his fingers down her cheek, then leaned back and tipped her face up to his. Her apparent reluctance to leave his embrace was gratifying—and boded well for his plans.

Easing her back so that she rested on the pillows piled against the headboard, he took both her hands in his. "There are several things I want you to understand. And to contemplate. A marriage between us would be very different from your first marriage. The first and most important difference is that I love you. I want to share your life and take care of you, and to love and cherish you as you deserve. I have no wish to control you, or to dictate what you can and cannot do.

"Second, you have far more experience as a wife than I do as a husband. Although I was married, I was never a husband to Marie *in any way*, so you will have to teach me how to be a proper husband."

Heartened by her amazed smile, he marshaled the rest of his arguments. "Four people now know that I have been here all week. Gossip is inevitable, so that number will soon increase. I do not want to be known as the man who married Marie Smalley so that her reputation would not suffer after she spent a few minutes alone with me, but who did not marry Madeline Graves after spending days as an unchaperoned guest in her home."

He raised her hands to his lips and brushed kisses across the back of each one. "I love you, Lynn, and I want to share the rest of my life with you. Please, my darling, will you do me the great honor of becoming my wife?"

"David, I—"

"You are a widow, so no one will know if we consummate our marriage on our wedding night or not. I swear to you, on my honor as a gentleman and on all that I hold dear, that we will not consummate our union until you are ready to do so."

She dropped her gaze, seeming to stare at their clasped hands. "What if I am never ready?"

David did not think that would happen, but saying so would sound the death knell to his hopes. Instead, he shrugged as if the matter were of little importance. "If you are never ready, then our marriage will forever remain unconsummated."

Her head snapped up, her eyes locking with his. "That is impossible!"

"No, dear one, it is not. My marriage to Marie was never consummated."

"But—"

He overrode her protest, smiling to counter the frown settling over her delicate features. "No one, other than us, will ever know if it is or not."

"But you must want children. An heir."

"I would like to have more children. And to give you children. But I don't have a title or entailed estates, so . . ." He shrugged again, then leaned forward and kissed her cheek, just at the corner of her mouth. "I love you, Lynn, and I want to share my life with you. If you are not ready to accept my proposal, will you at least agree to consider it?"

"Yes, I will consider it."

It was not the acceptance he'd hoped for, but it was a step in the right direction. "Thank you, sweetheart."

Progress was progress, no matter how slowly it was achieved.

Chapter Thirteen

*T*he bitter cold weather continued all the next week, preventing the snow from melting and making David's chores more difficult, since water buckets in the stable and barn froze solid in little more than an hour's time. Some days it seemed he spent most of his time watering the animals, chopping wood, and hauling it into the cottage, but he was determined to keep the fires blazing, so the frigid temperatures did not adversely affect Lynn's health. Her recovery was slow but steady, and by the end of the week, she felt well enough to spend most of the day out of bed, although she retired to her room for a mid-day nap.

Late Saturday afternoon, exactly one week after the squire's visit and the same length of time since David's proposal, he returned to the cottage after feeding the animals and found Lynn up to her elbows in bread dough, with a charming smudge of flour adorning her nose.

"Are you feeling robust enough for such violent pounding, my dear?"

She looked up and smiled. "Not pounding, kneading. And I feel well enough right now. A good thing, too, since we have eaten nearly all the bread my father brought."

"What can I do to help?" He doffed his greatcoat and hung it on a peg near the back door, then stood in front of the fire, warming his hands and feet.

"Would you make tea? The water should boil very soon."

"Of course I will." After washing his face and hands, he crossed to the dresser for the teapot and cups, spooned tea into the pot, then stepped over to the hearth and reached for the kettle. The water was boiling furiously, and apparently had been for some time, since the vessel was less than half full. Fortunately, enough liquid remained to almost fill the teapot. As the brew steeped, he refilled the kettle and hung it from a pot hook at the edge of the fire, then set the table and fetched the cream and sugar from the larder. Then, the preparations completed to his satisfaction, he turned to tell Lynn that tea was ready. And, unaware that she was standing behind him, nearly bowled her over.

Instinctively, he reached out to steady her. But within moments, his hands slid from her upper arms to her shoulders and then down her back, pulling her into an embrace.

It had been a week since he had held her this close, seven long days since he'd done aught but hold her hand, and he was determined to make the most of this opportunity. "Hmmm"—he rubbed his cheek against her hair—"if this is my reward for being clumsy, I shall have to make a habit of it."

Laughing, she looked up at him.

"You are so lovely. Especially with your beautiful hazel eyes alight with laughter, as they are now." He tucked a loose strand of hair behind her ear, then trailed the back of his fingers down her cheek. "I would like, very much, to kiss you."

She froze, then locked her gaze with his. "You would?"

The incredulity in her tone stabbed like a knife to the heart. *Does she not understand that I love her?* "Yes, I would," he affirmed. Stroking his fingers down her jaw to her chin, he traced the curve of her lower lip with his thumb. "May I?"

Her answer came a second or two later in the form of a nearly imperceptible nod.

He bent his head slowly, to give her time to change her mind—and prayed that she would not. Hovering with his lips a scant inch from hers, he looked into her eyes. No fear clouded the blue-green depths, so he closed the gap and brushed a soft, gentle kiss against her rosy lips.

Although he yearned for more, he lifted his head just far enough to see her beloved face. "Lynn?"

Her eyelids fluttered open, and the smile that blossomed on her countenance was as welcome, and as wondrous, as sunlight at dawn. "Hmmm?" she murmured, cuddling closer.

Delighted by her response, David was more than willing to acquiesce to her unspoken request. He nuzzled his face in her silky hair, shutting out the sight of the teapot. So what if the tea was strong enough to fell an ox? No doubt there were a number of salubrious benefits from drinking it at that strength.

When she stirred in his arms a minute or two later, he smiled down at her and, ever the optimist, asked, "Another?"

"Later" was the surprisingly saucy retort. Then, she rose on her toes and pressed a quick kiss to his cheek. By the time he recovered his wits, and control of his arms and legs, she was sitting at the table, calmly pouring tea.

His heart swelling with love and admiration, David took his seat beside her, vowing to do everything in his power to win Madeline Graves's heart. She had not yet accepted his second proposal—but she had not rejected it, either. It was time to initiate the next step in his campaign to woo and win her. And an ideal time to bring in the heavy artillery. He could only hope that Fortune would favor him, and that the ides of January would prove to be a far more auspicious date for him than the ides of March had been for Julius Caesar.

"Lynn, there is something I would like you to consider."

"Haven't you already given me enough?" she quipped.

Momentarily taken aback, until he realized she was teasing him—or half teasing—he did not respond immediately, although he matched her smile with one of his own. "Perhaps I have, but here is something else for you to ponder. When the roads are clear enough for travel, I would like you to return to Oxfordshire with me, so that you can meet my daughter."

"You want me to meet Isabelle?" The rising tones of the question indicated her surprise.

"Of course I do. When we marry—if we marry," he hastily amended, "you will be her stepmother. I thought you might want to meet her before you accept my proposal."

"I would like to meet Isabelle, but she will play little part, if any, in my decision."

David thought his delightful daughter might well play quite a significant role, but he did not demur. "Then, you will accompany me?'' If she agreed, he would need to hire a post-chaise. One could not ask a lady to ride such a distance. Especially not a lady whose only horse was nearly as old as she was.

"I will consider it."

"In addition to meeting Isabelle, you would also see the house of which you will be mistress."

"Tell me about your home."

"Hmmm." Not knowing if she would find a large house with a full complement of servants intimidating, he chose his words carefully. "Greendale is a manor house like many others. It was built about one hundred fifty years ago, and has been well maintained. The reception rooms, dining room, library, and estate office are on the ground floor, the bedrooms on the second floor, with guest rooms, the schoolroom, and the nursery above. The kitchen is in the basement, and the servants' quarters are in the attics."

"How many bedrooms are there?"

"Eight." *And six guest rooms.* But she had not asked about those and, discretion being the better part of valor, he wasn't going to volunteer the information.

She nodded, apparently unconcerned, so he concluded with an accurate, but decidedly vague, description of the estate itself. "There are six tenant farms, most of which have been worked by the same families for generations, as well as the usual outbuildings."

"Has estate management always been an interest of yours?"

"Yes, ever since I was a boy. My father always viewed my dirt-stained clothes and hands with equanimity and said I would make a good farmer." He smiled in reminiscence. "My aunt, however, was of a different mind."

"I daresay she was." Lynn's grin was as innocent, and as irresistible, as a child's. But he was even more captivated when her amusement bubbled forth in a peal of delighted laughter. "Although I could not have done so when we first met, now I can easily picture you as a grubby, but quite charming, boy."

His lips twitching as he attempted to restrain his laughter, David inclined his head in a bow. "Questionable though it may be, I shall take that as a compliment."

"Perhaps your boyhood . . . exploits are the reason—or a reason—why you enjoy working with the estate's tenants and laborers."

"Undoubtedly so, ma'am."

They smiled in perfect accord, then in unison reached for their teacups. David was delighted when, after a few sips, Lynn resumed her questions about his life. "How long have you been the estate manager at Greendale?"

"Since a few months after I came down from Oxford. More than five years now."

Judging by the frown that creased her brow, his answer was not the one she expected. "Isn't it unusual for a young man to hold such a position?"

"I don't really know. I suppose most are older, but . . ." He shrugged, seeking an answer that did not involve an explanation of exactly how he'd obtained the "position." He would, of course, tell her of his relationship to Bellingham, but he was hoping to defer that revelation until after she accepted his proposal. Or until he was certain the knowledge would not alarm her. The best answer he could contrive was "An older man would have more experience, but not necessarily a greater aptitude for the work."

"That is true." Her frown eased slightly but did not disappear.

Well, hell! Too late, he realized that his reply begged the very questions he'd been trying to avoid. Stifling a sigh, he marshaled arguments to convince his rather reclusive beloved that, despite his father's title and prominent social position, David Winterbrook was a simple, and rather unsociable, gentleman farmer.

But his worry, and his efforts, were for naught. At least for the moment.

"You were the estate manager at Greendale when you met your wife?" It was half statement, half question.

"Yes, I was." Anticipating her next question, he said, "If you are thinking that it is unusual for an estate manager to take part in the Season's social events, you are quite right. My participation, such as it was—I think I traveled back to Oxfordshire every other week—and the invitations I received were due to my father's position in the government, not to any particular merits of my own."

The frown disappeared as Lynn sipped her tea. To change the subject—and, hopefully, avert any queries about his father—David posed a question of his own. "Did you have a Season?"

"No. I was only seventeen when I eloped with Frank, and not yet formally out in Berkshire society."

The mention of her husband—or the thought of him—darkened Lynn's mood. Such musings were not likely to advance David's cause, so he placed his hand over hers, where it rested on the table, and prepared to bare a bit more of his soul.

"I am not Frank Graves, and marriage to me would be quite different from your life with him."

Surprise—or startlement—etched her features when she looked up at him and essayed a small, rather wobbly smile. "I know that, David. Truly I do."

"You know it, perhaps, but you don't yet believe it."

She appeared much struck by his words, so he pressed his advantage. "I believe in the sanctity of marriage, and I will honor the vows—all the vows—I make to you during the wedding ceremony. I will love you, comfort you, and honor you. I will be faithful to you."

Calling up the memory of his brother's wedding last summer, and the vows George had made to Beth, David continued, "I will care for you in sickness and in health—"

"You have already done that."

"I will love and cherish you always, and endow you with all my worldly goods. And when you give me leave, I will worship you with my body."

A blush tinged her cheeks with color, the rosy hue quite becoming. He hoped his were not as flushed, but the images conjured by his words had elevated his temperature a notch or two. And elevated other things, too.

Her eyes darted around the room, finally settling on the hand fisted in her lap. "What if I cannot?"

The muttered phrase was barely audible. Although he did not know if she'd intended to utter it, or if she was aware that she had, David would not—could not—ignore it. The question obviously troubled her greatly, since this was the second time she had raised it.

"Lynn." He waited until she met his gaze. "When I

kissed you earlier, and held you, I was worshiping you with my body. If that is all the intimacy you are ever able to allow me, we will still fulfill our wedding vows."

"Would you be happy with that, David? Could you truly be?"

What he wanted more than anything at this moment was to scoop her onto his lap and kiss away the wrinkle between her eyebrows. But such an aggressive action might well do more harm than good. Instead, he pushed his chair back from the table, patted his lap, and opened his arms. "Come here, sweetheart."

Then he prayed.

Lynn accepted his invitation. Not quite with the alacrity he hoped, but with gratifying swiftness. When she was comfortably ensconced on his lap and the tiny crease between her brows had disappeared, he was ready to answer her question.

"I could be happy with kisses and embraces. I hope that, in time, there will be more—and there will be, I think— but I could live very happily with only your kisses and embraces. They are rare, new pleasures for me."

Her eyes widened, and she leaned back to look at his face. "David, have you ever . . . lain with a woman?"

In an attempt to avoid answering her question, he reminded her, "I shared your bed the night your fever broke—"

"That isn't what I meant." She shot a disgruntled look at him before rephrasing her query. "Have you ever . . . um, known a woman in the biblical sense?"

This was soul baring, indeed! Had he not been holding Lynn, he would be squirming in his seat. "Yes, but not for many years."

"How many years?"

"Eight."

He felt her start of surprise, but he did not know if it was because he had been faithful to a wife who'd cuckolded him before they were wed or because he had been celibate for so long. Or both.

"Not since you were at university," she mused. "That is quite unusual for a man your age, is it not?"

"I don't really know how common or uncommon it is."

"When my brothers were that age, they bragged of their

conquests. Not to me," she clarified, no doubt in response to his appalled expression, "but to their cronies."

"Young men's boasts are often exaggerations, although they may contain a grain of truth."

"That is probably true." Grinning, she added, "I suppose it is a bit like the fish that was four inches long when it escaped Nick's line at the creek, but grew to a foot in length by the time he reached the house."

David laughed, as much at her story as at its unintentional analogy to another size of which men were wont to boast. When his chuckles subsided, he pointed out what was, to him, a very important distinction. "You said your brothers bragged of their conquests. For some men intimate relations between men and women may well be a series of conquests, but I cannot . . ."

He gathered his rather tangled thoughts and again tried to explain. "As a young man, I found physical intimacy without love to be . . . unsatisfying. Not physically, but emotionally. In all the years since, I have never been able to imagine being intimate with a woman I did not love. How can one bare one's heart, soul, and body to another without love and trust and commitment?"

Involuntarily, he shuddered. "Intimacy without love and trust would be like being forced to walk naked down Bond Street at noon. Or in Hyde Park at the fashionable hour."

"Unthinkable."

"Yes."

Lynn looped her arms around his waist and snuggled against his chest. He hoped that, having heard his disclosures, she could now believe his promise that they would not consummate their marriage until she was ready. But even if she had not yet reached that level of trust, David could not help but believe that the kisses and embraces they had shared this afternoon were an indication that she would eventually accept his proposal and make him the happiest of men.

They sat for a time in contented and companionable silence. Just as he was wondering if she had fallen asleep, she stirred and said, "When you said that I would have to teach you how to be a husband, I didn't realize that you meant it almost literally."

"Does it seem such a daunting task?" he teased.

"No." She sat upright, a smile curving her mouth and lighting her eyes. "I think I might enjoy it."

"I daresay we both will." He wiggled his eyebrows in his best attempt at a leer, then brushed a kiss against her laughing mouth.

After dinner, while David lit candles and the fire in the parlor, Lynn looked around the room, wondering how it appeared through his eyes. The sideboard and tables were polished to a shine, and although the blue-striped silk was a bit worn in spots on the arms of the wing chair in which she sat every evening, the fabric on its mate, which was still in her bedchamber, and on the camelback sofa looked as fresh as the day they had been re-covered. Picking up her sewing basket, she carried it to the sofa, wondering if David would sit with her or choose the wing chair across from her.

She felt as giddy as a schoolgirl in the throes of her first crush. And she was not at all certain she liked the trembly feeling.

David Winterbrook had blown into her life like a strong north wind, altering her opinion of gentlemen, causing her to question her resolve never to remarry, and initiating heaven only knows how many other changes. From him, she had learnt the pleasure of a man's touch, the comfort to be found in an embrace, and the delicious, delirious joy of a kiss. In his arms, she felt safe and protected and cherished . . .

And loved.

While she had no objection to being loved—there had been too little of that emotion in her life—she was not nearly as comfortable being the one who loved. Loving was a risk. When you loved, you gave someone the power to hurt you. And she had been hurt too often, and too deeply, in the past to want to risk her heart—and herself—again.

Not that she had much choice.

She loved David Winterbrook. There was no doubt in Lynn's mind, or her heart, about that. And she believed that he loved her. The question was whether or not she could trust his love. Whether or not she could trust him.

"A penny for your thoughts, my dear."

She started at the sound of his voice. She'd been so lost

in her musings that she had not realized that he'd crossed the room and seated himself beside her. "I have already taken a penny from you this week for thoughts that weren't worth the price."

"It was last week, and I received my money's worth."

He had paid her, too. There had been a shiny copper penny on her nightstand the next morning.

"I can afford a penny a week, sweetheart."

"Are you certain?" Flirting with him was much easier than attempting to explain her thoughts.

"Absolutely. A penny a week is only four shillings, four pence a year. Or a guinea and eight pence every five years, if you prefer a larger payment."

Curious, she stared at him. "Do you pay a number of people for their thoughts?"

"Only you, my love." He lifted her hand to his lips and kissed her fingertips. "Why do you ask?"

"How did you know the cost for five years?"

"I calculated it."

"In your head?" she gasped, incredulous.

"Of course."

"There is no 'of course' about it, dear sir. Most people would require a pencil and paper and considerably more time to figure the cost."

He shrugged. "My father is quite the mathematician. One of the founders of the Royal Mathematical Society, in fact. And George is one of its leading lights. Father played all sorts of numerical games with us when we were growing up, and most involved calculating things in your head as quickly and accurately as possible. George is much faster than I am. Maybe even faster than Father. But"—his grin was wicked—"Beth can calculate circles around them both."

His voice dropped to a conspiratorial whisper. "Beth calculates square roots in her head."

Lynn did not even know what a square root was. And fearing that she was in waters far above her head, she wasn't sure she wanted to know. But some response was required, so she said, rather weakly, "Does she really?"

"She does indeed."

"Do you do a lot of those sorts of calculations?"

"No." His smile was as cheerful as a schoolboy's on holiday. "Since leaving Oxford, I haven't done anything more strenuous than tally the estate and household accounts."

Relieved—accounts were quite unexceptional—Lynn smiled. Perhaps she was not in too deep, after all. She did, however, wonder how she would fare if ever she met the formidable Beth Winterbrook.

"Now, my darling Lynn"—David turned her hand and placed a penny in her palm—"about those thoughts?" Then, putting his arm around her shoulders, he drew her against his side.

Thoughts? Surely he did not expect her to think whilst he was kissing her temple and her eyelid and her cheekbone and . . .

"Lynn?"

She opened her eyes and found him peering intently at her, his handsome features unusually solemn. "Is something wrong?" Lifting her hand to his cheek, she felt the gentle prick of emerging whiskers and rubbed her palm against them, enjoying the little tingles that radiated to her fingertips.

"I was about to ask you that question." He covered her hand with his, then turned his head and kissed her palm.

Now her whole arm was tingling! She laid her head on his shoulder and tried to remember what he'd asked. "You asked about my thoughts, didn't you?"

"I did."

"I was thinking about love and trust."

"Very important considerations for people contemplating marriage."

"Indeed they are."

A few moments later he prompted, "Did you reach any conclusions?"

Had she? "No. Not really."

She did not hear him sigh, but his chest rose and fell a bit more deeply than usual. "I hope you will tell me when you do."

"I will."

"Good." He kissed the top of her head, then asked, "If you could have anything in the world, or do anything, what would you want most?"

"I . . . I don't know. I would have to think about it."

"Fair enough. When you decide, I would like to hear the answer."

She looped her arm around his waist and cuddled against him while she considered. The next thing she knew, he was scooping her up in his arms and carrying her down the hall.

"Time for bed, my darling. You are more than half asleep already."

After laying her down gently on her bed, he removed her shoes, covered her with a quilt, then bent over and kissed her. Twice. "Good night, sweetheart."

"Good night, David."

In the instant between consciousness and sleep, Lynn realized that she knew the answer to his question. What she wanted most in the world was David Winterbrook. But she still was not sure if she could have him.

Chapter Fourteen

*O*n Monday, January the seventeenth, a fortnight after David's arrival at Lynn's cottage, the temperature still had not warmed enough to melt the snow. It was as deep as ever, and now seemed permanently frozen in the drifts and mounds into which the wind had blown it shortly after it fell. Even so, he saddled his horse and attempted to ride, but he did not even reach the end of the drive before the horse foundered. Fearing injury to the animal, and possibly himself, if he persisted, David turned back with some reluctance. He did not want to leave Lynn, but he wished the roads were clear enough that they could travel to Greendale Manor. He missed Isabelle sorely. And he knew that she and Aunt Caro must be worrying about him.

When he entered the cottage, Lynn met him just inside the door. "I know you are disappointed, David, but perhaps it will turn warm tomorrow and the snow will melt."

He doffed his greatcoat, hat, and gloves, then stood in front of the kitchen fire, warming himself while she prepared luncheon. "I would like to think so, but at the moment, I feel like a little boy who wakes up on Christmas morning and finds his stocking empty."

As he sought to temper his frustration and disappointment, he was unaware of Lynn's movements until her arms slipped around his waist from behind and she rested her head against his back. Turning so he could embrace her, too, he rubbed his jaw against her silky hair. "You will travel with me to Oxfordshire when the roads are clear, won't you, sweetheart? I can no longer imagine my life without you in it."

"Yes, I will come." She turned her head and kissed his cheek. "I . . . I want to share your life, if I can."

"You can," he murmured, pressing a row of kisses along her jaw from ear to chin. "You can, and you will." He caressed her rosy lips with his, the soft, sweet kiss a declaration—and promise—of love.

On Tuesday, it snowed again. Not the heavy blizzard of two weeks past, but far more than a few flakes. Although it was impossible to distinguish the new from the old, by the time the skies cleared on Friday, David judged the snow on the path between the cottage and the stable to be six to eight inches deeper. And the weather turned cold again, ruling out the possibility of an immediate thaw.

The following week, on Wednesday, January the twenty-sixth, the temperature rose above freezing for the first time since David's arrival at the cottage. The snow melted a bit during the day, but froze again at night—a pattern that repeated daily until Sunday, February the sixth, when the weather finally began to warm.

That night, cozily ensconced on the parlor sofa with Lynn beside him, David proposed a plan to which he hoped, quite fervently, she would consent. Although she had agreed, more than a fortnight ago, to accompany him home, they had not discussed the matter since. Nor had she explicitly accepted his proposal. He had taken her softly expressed wish "to share his life if she could" as a sign that she would, in time, agree to marry him, but he was becoming increasingly anxious to hear a more definite—or, rather, a more binding—promise.

"Sweetheart, if the weather continues warm for the next few days, and I think this time it really will, I suggest we leave here Wednesday or Thursday morning and travel to your father's home. I am hoping that, after we inform him of our plans, he will loan us one of his carriages to take us to Tidmarsh, where I can hire a post-chaise. From there, we will leave the next day for Greendale Manor."

"Father may offer a carriage to take us all the way to your home."

"He might," David conceded, without any expectation of such an outcome, "but a post-chaise would be easier, if not quite as commodious."

"Why would a post-chaise—? Oh, because you would not have to worry about returning Father's carriage?"

"Yes." Not to mention that he wouldn't be beholden to the squire.

"How long will it take to travel from Tidmarsh to your home?"

"That will depend upon the state of the roads. If they are clear, we should be able to make the journey in one day."

"I hope they are. I know you are eager to see your daughter. Have you ever been parted from her for so long a time?"

As a tribute to Lynn's concern for a child she had never met, David raised their clasped hands to his lips and kissed the back of her slender hand. "The only other time we have been apart for more than a day was last year when she was kidnapped. She was taken on the eighth of February, and I did not see her again until the ninth of March— twenty-nine days later. This separation has been longer. I left on New Year's Day for what was supposed to be a two-day visit, and it will be at least Thursday before I see her. That is forty days. Possibly one or two more."

"Oh, David. I am sorry—"

"Hush, my love. None of this is your fault." He silenced her with a kiss. Several of them, in fact. And was more pleased than he could say when, for the first time, her lips clung to his.

Given the exhilaration in his heart and the pounding of his pulse, he had to rack his brain to remember what else he'd intended to say. "Since we will overnight at the inn in Tidmarsh, and it is possible that we will have to spend another night on the road, do you have a friend in the village who would accompany you? Or, perhaps, a maid from your father's house?"

"I daresay one of the maids would go."

With a gentle forefinger under her chin, he tipped Lynn's face up to his. "When we tell your father our plans, will I be able to say that you have made me the happiest of men?"

She looked so adorably confused that he dropped a kiss on her nose, then clarified, "Will I be able to tell him that you have agreed to marry me?"

Lynn studied his beloved features one by one, from the

lock of sandy hair that fell over his noble brow to his sky blue eyes to the blade-straight, rather patrician nose that bisected his face to the singularly sweet smile curving his wonderfully kissable lips. "Do you remember, a few weeks ago, asking me what I wanted most in the world?"

"Yes, I do."

Not certain if she could look into his eyes and complete her answer, she dropped her gaze and studied the tiny dimple in his chin. "And are you still willing to give me time before . . . before—"

"Before making you my wife in truth as well as in name?" he supplied, as always helpful and considerate. "Yes, my love, I am. You shall have as much time as you want. Or need."

Although she had not expected that he would have changed his mind, she was not absolutely certain of him—and of her answer—until he repeated his promise that they would not consummate their marriage until she was ready. She still did not know if she would ever again be able to offer her body to a man, but if she could, it would be to—and because of—David Winterbrook. The man she loved with all her heart.

She took a deep breath. "Then what I want more than anything in the world is to marry you and share your life."

His joyful whoop completely drowned the little squeal of surprise that escaped her when he scooped her onto his lap and squeezed her breathless. "Thank you, my darling. Thank you. I am surely the happiest man in England tonight."

Lynn was quite happy herself. How could she not be when he seemed intent on covering every inch of her face with kisses? But there was something else she wanted—or, perhaps, needed—to say. "You have made me very happy, too, and given me hope that I might yet fulfill my girlhood dreams. I love you, David Winterbrook."

The next two days were busy ones, and Lynn's emotions ran the gamut from joyful anticipation of the future to despair that she would not be ready to leave on Wednesday. There were all sorts of decisions to be made, too—some extraordinary and exciting, others quite mundane. Although she was accustomed to doing things for herself, and making her own choices and arrangements, Lynn found it extremely helpful, as well as vastly comforting, to be able to discuss her conclusions with David. She had come to value his judgment, and the calm manner in which he listened to her opinions, then suggested possibilities she had not considered, raised him even higher in her esteem. Quite often, they sat at the table for an hour or more after a meal while she debated her options. And there were some decisions she was quite content to leave to him.

"David, I need to know how long my visit to your home will be, so I know what—and how much—to pack."

The smile he gave her seemed just the tiniest bit wicked, and quite took her breath away. "Sweetheart, my choice would be for you to stay at Greendale Manor until the wedding. Speaking of which, do you want to be married here or in Greenfield?"

"Greenfield?"

"Greenfield is the town just south of the manor."

"So Oxfordshire has green dales and green fields?" she teased as she considered her answer.

"Aye. Not to mention ladies who will be green-eyed with envy when they met the shire's newest resident."

She rolled her eyes at his foolishness. "I imagine you would prefer the wedding to be in Greenfield?"

"Yes, I would, but it is not my decision to make."

"Why not?" Confused, she frowned, wondering if she had missed—or misunderstood—part of their conversation.

"Because, my darling"—he reached over, scooped her into his arms, and sat her on his lap, then kissed her puckered brow—"you are the bride."

"What does the bridegroom decide?"

"Any number of things, the most obvious being where we will live and what kind of ring to buy my beautiful bride."

"What kind of ring are you going to give your bride?" Lynn had discovered, much to her surprise, that she enjoyed flirting with him.

"I haven't decided yet. Do you have any suggestions?"

"No." Actually, she did have an idea. Not at all certain she could voice it without sounding like a ninny, she buried her face against his neck. "Well, perhaps."

"Are you going to share it—or them—with me?" She could hear the smile in his voice.

"One with a blue stone the color of your eyes."

"My eyes?" He reared back, trying to see her face, but she wrapped her arm around his neck and burrowed deeper beneath his chin. His hand moved from her hip and stroked up and down her back. After a minute or so, he asked, clearly puzzled, "Why would you want a ring with a stone the color of my eyes?"

"So I can look at it during the day when you are out on the estate and . . ."

"And?"

"And find comfort in the color," she whispered.

His arms wrapped around her tightly, hugging her closer to his chest, and he swallowed, hard. "Ah, my love," he murmured, his voice hoarse with emotion. "If that is what you want, I will do my best to find one."

They sat in silence for several minutes. Lynn pondered David's suggestion that she stay at his home until the wedding, as well as the question of where they should marry. He seemed content merely to rub his chin against her hair. When several additional, related questions occurred to her, she, with some reluctance, raised her head from its comfortable resting place on David's shoulder to ask his opinion.

"What should we do with the cottage?"

"Do with it?" His tone, as well as his arching eyebrow, made it clear that he did not understand her query.

"If I am going to stay at Greendale Manor until the wedding, then I will not live here again. That is, after we leave tomorrow, I won't live here. I need to find an estate agent to sell it."

"Are you sure you want to sell it, sweetheart? You could lease it instead. Or hire a caretaker to look after it." He smiled and kissed her cheek, then the spot under her ear that always made her shiver. "We might want to come here from time to time—to remember, or relive, our unusual courtship. Preferably," he added wryly, "without all the snow."

"It wouldn't be the same without the snow."

"Possibly not, but I am certain it would be just as wonderful." When he said things like that, and smiled at her just so, her heart melted. "You need not decide what to do about the cottage now. Besides, if you decide to have the wedding at the church in Tidmarsh, you may well spend another night or two under this roof. Or at your father's home."

"I would much rather stay here."

His eyes widened slightly at her emphatic declaration, but all he said was, "In that case, perhaps your father can suggest someone to serve as caretaker."

She nodded her agreement before launching her next series of questions. "When do you think we should be married?"

"I would marry you today if I could, my love. But since that isn't possible, my choice would be as soon after the banns are called as possible. I am hoping that when we are in Tidmarsh, we can meet with the vicar, so he can begin calling the banns on Sunday. After we arrive in Oxfordshire, we will meet with the vicar there, so he can call them, too."

"Must we decide where to have the wedding before meeting with the vicar?" She was hoping to see the church in Greenfield before making her decision.

"I don't know, but I wouldn't think so. The banns must be called in both parishes, so I imagine we can decide anytime in the next three weeks."

"Did you marry Marie in the church at Greenfield?"

He looked askance at her, no doubt surprised by the question, but answered readily. "No. We were married by special license in the drawing room of her father's London townhouse."

Rather diffidently, she explained the reason for her query. "I think it would be nice if this wedding was different from our previous one."

"I agree, sweetheart." If his kiss was any indication, David thought her idea was an excellent one. "Since our marriage will be very different from our first ones, our wedding should be, too."

Since she and Frank had eloped, Lynn had never planned a wedding. And she wanted this one to be perfect in every detail. "Do you think your aunt would be willing to help me with the wedding preparations?"

"I am certain Aunt Caro would be delighted to help. Beth, too."

"Beth?" Lynn did not think she and the mathematical Beth Winterbrook would have anything in common. Well, nothing but their love for Winterbrook men.

"My sister-in-law."

She shot him a disgruntled look and said, rather indignantly, "I know who Beth is—"

He laughed. "I realize that now, after being skewered by that bolt of pique from your beautiful hazel eyes. What I don't know is why you questioned Beth's willingness to assist you in planning our wedding. Since she and George were married less than a year ago, her experience is much more recent than Aunt Caro's. And Beth has a better memory for details than my aunt."

"But I thought your brother and his wife lived in Dorsetshire. Or Devonshire." It was one of the southwestern counties, but she did not remember which one.

"They live in Dorsetshire, but they were planning to go to London for the first month or so of the Season. And I know they would deem our wedding far more exciting than the most extravagant *ton* ball."

That brought to mind a new line of equally worrisome questions, but Lynn decided to defer them until later.

"Sweetheart, what about your stepmother? Won't she want to help plan the wedding?"

Lynn shrugged. "She may. But she and I have never been close. I would much rather ask your aunt. Or your sister-in-law."

"I am certain both Caro and Beth would be delighted to help."

A few moments later, Lynn realized that one of her most pressing concerns when she arrived in Oxfordshire would be finding a seamstress to make her some new clothes. She absolutely refused to marry David Winterbrook wearing one of her old gowns.

By Tuesday evening, Lynn's clothing was packed in her trunk, with her nightrail, her hairbrush and other toiletries, and a few changes of clothing in a portmanteau. Her furniture and other belongings would remain here for now. If

she decided she wanted or needed them at Greendale
Manor, they could be sent later, by carter.

David's lack of clothing was—and had been throughout
his stay—a source of concern to him, but there was no help
for it. She had washed his shirt, cravat, and linen, and had
brushed and cleaned his coat and riding breeches as best
she could, but she knew he must be heartily sick of wearing
the same clothes day after day. Her efforts ensured that he
would be presentable for their meetings tomorrow with her
father and the vicar, but David was worried that both men
would be offended by his informal attire.

With a weary sigh, she sank down on the parlor sofa.
David's arm immediately came around her shoulders, pulling her against his side, then guiding her head to rest on
his shoulder. They sat in silence for several minutes, content just to be together. But, still troubled by a number
of questions, Lynn eventually stirred and voiced the least
pressing of her concerns.

"Is there a lot of socializing in Greenfield?"

He shrugged. "A fair amount, I suppose. Perhaps I am
a bit of a recluse, but I decided years ago that one social
event a week was sufficient entertainment. I much prefer
to spend my evenings with Isabelle or, when his schedule
permits, with my good friend Dr. MacNeill."

One was good. Very good. Lynn's relief was so great that
she was, for a moment, unable to speak. She had worried
that there would be parties and such most nights of the
week—all of which would require her to converse with
strangers. Probably large groups of strangers.

"We may have to attend more than that for a while," her
husband-to-be blithely continued, unaware of her distress at
the unwelcome news he conveyed. "There are certain to
be parties given to celebrate our engagement, but once we
get through those, we will choose—together—which events
to attend."

*Ah, perhaps he was more aware than I gave him credit
for being.*

He turned his head and pressed a kiss against her temple.
"It may not be as bad as you fear, sweetheart. If the parties
are to celebrate our engagement, then I will be constantly
by your side, and I will be able to answer any questions
you have difficulty hearing."

She had not given him nearly enough credit. Shamed—she really did know better—she raised her head from its cozy resting place and kissed him. "Thank you, David."

Her murmured words halted him momentarily, and his usually smooth motion to lift her onto his lap splintered into two distinct movements. Once she was settled to their mutual satisfaction, he arched a brow and inquired, "For what?"

"For being the wonderful man you are."

"Could you be a bit more specific?" A grin twitched the corners of his mouth as he added, "If I know exactly what I did to earn that kiss, I can endeavor to repeat it. Frequently."

Feeling the hot flush of color in her cheeks, she tucked her head under his chin. "You realized that social events are difficult for me, especially among strangers. Or people I don't know well."

"I believe you told me that." Then, in a slightly teasing tone, "Alas, that particular realization will not garner me many kisses. Have you no dragons for your gallant knight to slay, Fair Maiden?"

She shook her head, smiling at his foolishness. "No dragons today, Sir Knight. I do, however, have a number of questions for which I seek answers."

"Ah, a questions quest. I will do my humble best to provide the answers you seek, my lady."

"David—"

"It is customary for a lady to bestow a favor upon a knight before he begins a quest."

"Unfortunately"—she sighed with mock regret—"I am not wearing any ribbons today."

"They make rather paltry favors anyway."

"Do they really?" She smiled, well aware of the "favor" for which he was angling. "What would you suggest in lieu of a ribbon, Sir Knight?"

"Hmm . . . Perhaps a kiss?"

Feigning surprise, she lifted her head and stared at him. "A kiss in lieu of a ribbon?"

"Yes."

"But a kiss is not tangible. You cannot tie it on your lance or your arm like you could a ribbon."

"That is true, my lady, but a kiss will inspire my dreams."

Lynn opened her eyes wide and lifted her brows in what she hoped was a skeptical expression. After a moment she said, as if unconvinced, "If you are certain . . ."

"Absolutely certain, my lady."

"In that case . . ." She framed his face with her hands and brushed a light, quick kiss against his smiling mouth.

"Trifling, madam," he muttered. Then his lips captured hers, caressing them with a series of light, sweet kisses.

"Oh my." Tingling from head to toe, she leaned back against his arm. "A kiss can, indeed, inspire dreams."

"Yes." Mischievousness replaced the tender expression in his eyes. "Kisses are also an excellent reward for a knight who successfully completes a quest."

"I will keep that in mind."

Serious again, he asked, "You have some questions, sweetheart?"

What were the questions? "David, what if your aunt and Isabelle don't like me?"

His shout of laughter greatly decreased his chance of being rewarded with a kiss. After a few moments, perhaps realizing she did not share his mirth, he tilted her face up to his. "I do not believe there is the slightest chance of that happening. You are a kind-hearted, generous, intelligent woman. Sweet natured and even tempered. You are a good conversationalist, and an even better listener. How could they possibly not like you?"

"But—"

"But if for some bizarre, inconceivable reason they don't, we will deal with it. Together."

"I cannot imagine what your aunt will think when you arrive home with me in tow. Especially when you tell her you are going to marry me."

After a slight hesitation, either to consider his aunt's likely reaction or to find a tactful response, he said, "When she learns that I stayed here with you, I suppose it is possible that Aunt Caro will wonder if compromising circumstances prompted my proposal. If that proves to be the case, I shall quickly disabuse her of the notion."

Hearing her fear voiced made it seem more real, somehow. But even so, Lynn mustered a smile for the man she loved. "Shall you, indeed? I cannot help but wonder how you intend to do that."

"By telling her why I accompanied you home."

"I don't believe a mud-splattered greatcoat, even one as filthy as yours was, is a compelling argument."

He smiled and dropped a kiss on her nose. "My muddy coat was the reason for your invitation, but not for my acceptance of it."

"No? Then why did you agree?"

"Because the moment I saw you, I knew that you were the lady I would love for the rest of my life."

A thrill shivered down her spine at his words. "Your aunt will dismiss that as melodramatic nonsense."

"No, she won't." There was not a trace of uncertainty in his voice.

Cupping his cheek in her hand, Lynn smiled into his eyes. "If I don't believe it, dear one, why would she?"

"You should believe it, it is quite true. Caro will believe it because it is part of the tradition."

"The tradition about the members of your family marrying for love?"

"Yes. Winterbrooks, with the obvious exception of my marriage to Marie, marry for love. And they have all claimed to know their loves at first sight. Well, all except George"—he smiled in reminiscence—"who was so exhausted when hit by his thunderbolt that he didn't realize its significance until months later."

"You felt a thunderbolt when you first saw me?" Lynn could hardly believe that she was asking such a question.

"No, not a thunderbolt. It was more like a shiver up my spine. Not like a cold shiver—it was a different, deeper feeling."

Her expression must have reflected her skepticism, for he continued his earnest, rather impassioned explanation. "As I walked toward you on the road, you had your back to me. When I spoke to you and you turned so that I could see your face, I felt the shiver, and I *knew*, absolutely and with utter certainty, that you were the lady I would love for the rest of my life. The other half of my heart and soul."

Lynn's pulse accelerated at his description, or because of the love shining from his eyes, but she was greatly discomfited by the thought that Fate might have played a role—any role—in his decision.

"Do you think I am a sensible man?"

"Yes, of course I do."

"Given what you know about my first marriage, do you think I would let a tradition, or anything else, lead me into another unhappy union?"

"No, I don't." After a slight hesitation, she added, "It amazes me that anyone who was unhappily married even considers marrying again."

"Even us?" A bit of amusement sparkled his sky blue eyes.

"Especially us. Me more than you."

"You haven't changed your mind, have you?" David's anxiety was almost palpable.

Lynn cupped his jaw, rubbing her thumb back and forth across his lips. "No, dear one. I have had second thoughts—and third and tenth and fiftieth thoughts—but I have not changed my mind. I love you, and I want to share your life."

Then she leaned forward and replaced her thumb with her lips. "Thank you, O Gallant Knight, for successfully completing your quest."

Chivalrous knights were resourceful gentlemen with much to recommend them. And rewarding them had rewards of its own.

Chapter Fifteen

Wednesday morning shortly after nine o'clock, David and Lynn departed from the snug little cottage in her gig, with his mount trailing behind. He hoped the ancient conveyance and its equally aged horse would withstand the journey to the squire's home, but never before had a trip of five miles seemed such a long and arduous prospect. The *plink, plink, plink* of melting snow dripping from tree branches and hedgerows formed a pleasing counterpoint to the plodding of the old mare's hooves, and harmonized with the joyful melody singing in David's heart. The road, although snow-packed, was not as icy as he had feared, and while they set no speed record, they completed the journey without mishap, arriving at Beechwood Grange about half past eleven.

David halted the gig in front of the house, then jumped down and turned to assist Lynn. Before her feet touched the ground, a groom stood at the mare's head and an elderly retainer opened the front door and peeked out at the visitors.

Lynn greeted both men by name. The butler stepped out onto the porch, his face lit by a smile. "Miss Maddie, it has been much too long since you were here."

"It has, indeed, Hatcher, but the weather made travel impossible. If you recall, you predicted that snow when last I was here."

"Aye, miss, I remember. Several days of wet, heavy snow, I said. And I was right."

"Couldn't you have warned me about the cold to follow?" she teased.

"I wish I could have, miss." The old man's sigh clearly indicated that he felt he had failed her.

"We are here to see my father."

"I believe he is in the book room." With the familiarity of an old retainer, the butler arched an eyebrow at Lynn—a subtle reminder that he was not acquainted with her companion.

She, however, did not appease his curiosity. Instead, after informing the elderly manservant that he need not announce them, she led David down the hall, knocked on the last door, and, when bidden, entered on his arm.

Squire Henry Patterson rose from behind his desk to greet them. "You are looking much improved, Maddie. I hope you are feeling better?" He motioned toward the chairs in front of his desk, but Lynn led David to a sofa and pulled him down beside her.

Her father had little choice but to follow, and seated himself on an armchair opposite the sofa. "Are you in need of more food, daughter? You did not have to disturb me for that."

Lynn glanced from her parent's face to the account book open on his desk then back. "I am sorry if we *disturbed* you, Father." The squire flushed and blustered, but she gave little credence to his apology. "We came here today—"

Covering her hand with his, David took over the explanation. "We are here today, sir, to inform you that Lynn has agreed to marry me. And also to request a favor."

Patterson studied his daughter's face. "Do you truly want to marry him, child? If not, I daresay that, as a widow, your reputation can withstand a bit of gossip."

She twined her fingers with David's and smiled at her father. "Yes, sir, I want to be David's wife."

The squire leaned back in his chair. "Well, I own I am surprised—I did not think you would ever remarry—but 'tis obvious that you are happy. I wish you well. When will the wedding be?"

"We have not yet set a date, sir," David informed him. "Lynn hasn't met my daughter, so she is going to travel with me to my home in Oxfordshire. There, with my aunt's help, we will make our plans. We do, however, hope to meet with the vicar this afternoon and arrange for him to begin calling the banns on Sunday."

Patterson frowned. "How are you going to plan the wedding if you're in Oxfordshire?"

"We *may*," Lynn emphasized delicately, "decide to have the wedding there. We haven't decided yet. And won't until after I have seen David's parish church."

"But, Maddie, you have attended the church in Tidmarsh since you were a babe!"

"Yes, I have," she agreed. "And I may well choose to be married there. We have not yet decided which location would be best."

The squire was not pleased, but the reason for his displeasure was unclear. It was time to cut to the chase, David decided. "Would you attend the wedding if it were held in Oxfordshire, sir?"

"Of course I would come!" Patterson thundered. "Maddie is my only daughter."

Lynn smiled at her father. He crossed his arms over his chest and scowled. "But how the devil is your stepmother going to arrange a wedding breakfast in Oxfordshire?"

Ah, so that was the problem! David hastened to reassure the squire that his daughter would be properly feted. "If we decide to have the wedding in Oxfordshire, my aunt will make the arrangements for a wedding breakfast. After consulting with your wife, of course."

"Maddie, perhaps you should inform your stepmother of your plans whilst I discuss the settlements with Winterbrook."

Lynn opened her mouth to protest her dismissal, but David was quicker. "If you will give me the name of your man of business, sir, I will have my solicitor contact him. Lynn will have a generous allowance and jointure. My only condition is that if she has a dowry, the money must be placed in a trust for her sole use. Or for our children."

There was a reason, one very important reason, for David's unusual stipulation. Judging from the stunned expression on Patterson's face—and Lynn's—he had achieved his goal. Both were convinced that David Winterbrook was *not* a fortune hunter.

*   *   *

Before luncheon was served, the squire arranged the transfer of Lynn's animals to his own barns and stable, installed a caretaker who met his daughter's approval in her cottage, and volunteered his carriage to convey David and Lynn to Tidmarsh. Lynn also had the squire's housekeeper, Mrs. Baxter, as her chaperone, that venerable lady having volunteered for the role when called upon to suggest which of the maids would be suitable—and then bullied Patterson into agreeing that the household would manage well enough if she were absent for a few days.

By the time David, Lynn, and the redoubtable Mrs. Baxter sat down to supper in a private parlor of Tidmarsh's Duck and Drake Inn, they had accomplished all they'd hoped to achieve that day. David had hired a post-chaise for the morrow, and he and Lynn had met with the vicar and arranged for the banns to be called for the first time on Sunday.

The journey from Tidmarsh to Greenfield Manor was blessed by good weather, moderately clear roads, canny postillions, and a bit of luck. When they turned between the gateposts of Greendale Manor just after three o'clock on Thursday afternoon, Lynn reached out and clasped David's hand tightly.

"Nervous?" he queried just loud enough for her to hear.

"Nervous? Ha!" She huffed out a breath. "I am scared to death."

"There is no reason to be, sweetheart. Isabelle and Aunt Caro aren't going to eat you."

"Not in your presence, they won't," she muttered. "Isabelle probably wouldn't anyway, but I am not so sanguine about your aunt."

David silently vowed not to leave Lynn's side until he was certain his aunt and daughter accepted her. Not just a token "grit your teeth and endure what cannot be changed" acceptance, but a warm, welcoming one. The same sort of friendly "we are delighted to have you as a member of our family" welcome they had given Beth last year.

The post-chaise slowed as they approached the house, then came to a smooth stop just short of the double doors. Two footmen ran down the front steps, and David had no doubt that an equal number of grooms had raced from the stables.

One of the footmen opened the carriage door and lowered the step. "Welcome to Greendale Manor." Then he glanced at the vehicle's occupants, his face lighting in a smile when he saw David. "Welcome home, my lord!"

As he stepped out of the vehicle, David returned the smile and the greeting. "Thank you, James. It is very good to be home." Then he turned to help Lynn and Mrs. Baxter alight.

Word of his return spread like a flash of lightning. By the time his traveling companions were standing on the drive, he heard Isabelle's joyous "Papa! Papa!" David spun around in time to see her headlong dash down the front steps, then he ran toward her, catching her in his arms and hugging her tightly. *Now I am home!* Nuzzling his cheek against the petal-smooth softness of hers, he kissed her. "I love you, Isabelle."

Clinging to him like a limpet, she kissed his cheek again and again. "I love you, Papa." She drew her head back and scolded, "You must never again visit someone when it is snowing. I miss you too much when you are gone."

"I missed you so much, poppet. I would have come home if I could, but the snow made traveling impossible."

"I know, Papa. That is why you must never again go away if it is going to snow!"

Tears sprang to Lynn's eyes as she watched David's reunion with his daughter. *How wonderful it must be to be loved so deeply!* The squire had never demonstrated a fraction of the affection for her that David had just shown his daughter. Lynn knew her father loved her in his own aloof way, but the most telling display of his feelings had been his trip through the snow to bring food to her cottage. Would her life have been different if she'd felt more certain of his affection?

Before she had her emotions under control, David turned to her, still holding his daughter, and extended his hand. "Lynn, I would like to introduce you to my daughter, Isabelle."

Lynn smiled at the little girl. "I am very pleased to make your acquaintance, Isabelle. Your father has told me quite a lot about you, and I have been looking forward to meeting you." The child was a beauty, her curly blond hair and deep blue eyes drawing attention to her delicate features.

"Isabelle, this is Mrs. Graves. She is a very nice lady, and she let me stay at her house when the blizzard made traveling dangerous and I could not come home."

Lynn was subjected to a very thorough scrutiny by the delft blue eyes. "Thank you for taking care of my papa, Mrs. Gwabes."

A bit surprised by the maturity of the child's response and amused by her mispronunciation, Lynn offered the little girl another smile. "You are quite welcome."

David inclined his head toward the house. "Let's go inside before we all catch a chill."

There was a crowd of people in the entry hall, all of whom were calling greetings to David. To Lynn, it sounded remarkably like the biblical Tower of Babel—a horde of people all talking at once, saying things she could not understand. The drone of voices was quite loud, rather like the buzzing of a huge swarm of bees. For the most part, individual voices were indistinguishable, although she grasped words or phrases here and there. And those she did comprehend convinced her that this was the rudest, most blasphemous group of people she had ever encountered. Every comment she heard began "Lord, David."

Several minutes passed before the prattling finally ceased. David thanked them for their effusive welcome, introduced her simply as "Mrs. Graves, who will be staying with us for a time," then set Isabelle on her feet and helped Lynn remove her cloak before doffing his hat, gloves, and greatcoat. Mrs. Baxter was introduced to Greendale's housekeeper, Mrs. Finch, who promised to show her about as soon as a tea tray was sent to the drawing room. With a smile of thanks, David dismissed the throng, picked up his daughter and hugged her again, then turned to Lynn and silently offered his crooked arm.

As they moved toward the stairs, a figure approached from the back of the hall. Lynn discovered that she was, once again, being thoroughly scrutinized. The woman studying her so intently was undoubtedly David's Aunt Caro, although she was much younger than Lynn had expected.

The lady's identity was confirmed a moment later when David leaned forward and kissed her cheek. "Good afternoon, Aunt Caro. I cannot, at the moment, offer you a hug or an arm, but if you will lead us up to the drawing room, I will greet you properly there and formally introduce you to my companion."

Ascending the stairs, Lynn studied David's aunt quite as closely as she herself had been inspected. Approximately two inches taller than Lynn's five feet and three inches and almost equally curvaceous, Aunt Caro (Lynn knew no other name for her) was about forty and very lovely, her dark brown hair and chocolate brown eyes a pleasing contrast to her porcelain complexion. Her elegant, rose-colored silk gown was in the first stare of fashion, making Lynn feel extremely dowdy in her unadorned, woolen round gown, even though it was her favorite color—sky blue.

Upon reaching the drawing room, which was furnished in shades of green and gold with a thick, patterned Aubusson carpet underfoot, David lowered his daughter to a seat on a camelback sofa with green brocade cushions. Lynn slipped her hand from his elbow and, since she had not yet been invited to sit, stood near the child. Isabelle, however, had eyes only for her father.

Turning to his aunt, David enveloped her in an embrace. "I have missed you, dear Caro. I hope you and Isabelle were not too worried when I did not return as expected."

"Of course we were, my dear." The affection between aunt and nephew was quite obviously mutual. "We assumed that the snow delayed you, but since we did not know where you were, or with whom, of course we worried. Especially after your coachman returned Tuesday afternoon and told us that you had chosen to ride cross-country. And"—she inspected him from head to toe—"that you had nothing with you but the clothes on your back."

"Yes." David's laugh was rueful. "Next time I take such a jaunt, I will be certain to pack several changes of clothing into a pair of saddlebags." He kissed his aunt's cheek, then stepped back, turning toward Lynn. "As for where I have been staying . . ."

Smiling, he extended his hand and drew her toward them. "Caro, may I present to you Mrs. Graves—Madeline Graves—who has made me the happiest of men by agreeing to be my wife."

He ignored his aunt's gasp of surprise. Or, perhaps, shock. "Lynn, this is my late uncle's wife, Caroline, Lady Richard Winterbrook."

Biting her lip to confine her own startled gasp, Lynn curtsied. "It is a pleasure to meet you, my lady. David has spoken highly, and fondly, of you."

Her mind awhirl as David took her arm and escorted her and his aunt to a seat, Lynn darted a quick, dismayed glance at the man she loved. "Lady Richard" was the proper form of address for the wife of a younger son of a duke or marquess. And if David's uncle was a son of such a high-ranking peer, then his father was also. Perhaps his father *was* the duke or marquess now. Suddenly, the greetings she'd earlier thought rude and blasphemous were revealed as neither. People had not been saying "Lord, David," they had been addressing him by his title—"Lord David." Her knees buckled at the revelation, and Lynn sank down on the green brocade sofa gratefully, but rather gracelessly.

Why didn't he tell me? How could he possibly think me a suitable wife? I could never fit into a family of such exalted rank and social position. She wondered if the marquess who owned this estate was his father or his brother. Not that it mattered . . .

She was jolted from her dizzying spiral of questions and recriminations when David's aunt expostulated, "David, you cannot—"

The look he sent her must have been a quelling one. "We will discuss this later, Aunt Caro," he said, his tone so firm that it brooked no possibility of refusal. He inclined his head toward his daughter, indicating that he did not want her to hear whatever his aunt intended to say.

Thankful for the reprieve, temporary though it would be, Lynn sought her voice—and a neutral topic of conversation. She smiled pleasantly at David's aunt, who was seated in an armchair to her left. "Lady Richard, I saw there was still some snow on the ground. How deep was it initially? Did it make the roads here quite impassable?" Then she prayed, fervently, that she would be able to hear the answer. Or deduce it from the movement of the lady's lips.

"The first snowfall—and it snowed without pause for three days—dropped more than a foot of snow. Isabelle was in alt at first, until she realized her papa would be delayed because travel was impossible."

Since David had ranged himself, his daughter, and Lynn on the sofa, she had to lean forward and peer around him to see the child. "I imagine you were very disappointed when you realized that the snow, which is so much fun to play in, would postpone your papa's homecoming."

The first word of the soft-spoken reply was yes, but Lynn could not hear the rest. Nor could she discern it, since she saw Isabelle in profile.

'Tis best to begin as you mean to go on. The proverb offered good advice, but Lynn did not relish implementing it. Especially since it seemed impossible that she would ever have a future here. But for now, despite her uncertainty, she would act as if nothing had changed. As if her dreams had not been shattered into a million pieces.

It was, she supposed, remotely possible, albeit highly unlikely, that she might have a future with the man she loved. After all, David had known who he was when he proposed, and he knew all of her deficits and limitations. *Had he begun as he meant to go on?* She did not know; they would have to discuss it later. Right now, she must contend with a different, and more immediate, problem.

Slipping from her seat, Lynn knelt in front of Isabelle and launched into an explanation, couching it in simple terms so the child could understand. "Because of an accident several years ago that hurt my ears, I cannot hear very well. I can hear what people say if they are sitting or standing near me, and quite often I can figure out what someone is saying by watching their lips move. Unfortunately, I was a bit too far away to hear you. And since I could only see part of your mouth, I couldn't figure out the words. Would you please tell me again?"

The little girl nodded, then said, a bit louder this time, "I was unhappy when the snow kept Papa from coming home, but I made a snowman and pretended it was Papa."

"That was very clever! You could talk to the snowman just like you would your papa. But the snowman could not answer. I daresay it didn't give hugs or kisses, either."

"No, he didn't." Isabelle tilted her head to the side, a frown creasing her tiny brow. "Do your ears hurt?"

"No, they don't hurt now, but they did when they were

injured. When they got hurt," Lynn amended, not certain a four-year-old would know the meaning of "injured."

"If you say something to me and I don't answer, it is because I did not hear you. You just have to come closer and tell me again." Lynn smiled, hoping that she was encouraging, not frightening, the little girl. "Sometimes I hear a person's voice, but I don't quite hear all their words, so I have to ask them to repeat what they said. Some people get upset or even angry when I do that, but—"

"I won't be angry." It was a child's solemn promise.

"Thank you, Isabelle." Given the ease with which David had acknowledged her hearing deficiency, Lynn was not surprised by his daughter's ready acceptance. *Like father, like daughter.* His aunt's reaction was another matter entirely, especially in light of her shock at his announcement. Although not yet ready to discover how her revelation had affected Lady Richard's opinion, Lynn was given little choice when David stood and offered his hand to assist her to her feet.

He raised her hand to his lips, then leaned over to whisper, "You are a strong, courageous woman, Madeline Graves. I love you, and I am very proud of you."

"And I love you, David Winterbrook. But we need to talk about a number of things, *my lord*." With that softly spoken but pointed rejoinder, she sat down on the sofa again.

"Yes," he agreed, albeit a bit sheepishly, resuming his place beside her.

The arrival of the butler with the tea tray, followed by two maids with plates of sandwiches and cakes, provided a welcome reprieve—and afforded Lynn an opportunity to surreptitiously study David's aunt.

The lady was all politeness as she inquired how Lynn drank her tea, and as she served sandwiches and cakes. With the ease of an experienced hostess, Lady Richard kept the conversation flowing, asking general questions about David's visit to Berkshire and his cross-country attempt to hasten home, then about the journey from Tidmarsh to Oxfordshire. She also gave a concise accounting of all that had occurred at Greendale Manor during his absence. But as soon as Isabelle's nanny appeared and led the little girl up to the nursery—indeed, not two seconds after the draw-

ing room door closed behind them—David's aunt dropped
all pretense of social chit-chat in favor of a pointed, and
remarkably blunt, interrogation.

"Now, David, since you have never mentioned Mrs.
Graves before, I assume your acquaintance with her is a
relatively recent one?"

"Yes, it is." He clasped Lynn's hand in his. "I met—"

"And since you alluded to Mrs. Graves earlier, in regard
to where you were staying, I assume you were stranded in
the same inn?"

"We were staying in the same place, but—"

"You cannot know much about Mrs. Graves after such
a short acquaintance," Lady Richard opined. "Nor under
such unusual conditions. Are you certain that your heart, or
your reason, was not unduly swayed by . . . other factors?"

The assumption was so far from the truth that Lynn did
not know whether to laugh or cry. Or scream. She felt the
increased tension in the muscles of David's arm, but his
voice was as amiable as before. "It was not. My decision—"

"Men often mistake . . . desire for love. Are you certain—"

But even David's seemingly inexhaustible patience had
its limits. "For the love of God, Caro! If you are determined to ask so damned many questions, you ought to listen to the answers. You might even," he added, his voice
edged with sarcasm, "show a modicum of courtesy and
allow me to complete one answer without interruption."

Hot color flushed his aunt's face. Lynn did not know if
Lady Richard was embarrassed by her lapse of manners or
mortified by her nephew's reprimand. After an uncomfortable moment during which both women shifted in their
seats, Lady Richard apologized. "I beg your pardon, David.
And yours, too, Mrs. Graves. If you can overlook my rudeness, I would like to know how and when you met, and
why you decided to marry."

David nodded. "I will attempt an explanation that answers all your questions."

"I promise that I will listen. And not interrupt."

"I met Lynn during my cross-country ride, not long before the snow forced a halt to my journey. I was on a
road—and had been for several miles—in search of an inn.
The road was quite icy, and Lynn's gig had slid into a

ditch. I stopped, of course, and offered my assistance, and between us we got her vehicle back on the road."

"It would be more accurate," Lynn interjected, "to say that David got it back on the road. All I did was guide the horse forward. He climbed down into the ditch and pushed the gig out. The ditch water ruined his boots, and his greatcoat was muddy from collar to hem."

"That it was." David smiled into her eyes and squeezed her hand. "Lynn told me the nearest inn was twelve miles away, but I knew the snow would force me to stop long before that, so I asked who the nearby landowners were, thinking I could beg a night's hospitality. The local squire lived about five miles away, and I thought I could travel that far, but given my mud-splattered appearance, Lynn was quite certain he would turn me away."

"So," Lynn took up the tale, "since David had been kind enough to stop and help me, I sought to return the favor by inviting him to my home, which was nearby, so that he could warm himself with a cup of tea and dry his boots whilst I attempted to clean his greatcoat."

Lady Richard's mouth flattened into a thin line, but she did not interrupt. David ignored her obvious displeasure, as well as the conclusions to which she had all too clearly jumped. "Before we reached her home, the snowstorm grew into a blizzard. The temperature must have dropped, too, because the road became even more treacherously icy. I could not have ridden safely to the end of the drive, much less the five miles to the squire's home, so Lynn had little choice but to extend her invitation to include a meal and a night's lodging."

"Of course," Lynn interposed, "neither of us knew that the storm would be so severe. Nor that it would be weeks until the roads cleared enough for safe travel."

David resumed his narrative, addressing his aunt's next question. "When two people are stranded together, they come to know each other very well. Both good and bad traits quickly become apparent, as do strengths and weaknesses. We had to rely on each other's skills to survive, and once the chores were completed—"

"Chores?" From Lady Richard's tone, one might think she had never heard the word before. "Were there no servants?"

"No, there were not," Lynn answered at the same time

that David said, "Lynn's only servant returned to his family's home before we arrived.

"Once the chores were completed," he continued, "conversations and games of chess or cards were our only entertainment, so we learnt everything worth knowing about each other's life and history."

"Not everything," Lynn muttered.

David smiled an apology and twined his fingers more snugly with hers. "In such isolation, one learns far more about another person than one would in a Season of morning calls, drives in the park, and dances."

"I expect that is true," Lady Richard conceded. "But regardless of how much you have learnt about each other, the long and short of your tale is that you offered for Mrs. Graves because your presence in her home compromised her reputation."

"When, dear Caro, did you develop this deplorable habit of leaping to unsubstantiated conclusions?" The question was obviously rhetorical because David gave his aunt no chance to answer. "The long and the short of the tale is that Lynn and I spoke of marriage several days before my presence in her home was discovered."

"Because you felt honor-bound to propose." It was more statement than question.

"No. Because I knew I loved her, and had fallen in love with her." David's choice of words, as well as the conviction with which he uttered them, rendered the declaration unequivocal.

"But—"

David interrupted his aunt, anticipating her final question. "It was a well-reasoned decision of the heart. Uninfluenced by any other factors."

Lady Richard pursed her lips and attempted, without success, to stare her nephew out of countenance. Then, apparently still unconvinced—or, perhaps, not yet willing to concede defeat—she set her sights on a new target. "And you, Mrs. Graves?" she inquired silkily. "Was your decision to marry David a well-reasoned decision of the heart, uninfluenced by any other factors?"

"It was certainly a decision of the heart. One made after a great deal of thought and discussion. But it was influenced by fewer factors than, perhaps, it ought to have been."

"What does *that* mean?"

David answered his aunt's sharp-voiced question, despite the fact it had not been addressed to him. "What it means, Caro, is that Lynn chose to marry plain David Winterbrook, a man she believed to be nothing more than an estate manager."

"Gammon!"

Stung by the scorn in Lady Richard's voice, Lynn asserted, "It is quite true, my lady. He introduced himself as David Winterbrook—"

"He always does." Lady Richard clearly thought this quirk foolish beyond permission.

"When I addressed him as Mr. Winterbrook, he did not correct me. He told me that he managed an estate for the Marquess of . . ."

"Bellingham," David supplied.

"And our conversation, coupled with the fact that David volunteered to do—nay, insisted upon doing—my absent stable boy's chores, led me to believe he was employed by the marquess. Now, however, I believe the marquess is either his father or his brother."

"My father," David confirmed.

"And when did you realize your error, Mrs. Graves?"

Lynn chose to ignore the insinuating tone; Lady Richard would realize *her* error as soon as Lynn answered. "When David introduced you."

"I don't believe it!"

"Your belief or lack thereof does not alter the truth, my lady." Lynn was rapidly reaching the limits of her patience, but she managed, just barely, to maintain a civil tone.

Remembering their arrival, she turned to David and smiled. "When we were in the entry hall, I could understand very little of what was said. There were too many people talking at once. But from the bits and pieces I heard, many of which began 'Lord David,' I deemed your servants the rudest, most blasphemous group of people I had ever encountered."

After a moment of shared mirth, he sobered. "As Aunt Caro said, I never use my title when I introduce myself. I hate all the fawning and toadying it inevitably evokes. Most people soon become aware of my identity—or, more accurately, my relationship to Bellingham—especially in London. I never know whether they seek my company because they enjoy it or because they hope to gain some advantage. To curry favor with my father or some such thing."

"How horrible for you!"

"You cannot know how delighted I was when you agreed to marry plain David Winterbrook."

"You are not plain," Lynn objected. "You are quite handsome. The most handsome man I have ever met."

A pleased smile lit David's eyes and curved his mouth. "Do you really think so?"

She motioned toward the pier glass above a side table set between two windows. "You don't need me to tell you that. Look in the mirror."

"I wasn't fishing for compliments, sweetheart. It just seems . . . fitting somehow, since you are the most beautiful woman I have ever met. Beautiful inside and out."

She rolled her eyes. "Spanish coin, my lord."

"Indeed it is not."

"Then your vision is faulty." After a moment she laughed, but there was no amusement in it. "What a pair we make! A woman who cannot hear and a man who cannot see what is in front of him."

Slipping her hand from his, she took a deep breath and gathered her courage. "Except that we will not be a pair. I cannot marry you, Lord David."

With that, she stood and strode swiftly from the room, unable to view the devastating destruction that follows in the wake of shattered dreams.

Chapter Sixteen

*F*or a moment David sat as if turned to stone, paralyzed by the shock of Lynn's totally unexpected pronouncement. Then he was on his feet, running after her.

"Lynn!"

His call did not stop, or even slow, her headlong flight. He increased his pace, grabbing her arm just in time to prevent her from tumbling down the stairs.

She flinched at the contact. David swore under his breath.

"Look at me, Lynn," he commanded, stepping in front of her. "Look at me and see that I am David Winterbrook, not Frank Graves." More gently, he continued, "I will never hit you. Never do anything to hurt you. You will always be safe with me, no matter how angry I might become."

She did not look up. Perhaps his words, or the sound of his voice, were sufficient to recall her to her surroundings for she leaned toward him and rested her forehead against his chest.

He wrapped his arms loosely around her, wanting her to feel safe but not confined. Then, for his comfort, he rubbed his jaw against her silky hair. "I have just realized something. A rather important something I ought to have seen before."

"What have you realized?" The words were muffled by his coat as she stepped closer.

"Every time you have said something you think might anger me, you have run from the room. It is instinctive, I think. A behavior learnt during your marriage to protect yourself, but now so ingrained that you do it without conscious thought. You flee to avoid the risk of being hit."

After a beat of silence, Lynn looked up at him. "I daresay you are right." She looped her arms around his waist. "I know that you will not hurt me, David. Truly I do."

"Good." He pressed a kiss to her forehead. "Now, we need to discuss the startling declaration you made just prior to your flight from the drawing room. We can either return there so you will have Caro's presence as protection, or we can discuss it in private."

"Protection?" A frown creased her brow. "Protection against what?"

"My annoyance."

"You don't seem vexed."

"Well, I am." He cupped her chin, tilting her head so he could kiss her. "I love you, Lynn. I am the same man you agreed to marry a few weeks ago. The fact that I have a courtesy title changes nothing."

"As much as I love you, David—and I do—the fact that you have a title changes everything."

"Why? It hasn't changed me."

"No, but it has changed your situation."

"How?" His bewilderment, and rising frustration, echoed in his voice.

"My dears." Both he and Lynn started at the sound of Caro's voice. David looked over his shoulder and saw his aunt standing in the drawing room doorway. "Kiss your fiancée, David, then come in here so we can discuss her concerns. I will ring for more tea."

He grinned down at Lynn, then touched a finger to the crimson flags riding her cheekbones. "I have been instructed to kiss you, my love. And since I believe in following instructions, I shall do just that."

He brushed kisses against her eyelids and cheeks before moving to her mouth. It required a conscious effort to keep the kisses soft and gentle, but he feared that a more passionate demonstration of his love would frighten her. And God knows, she was already skittish enough. He felt amply rewarded for his restraint when her lips clung to his as he raised his head.

"Just let me hold you for a minute, love, then we will

talk." He rested his forehead against hers—and willed his body to calm.

Quite willing to hold and be held by David for far longer than a minute, Lynn cuddled closer. Then froze.

"There is nothing to fear, sweetheart." His hand stroking up and down her back was as soothing, and as calming, as his voice. "I cannot control my body's response to your sweet kisses, but I can and will control my actions."

This is David. Kind, gentle David. Not Frank. "I know. I was just . . . surprised." She brushed a kiss against his mouth as proof of the sincerity of her words.

"Another instinctive reaction, I imagine."

"Yes." She rewarded his perspicacity with another kiss.

He groaned, then captured her lips with his. Several seconds later he broke off the kiss and muttered, "Sweetheart, this is not helping," then rested his forehead against hers again.

Smiling, she nestled deeper in his embrace. "It may not be helping you, but it is doing wonders for me."

His head jerked up as if her words surprised him. "Is it?" When she nodded, he said, rather pensively, "I hadn't considered that lack of action could be a proof of character."

Lifting his hands to her shoulders, he set her away from him. "We will pursue this later. For now, my darling, please go into the drawing room and divert Caro for a few minutes. I will join you as soon as I am . . . presentable."

"Of course I will, if that is what you wish."

"It isn't necessarily what I want, but it is essential all the same." He dropped a kiss on her nose, then turned on his heel and strode down the corridor to the window at its end.

Lynn took a deep breath and let it out slowly, then squared her shoulders for battle with the dragon.

David gazed out the window, but his thoughts were not on the familiar scenery outside. Instead, he was reviewing the merits and disadvantages of an idea triggered by Lynn's surprising statement. Her second surprising statement, to be precise, since she had uttered more than one this afternoon.

So, my darling Lynn, my presence is helpful to you, even when aroused, eh? In that case, I shall be certain you receive

large doses of my company, regardless of my condition. As-
suming, of course, I can convince you that my title does
not make me a whit different from the plain "Mr." David
Winterbrook you agreed to marry.

He smiled. It was a brilliant plan, if he did say so himself.
He would convince her she had nothing to fear from him,
whether they were in a parlor, a kitchen, or a bedchamber.
Despite her instinctive, self-protective behavior, David
knew she was already comfortable with him in the first two
venues. It was the latter that would be the biggest hurdle—
and bestow the greatest rewards.

Making his decision, he slapped his hand against the window frame. *From the day we wed, my darling Lynn, you*
shall share my bedchamber. And when we finally consum-
mate our marriage, I shall do everything in my power to
ensure that you never want to leave my bed.

It was, perhaps, a foolish vow for a man with less experience of intimacy than his bride, but David believed that
love could overcome any obstacle, and he loved Lynn with
all his heart and soul. But to weight the odds in his favor,
he would solicit his brother's help and advice.

Lynn could not have been more surprised when she reentered the drawing room and found the dragonish Lady
Richard had been miraculously transformed into an amiable, concerned woman. One, moreover, who appeared to
genuinely want to help.

"Mrs. Graves, from what you said earlier, I have the
impression that learning David has a title caused you to
rethink your decision to marry him. May I ask why you
think the title changes him?"

"It doesn't change him, ma'am, it changes his
circumstances."

"Perhaps I am particularly obtuse this afternoon, but I
don't understand what you mean. Could you explain a bit
more, please?"

Lynn glanced down at her hands, which were clenched
so tightly together that her knuckles appeared white, and
sought words to clarify her chaotic, and regrettably muddy,
thoughts. "I know I am not a prize on the Marriage Mart—
not that I ever thought of remarrying. I am five-and-twenty,
extremely hard of hearing, and have few social graces. I

might be an acceptable wife for an estate manager, but not for a son of Lord Bellingham. Even I, isolated as I live, have heard of the marquess. He and his family move in the highest circles of Society—a sphere in which I would not fit at all."

"I do not agree that you have few social graces, but we will save that discussion for another time." Lady Richard's smile was kind. "While it is true that Bellingham moves in the highest circles of the *ton*, as does Weymouth—"

"Weymouth?" Lynn had never heard the name. Or title, if that is what it was.

"David's brother, as Bellingham's heir, has the title Earl of Weymouth."

"Oh, of course." She felt remarkably foolish. "David always refers to his brother as George."

"He does," Lady Richard agreed, smiling. "They are a close-knit family, and not at all high in the instep.

"Now, what was I saying?" She tapped a finger against her lip. "Ah, we were talking about social circles as regards the family. While it is true that Bellingham and George are frequently seen at social events in Town, David has always preferred the country. In the eight months I have lived here with him and Isabelle, I don't believe David has attended more than one entertainment in any week. He is quite content to spend his evenings at home, playing games with Isabelle or reading or, occasionally, matching wits over a chessboard with the local physician."

"He told me that, but . . ." Lynn spread her hands, palms upward in supplication. "Does he never go to London? I might be able to make my way in local society without disgracing him and embarrassing myself, but not in Town."

"He went to London for a week or two last year after—" Lady Richard stopped abruptly, looking quite conscious. "Has David told you what happened last year about this time?"

"I know that Isabelle was kidnapped. As was George—Lord Weymouth, I should say. And that they were rescued by the lady who is now his lordship's wife."

"Yes. And thank God they were!" She shivered as if the memory chilled her, then poured them both a cup of tea. "To answer your question, David went to London for a week or two last year whilst awaiting George's and Isabelle's return, but he did not attend any social events. The only other time I can recall that he was in Town for any part of the Season was five years ago."

"The year he met his wife."

"Yes." The look Lady Richard shot her was rife with curiosity. No doubt she wondered how much Lynn knew about David's marriage.

"If David restricts himself to local society—and a limited amount of that—perhaps I can manage well enough . . ."

"David may well want to go to Town for a few weeks this year, so that you can be presented."

"Indeed he will," that gentleman confirmed as he entered the room and crossed to sit beside Lynn. "I want everyone to know what a fortunate fellow I am."

Oh, David! Lynn's soaring hopes turned to anguish, plummeting back to earth and crashing like waves against a rocky shore. Despite her determination not to show her despair, the smile she mustered for him wobbled a bit. "You have just put paid to all your aunt's efforts on your behalf."

"I can't imagine why." He clasped her hand in his, rubbing his thumb across her knuckles and up and down her fingers.

"People will be curious about me, won't they? They will want to know how we met, and once they learn that, they will think you were forced to marry me."

"People will be curious, of course. But I have no intention of revealing the exact circumstances of our meeting. I can, with perfect truth, say that we met during the course of a visit I made to a friend's home to look at some horses he was selling."

"That should serve very well," Lady Richard said.

"Will they not want to know who you were visiting and how we met?" Knowing that the people in Berkshire would ask those questions, Lynn did not believe that Londoners would be less curious.

David shrugged. "Some probably will ask. If they do, I will say I was visiting Bancroft."

"But—"

He anticipated her question. "If anyone is rag-mannered enough to inquire how we met, I can, again truthfully, say that I met you while I was out riding."

"Quite unexceptional. I am certain there must be several members of the *ton* and of local society who met their spouses whilst out riding," Lady Richard commented.

"But if the actual circumstances become known, either before or after we are married, people will think you were forced to wed me." Lynn found it hard to believe that the truth would not become known, even though only a handful of people knew it.

"Sweetheart, you and I know that ours is a love match. Does it really matter what other people think?"

Lynn did not know the answer to David's question. Most of her experience was with regimental society, and the opinions of others held great sway there.

"I cannot claim to be an expert on Oxfordshire society"—Lady Richard's moue clearly indicated that she did not consider acquiring such expertise a worthy goal—"but traveling with my husband to various and sundry Diplomatic Corps postings, I learnt that people are much the same everywhere. They will think whatever they want to think, regardless of what you say or don't say."

"Even if the truth becomes known, my darling, you would likely be lauded as a Good Samaritan."

Lynn thought David's opinion was unrealistically optimistic. Apparently his aunt did, too, because she said, "I am not so certain about that."

"Society embraced Beth when it learnt of her role as a Good Samaritan," David reminded his aunt. "Lynn's invitation was no different."

Lady Richard shook her head. "While I agree that Mrs. Graves rescued you in much the same manner Beth rescued your brother, Society will view the ladies' roles differently. Beth and George conducted their courtship under the *ton*'s watchful eye. And even before that, during their journey from Scotland, Beth had a maid as chaperone. Not to mention the ever-curious Isabelle." She smiled at the thought of her great-niece as a chaperone.

David's chuckle blossomed into a rich, full laugh. "The presence of Isabelle the Inquisitive would put a damper on any impropriety."

After several moments, he looked from one lady to the other. "Since I reentered the room, you have not been playing the roles I expected. I thought Caro would be the doubting one, and Lynn answering her questions."

"If not for your title, that might well have been the case." Lynn, too, had been wondering about Lady Richard's change of heart.

David and Lynn turned as one to look at his aunt, who met their inquiring gazes with a smile. "I confess, I had doubts at first. I feared that David had either been compromised into making an offer or . . . uh, lured into proposing. But now, despite the unconventional nature of your acquaintance, I am absolutely certain that both of you are marrying for love."

Lynn's curiosity was not appeased. "May I ask what changed your mind, my lady?"

"I saw you together in the hallway, and overheard a portion of your conversation."

Although she hoped Lady Richard had not heard everything, Lynn decided she would be happier not knowing exactly what David's aunt had overheard.

He smiled at his relative. "In case you are wondering, Caro, I knew before I accepted Lynn's invitation that she was the lady I would love for the rest of my life, so I was not concerned about the possibility of being compromised."

Lady Richard's eyes widened. "Did you? Oh, how wonderful!"

Lynn found it almost impossible to believe that anyone, much less an entire family, could put such credence in a legend. "My lady, did you know from the first that your husband would be the love of your life?"

"No, my dear, I did not. The phenomenon only affects Winterbrooks. Neither Bellingham's wife nor Lady Matilda's husband knew immediately, either. Nor did Beth— George's wife."

Since she did not believe in the legend's purported power, Lynn knew it was ridiculous to feel relieved that other Winterbrook spouses had not experienced its effects, but foolish or not, she was comforted by the knowledge.

David rose and crossed to the far corner of the room, where glasses and several decanters reposed upon a side table. "Aunt Caro, have we answered all your questions?"

"Yes, I believe you have. No, wait! You have not said when and where the wedding will be."

As one, aunt and nephew turned to Lynn, but it was David who asked, "Is there going to be a wedding, my darling?"

Before Lynn could answer, Lady Richard offered several essential assurances. "I don't believe you will have the slightest difficulty fitting into society here, Lynn. Balls and routs in London may present more of a problem—some are quite noisy—but since David rarely goes to Town, you need not worry overmuch about that."

David returned carrying three glasses of sherry, which he set on the table next to the tea tray, then resumed his seat on the sofa beside Lynn. Locking his gaze with hers, he took her hand, raised it to his lips, and kissed her fingertips. "I love you, Madeline Graves, and I want to share my life with you. Are you going to make me the happiest of men by marrying me and taking on the title of Lady David?"

Love and trust go hand in glove. David trusted her so profoundly that he had already brought the sherry for a celebratory toast, but he loved her enough to reassure her that in this, as in everything, the choice was hers to make. With that realization, Lynn's answer was as clear-cut as the facets of the crystal goblets. "If I can trust you with my heart and my self, then I can trust your certainty that I will fit into, and be accepted by, your family and local society. So, yes, Lord David, I will marry you."

His delighted smile was as bright and as warming as the sun. "You can trust me, my love. Always." He kissed her hand again, more lingeringly than before, and her cheek, quickly. In his eyes she read the promise of more later, when his aunt was not present.

Rising to his feet, he distributed the sherry. Then, with eyes only for Lynn, he raised his glass. "To love and marriage and many, many years of happiness."

A short nap restored Lynn's flagging spirits. The emotional upsets of the afternoon were a compelling argument that a lady should not hastily change her mind. Not until *after* she had carefully analyzed all the facts and thoroughly considered the consequences of her decision. Now, secure in the knowledge of David's love and with dreams of their bright future still dancing in her thoughts, Lynn dressed for dinner. Deciding what to wear was not difficult; she had only one evening gown, a blue watered silk that neither flattered nor flaunted her figure, and which had not been particularly fashionable five years ago when she'd bought it. Time had not improved it in that regard.

As she reached up to place the last hairpin in her coiffure, a knock on the door so startled her that she dropped the pin.

"Come in," she bid, bending to search for it as she held the unpinned lock of hair in place.

"Good evening, my love." Then, clearly amused by her contorted position, David inquired, "What *are* you looking for?"

Picking up the pin, she turned to show it to him—and her breath clogged in her throat. "A hairpin," she choked, jabbing it into place. *Lud, he was even more handsome in evening attire than in the riding clothes he'd worn in Berkshire!*

She glanced away—ostensibly to check her appearance in the mirror, but really to gather her scattered wits. In the glass she saw him push away from the door frame and cross the room to stand beside her.

With a gentle hand on her arm, he turned her to face him. "You look lovely, sweetheart." Circling his arms around her, he pulled her closer and kissed her.

She slid her hands up the lapels of his coat until they encircled his neck. "And you," she informed him between kisses, "are even more handsome than usual. Devastatingly so."

He lifted his head and smiled down at her, one sandy eyebrow rising. "Devastatingly so, you say? You don't appear devastated, my love."

"Dazzling so, then. I am most definitely bedazzled." She tugged him down for another kiss. Or four.

"Not that I would ever object to being the recipient of your kisses, but I did have another reason for coming here."

How unfortunate! Lynn would have been perfectly happy to spend the evening in his arms. "Did you?" She kissed him again, wishing she could cuddle closer but fearing that, if she did, she would wreak havoc on the pristine folds of his starched cravat.

"Hmmm, yes. I want you to accompany me when I tell Isabelle that we are getting married."

"Very well. When do you plan to tell her?"

"Before dinner," he murmured against her neck.

"Now?" Lynn pushed away from his chest just far enough to look up at him.

She caught a glimpse of his slightly wicked grin before he pulled her close again. "Not right at this moment."

All too soon they ascended the stairs to the nursery. When they entered, Isabelle leapt up from the center of a circle of dolls on the carpet and raced toward them. "Papa!"

David crouched down and opened his arms, hugging and kissing his daughter as he straightened. As he held her and listened to her chatter, it was apparent that neither gave a thought to the state of his cravat.

There's a lesson for you, my girl. If David does not worry about his attire, why should you? Lynn smiled at Isabelle's nanny, Mrs. Abbott, a plump, kind-looking woman of about fifty, who motioned her to a wing chair in front of the fire. When David joined them, still holding Isabelle, he suggested that the older woman go down to the kitchen and enjoy a cup of tea. Bestowing a smile upon them all, she departed.

He angled a matching chair toward Lynn's, then sat, settling Isabelle, who was still prattling, on his right thigh so Lynn could see her.

The stream of chatter halted abruptly, and the child's eyes darted from her father's face to Lynn's. "Did I do something bad, Papa?" The girl's lower lip wobbled before she completed the question.

David pressed a kiss to his daughter's forehead, and the arm he'd wrapped loosely around her hugged her close. "No, poppet. Mrs. Graves and I are here to talk about good things."

Instantly, Isabelle brightened and relaxed against her father's supporting arm. "Then tell me." A moment later, remembering her manners, she added, "Please."

David smiled at Lynn, then addressed his daughter. "In the drawing room, you heard me tell Aunt Caro that Mrs. Graves has agreed to be my wife. Do you know what that means?"

A frown pleated Isabelle's forehead for a moment, then her delft blue eyes widened. "Like Uncle George and Aunt Beth, right? Since the wedding, Aunt Beth has been his 'darling wife.' And she lives at his house now."

David nodded. "Exactly so."

"But"—Lynn smiled at the little girl—"I am luckier than your Aunt Beth because, in addition to becoming your father's wife—"

"My darling wife," he corrected.

Lynn darted a fleeting but smiling glance at him, then returned her gaze to Isabelle and continued, "I also will become your stepmother."

The tiny brow creased again in a pensive frown. "What does a stepmother do?"

"A stepmother," David informed his daughter, "does all the things a mother would do. Mrs. Graves will play with you, read stories, give you hugs and kisses, help me tuck you in bed every night, teach you how to embroider lovely samplers, as well as everything else you must know to grow up to be a proper young lady."

"Not like in the stories?" Isabelle looked worriedly from one adult to the other.

"What stories?" Lynn and David asked in unison.

"Like in *Cinderella*?"

Laughing, David hugged his daughter. "No, poppet. Mrs. Graves will not be at all like the stepmother in *Cinderella*. That stepmother was a wicked one."

Apparently not entirely convinced, Isabelle scrambled off her father's lap and stood in front of Lynn. "Mrs. Gwabes—"

"Mrs. Graves," David corrected. "Her name is Mrs. Graves."

Intent on something she obviously considered far more important, Isabelle hunched a shoulder at the interruption. "Do you like little girls?"

"Yes, I do. For years and years, I wished for a little girl of my own, so I am very happy that your father has agreed to share you with me." Lynn lifted Isabelle onto her lap. "Since my present name is difficult to pronounce, why don't you call me Lynn instead?"

"Miss Lynn," David amended.

"Miss Lynn, then." She smiled at the little girl. "That is much easier to say than Mrs. Graves, isn't it?"

Isabelle nodded, then with a perspicacity Lynn would not have expected from a child of four asked, "Miss Lynn, is your name going to change?"

"Part of it will change when I marry your papa. My given name will still be Lynn—or Madeline—but instead of being Mrs. Graves, I will be Lady David Winterbrook."

"If you want," David told his daughter, "after the wedding, you can call Miss Lynn 'Mama.' "

"But only if you want to," Lynn insisted. "You can call me Miss Lynn if you prefer."

Isabelle nodded again. Wanting to get to know the little girl and knowing that it was essential for Isabelle to become comfortable with her, Lynn suggested, "Perhaps tomorrow you will let me play with you for a while, or take you for a walk, or read a story to you."

"Yes!" Clearly, Isabelle was in favor of the idea.

"Every day, we will do something together. You will get to know me, and you can teach me everything a stepmother—a *good* stepmother—needs to know."

Isabelle giggled. "Me, teach you? I thought you were supposed to teach me."

"We will teach each other." Lynn smiled and ventured a hug. To her great delight, she received one in return, as well as a kiss on the cheek.

In London the following afternoon, while George Winterbrook, Earl of Weymouth, was taking tea with his wife, Beth, in the drawing room at Bellingham House, the butler entered the room carrying a silver salver.

"We are not at home to callers, Hargrave," the earl said in a tone that hinted of annoyance at the interruption.

His statement did not, however, halt the servant's approach. With a bow, Hargrave extended the tray. "It is an express from Lord David."

Alarm vanquished annoyance as George grabbed the letter and quickly broke the seal, oblivious to the fact that in his haste he splintered the wax, which now adorned his biscuit-colored pantaloons and one sleeve of his blue super-fine coat.

As his eyes scanned the page, his wife gripped his arm. "Is something wrong, George? Are David and Isabelle and Caro well?"

Despite the anxiety that quivered in her voice, George did not respond. Not until after he finished reading the missive and dropped it in his lap.

He smiled to reassure her. "All is well, my love. David has written to request two favors."

"He sent an express to request a favor?" The rise of her golden brown eyebrows, as well as the tone of her voice, eloquently expressed her incredulity.

"Two favors," he teased.

When she rolled her eyes at him, he grinned—and re-lented. "He writes to request our presence in Oxfordshire as soon as your delicate condition permits"—he placed his hand on the blue sprigged muslin covering her gently rounded abdomen—"and after I have completed a commis-sion for him, so that we can welcome his fiancée—"

"His fiancée?"

George nodded. "So that we can welcome his fiancée into the family, and so that you can help with the wedding plans. If you are agreeable, of course."

"Of course I will help!"

"Are you certain you and my heir are up to the trip?" He lifted her onto his lap.

"Your daughter and I will be just fine," she riposted. "Probably." She ran her fingers through his hair. "Riding in a carriage doesn't bother me in Mayfair, so I will just have to hope that the road to Oxfordshire is smoother than the route between Dorset and London."

"We will pray for smooth roads."

"When is the wedding? And when do you wish to leave for Oxfordshire?"

He consulted his brother's letter. "He doesn't state the wedding date, only that the banns will be called for the first time on Sunday. The bride—"

"What is her name? Do you know her?"

"I don't know her. Apparently she lives—or lived—in Berkshire. Her name is Madeline Graves, but she prefers to be called Lynn. She is a widow—no children—and, due to an accident several years ago, has difficulty hearing. David says that we must stand quite close in order for her to hear us, but that she is very skilled at discerning what is said by watching the movement of the speaker's lips."

"Will the wedding be in Berkshire, then?"

"He didn't say. His main concerns are that we come post-haste to welcome her into the family, and that I make a purchase for him. What color are David's eyes?"

"Blue."

Now it was George's turn to roll his eyes. "I know they are blue. What shade of blue, exactly? He has asked me to find an engagement ring with a stone the color of his eyes."

"Lynn must have made that request!"

"I imagine so. Now, how would you describe the color of his eyes?"

"Not so deep a blue as yours, but a bit darker than mine. His eyes are the color of the sky on a bright summer day."

"Thank you, darling." He rewarded his wife with a kiss. "I will go to Rundell and Bridge tomorrow morning. Do we have any pressing engagements in the next few days? Or could we leave for Greendale Manor the day after tomorrow?"

"The day after tomorrow is Sunday. As for engagements, the only one *I* have"—she patted her abdomen—"is dinner with Elston and Karla next Tuesday, and given the circumstances, they would be the first to urge us to forego it."

"Could you be ready to leave around noon tomorrow? Assuming, of course, that I find a suitable ring in the morning."

"Leave tomorrow for a stay of three weeks or more?" she queried in shocked disbelief. When he nodded—warily—she responded, "Only if I start packing this instant."

"Thank you, darling." He kissed her nose, then lifted her to her feet. "Unless we get an early start, we won't be able to travel all the way to Greendale tomorrow. But if the roads are clear—and smooth—we should be able to cover at least two-thirds of the distance, then complete the trip Sunday morning."

Her eyes widened in surprise, but she did not question his haste. Or his decision to travel on Sunday. As he watched this beloved wife leave the room, George wondered what his brother's third request—the one "too delicate to explain in a letter"—would be.

Saturday was an extremely eventful day. In the morning, Lynn and David met with the vicar, then Lynn and Caro (already on such friendly terms that they addressed each other thusly) spent the afternoon at the dressmaker's shop. Lynn's intent was to order one new gown—her straitened circumstances would not permit more—but when David's aunt selected four others, each one lovelier than the last, and informed Lynn that they were a bride gift, she could not graciously refuse. Nor, in her heart of hearts, did she really want to do so. Instead, she thanked Caro prettily, and quite sincerely, for her kindness and generosity.

Saturday evening, just about the time David, Lynn, and Caro were beginning to think of seeking their beds, the Earl and Countess of Weymouth arrived. Lynn, who had been dreading the meeting with the redoubtable Beth, was delighted to discover that the lovely countess was not the least bit formidable. Lynn had not known that her soon-to-be sister-in-law was an American, but aside from some initial difficulty with Beth's lilting accent—the drawled vowels made it impossible for Lynn to discern Beth's words by the movement of her lips—the two women were fast friends in next to no time. The very tall, handsome, gregarious, earl soon had Lynn calling him George—and wishing she had a brother like him.

Sunday morning, shortly before they were to leave for church, David asked Lynn to accompany him to the conservatory. After seating her on a marble bench, he knelt and took her left hand in his. "I love you, Lynn. And Isabelle, Caro, George, and Beth all think you are quite wonderful—and the perfect bride for me. Which, indeed, you are." Smiling, he withdrew something from his waistcoat pocket. "I hope you will wear this ring"—he slid it on her fourth finger—"as a symbol of my love for you."

Tears filled her eyes at the sight of the large, square-cut sapphire—the exact color of his eyes—surrounded by diamonds. "Oh, David!" she choked.

"If you don't like it—"

"It is the most beautiful ring I have ever seen!"

Pulling out his handkerchief, he dabbed at the tears spilling down her cheeks. "Then why are you crying, my love?"

"Because the ring is so beautiful." She leaned forward just far enough to rest her forehead on his shoulder. "And because I am happier than I have ever been in my life."

His arms came around her in a comforting embrace. "I thought tears were a sign of sadness," he muttered.

"Sometimes they are."

"How can a man distinguish happy tears from sad ones? They look the same to me."

"I daresay they do look the same."

His hand stroked up and down her spine, offering further comfort, and his patient acceptance of her foibles soothed her to the depths of her soul.

"I love you so much, David. But sometimes I fear that this is a wonderful dream from which I will soon wake—"

"It isn't a dream, sweetheart."

"I would be desolate—devastated—to find myself without you and your love." Just the thought of life without him wrested uncontrollable sobs from deep inside her.

"Hush, my love. You will make yourself ill." He gathered her close to his chest, lifted her, and somehow maneuvered himself from his kneeling position to a seat on the bench, with her on his lap.

"It isn't a dream, sweetheart. You are worrying about something that will never happen." He continued his soothing caresses along her spine. "You will always have my love—nothing can, or will, take it away from you—and in three weeks and three days, you will be my wife." Hugging her tightly, he added, "In my heart, you already are, but when Greenfield's vicar makes it official, all the world will know."

He nuzzled his face against hers, pressing kisses against her temple and along her jaw. "No one will ever hurt you again. You are here with me, safe and loved, and nothing will ever change that. Nothing."

Blindly, she sought the comfort of his kiss, and finally she calmed. In the shelter of David's arms and his love, she had found a safe harbor, a port in which she could weather any storm.

Chapter Seventeen

*W*ord of the impending nuptials spread quickly, as such tidings always do, and throngs of callers flocked to Greendale Manor's drawing room every afternoon to meet the future Lady David. The dinner party that Caro, Lynn, and Beth were planning to introduce Lord David's bride to the local gentry seemed quite unnecessary; Lynn was convinced that she would meet all the guests, as well as every other person of note in the district, before then.

The three weeks between the first calling of the banns and the final one sped by on winged feet. Lynn spent time every day with Caro, familiarizing herself with the household and its routines, learning the servants' names, and acquiring every bit of knowledge that might be the least bit helpful when she was mistress of the manor, Caro having announced her intention of leaving with the Weymouths, to provide companionship for Beth as her activities became more limited and to help out after the baby was born. Lynn also spent an hour or two each day with Isabelle, to their mutual pleasure, and now knew firsthand why the little girl had earned the nickname "Isabelle the Inquisitive." Most of the rest of Lynn's time was spent with Beth. The two almost sisters-in-law genuinely enjoyed each other's company, and they shared several interests, especially music, reading, and needlework. Lynn had not played the pianoforte for two years, but with Beth's help, she was learning several new pieces. In return, she was teaching Beth the art of lace making.

After having spent five weeks solely in David's company, Lynn found it disconcerting that they now had so little time

together. He devoted many hours each day to dealing with
the estate business that had accumulated during his absence, but he also spent a great deal of time with his
brother. There were days when she saw David only at
meals and in the drawing room after dinner, and although
she tried not to resent the fact that he spent so little time
in her company—almost none of it alone with her—she
was powerless to halt an increasing feeling of ill use at
his neglect.

When her distress grew to the point that she could hardly
think about anything else, Lynn knew she had to discuss
her concerns with David. The wedding was only five days
away, and if the dearth of his company she'd experienced
the past few weeks would be the pattern of their marriage,
she wanted to know now.

Confrontation was not Lynn's wont—indeed, in the past
she had gone to great lengths to avoid it—but after a night
made sleepless by worry, she knew the matter was important enough to risk provoking David's wrath. And if her
innocent question roused his ire, it was best she know that
now, too.

Thus resolved, after breaking her fast, she squared her
shoulders and knocked on the door of the estate office and,
when bidden to do so, entered.

When David looked up and saw her, he smiled with delight, rising from his seat behind the desk and hurrying
around it to greet her. "Good morning, sweet—"

"I know you are busy, David—"

"I am never too busy to talk to you." He bent to kiss
her cheek, then seated her on one of the chairs in front of
his desk. After turning the other so it faced her, he sat
down and crossed one buckskin-clad leg over the other.
"What may I do for you this morning, my love?"

"You may answer a question, if you would. About something that has been . . . troubling me."

"Of course I will. Provided I know the answer."

Lynn looked down at her hands, wondering how best to
phrase her query. "I know you have been very busy with
estate matters since we have been here. And I know that
there have been guests to entertain, and . . ." She gritted
her teeth against a moan of pure frustration. *Are you going
to make excuses for him or ask your question?*

She started anew, speaking so rapidly the words almost tumbled over one another. "A moment ago, you said you are never too busy to talk to me, but since we have been here, we have spent very little time together. Perhaps it just seems so in comparison to our days at my home, but I . . . I have been disconcerted by the change. I want to know if, when we are married, I will see as little of you as I have the past few weeks."

"Sweetheart, I hope you don't think I have been avoiding you. I have not. For the past few weeks, estate matters have occupied a great deal of my time, much more so than usual. Initially, I had to deal with everything that cropped up during my absence, but more recently, I have been trying to do some work in advance, so that I will be able to spend more time with you after our wedding. There were also some pressing concerns I needed to discuss with George."

He leaned forward, reaching his hand toward her. When she clasped it, he twined his fingers with hers. "I won't be able to spend as much time with you every day as I did at Larkspur Cottage—I have more responsibilities here. Normally, I spend the morning on estate business. My afternoons and evenings will be devoted to you and Isabelle. Can you be satisfied with that?"

She smiled, feeling enormously relieved. "I will be very happy with that."

"I am sorry if you have felt neglected, sweetheart. I ought to have explained—" Shaking his head, he broke off the explanation. "I am sorry, Lynn."

He uncrossed his legs, planting his booted feet flat on the floor, and tugged on her hand. "Come here, please."

Once she was settled on his lap, reveling in the feel of his arms around her and in the comfort she derived from his embrace, he slipped a crooked forefinger under her chin and tilted her face up to his. Well aware that her sleepless night had left its mark upon her countenance, she was not surprised when he asked, "How long have you been worrying about this?"

"For a few weeks."

"*Weeks?* Why didn't you say something before now?"

Unwilling to meet his gaze while she confessed, but unable to hide her face with his finger beneath her chin, she closed her eyes. "Because I am a coward. And I dislike confrontation."

Sliding his hand along her jaw and through her hair to cup the back of her head, he hugged her close to his chest. "You are *not* a coward. If you were, you wouldn't be here. Not just in this room—you wouldn't even be in Oxfordshire. Would a cowardly woman have agreed to risk her heart, and her self, again in marriage?"

"I suppose not."

"Most definitely not," he corrected. "As for disliking confrontation, in the past you had good reasons to avoid it. But those reasons no longer exist, do they?"

"Only in my mind. And in my nightmares." Involuntarily, she shuddered.

"Ah, my love." His hand began a soothing caress up and down her spine. "I wish I could do something to make them disappear. To ensure that all your dreams were pleasant ones."

"You already have. The nightmares are much less frequent now."

"Good." After several moments of companionable silence, he asked, "What else would you like to discuss?"

Loath though she was to end this interlude, her other concern was not one she was willing to admit. "Nothing."

The quiver in her voice gave lie to her response. Once again, he tilted her face up to his. "What?"

When she did not respond, he asked again, without the slightest hint of impatience in his voice, "What is it, Lynn?" Then, after another beat of silence, "I cannot do anything unless I know what the problem is."

"It isn't a problem, exactly."

At her begrudging admission, his lips twitched as he suppressed a smile. "Why don't you tell me what, exactly, it is and let me decide whether it is or isn't a problem?"

"You will think I am foolish."

Instead of the polite denial she half expected, his response was, "I will think you far more foolish if you don't tell me."

She grabbed his finger, freeing her face from his scrutiny, and tucked her head against his shoulder. "It bothers me a bit that I have never seen you angry."

"Given your history, that is a very valid concern." Pulling

his finger from her grasp, he stroked his hand over her hair. "Unfortunately, I cannot easily alleviate your anxiety. I am an even-tempered man, slow to anger, and my ire, when roused, is quickly spent.

"You already know my opinion of men who hit women and children. Needless to say, I am not one of those men, but proving it . . ." His hand stilled, then he resumed the gentle caress. "You might try to provoke my wrath, so that you can see how I behave when angry."

"No! Not on purpose."

"Why not? It might ease your fears."

"Maybe so. But I don't want you to be angry at me."

"You could ask George or Caro or Aunt Tilly how I act when I am angry. Or my father, when he arrives on Monday."

"I don't want them to think me foolish. And they would," she insisted, "unless I explained my reasons for asking."

"And you are unwilling, or unable, to do that." He exhaled a long breath, more an admission of defeat than a sigh. "I daresay I would be, too, if the situation was reversed."

"I am sorry, David—"

"Hush, love. There is nothing for which you need apologize."

She allowed herself another minute or so to enjoy his embrace, then, reluctantly, sat upright. "I should leave so you can get back to work."

"I am not quite ready to forego the pleasure of your company. I have had too little of it lately. What else would you like to discuss?"

"Nothing." When he quirked a brow, she asserted, "Nothing. Truly."

"Will you promise me something, sweetheart?"

"Of course. If I can."

"Promise me that any time you are the least bit bothered by something I do—or don't do—or by something I say, you will tell me before the end of the day. So that we can discuss your concerns long before they cause sleepless nights." He cupped her cheek and gently traced the circle under her left eye with his thumb.

It was a reasonable request. More than reasonable; it was

also sensible. Caring. Perhaps even loving. *But surely he did not mean . . . ?* "Anything? No matter how trifling?"

"If it bothers you, even a little bit, it is not trifling."

Definitely loving. "I promise," she vowed, her heart overflowing with love. "On one condition."

"What condition?"

"That you make the same promise to me." She bracketed his beloved face between her hands. "I am out of my element in your world, I can hardly hear, and I am . . . not wholly free of the past. It is far more likely that I will do or say things that annoy you."

As he listened to Lynn's litany of "faults," David's heart felt like it was being squeezed by a giant's fist. But now was not the time to argue with her, not after she had so bravely sought him out and voiced her concerns. Instead, he offered her something far more pleasurable than dispute, closing the distance between them and brushing a quick kiss against her rosy lips. "I promise. I disagree with your assessment, but I promise that if you ever do or say anything that bothers me, I will tell you by day's end."

"Thank you, David." She rewarded him with the rare, sweet gift of her kiss—a longer one than he had given her, lingering enough to increase his heartbeat. "I promise the same."

"No matter how trifling," he reiterated.

Solemnly, she nodded. "No matter how trifling."

He did not want her to leave, so he cuddled her against his chest, feeling blest by the presence of this special woman in his life. Blest and . . . enriched was the best description, he thought. His life was fuller, with more meaning and purpose than it had before he met her.

"I know you have work to do, but I don't want to leave. I just want to sit right here and . . . savor you and your presence in my life."

"I was thinking much the same thing, my love," he murmured, pressing kisses along her jaw in search of her mouth.

Soft, sweet kisses gradually progressed to nibbling ones. When Lynn's lips parted slightly beneath his, David shouted a silent "hallelujah!" and slowly stroked his hand up her side, stopping several inches below the bodice of her gown. But since all the blood seemed to have left his brain and traveled south to his loins, he was finding it diffi-cult to recall his brother's advice—hell, he was having trou-ble remembering to breathe!—so after a few more sweet, gentle kisses, he wrapped his arms around her and just held her close to his heart. A heart that was pounding as if trying to beat its way out of his chest.

Nuzzling his face in her hair, he said softly, "I love you, Madeline Graves."

She hugged him tightly and returned the pledge. "I love you, David."

After a few—or, possibly, many—minutes, he confessed, "I can summon no enthusiasm to send you on your way. Especially not in favor of balancing ledgers."

Tipping her head back against his shoulder, she looked up at his face. "I thought you liked mathematics and nu-merical games?"

"I do." He could not resist the urge to kiss her again—not that he tried very hard. "But I like you more."

"I am very glad to hear it, sir." Her smile was as bright as sunshine. "But if you are not feeling diligent, Mr. Estate Manager, then it is my duty as your wife—almost wife—to leave, so that you have no choice but to work."

He circled his hands around her waist and lifted her to her feet, then stood and hugged her, holding her closely, but not tightly, against him. *Are you finding this beneficial, my love? I hope so, because I am finding it tortuous.*

Releasing her, he started to step back, but she wound her arms around his neck and rose on her toes to kiss him. "Thank you, Sir Knight, for successfully completing another questions quest."

Smiling, he offered her a deep bow worthy of a courtier. "It was my pleasure, my lady."

"In five more days, I will truly be your lady," she mur-mured, awe in her voice and expression.

When she left, he did not even glance at his desk. In-stead, he stood for a time with teeth gritted and fists clenched, then walked out the door, snagged a towel from the laundry, and headed toward the lake. This early in March, the water would be demmed cold, but his brother had assured him that cold baths quenched desire.

David had a feeling that he would be doing a lot of swimming this spring.

*   *   *

Lynn was in alt after her conversation with David. Had her life depended on it, she could not have said what heartened her more: his words or his kisses. Just thinking of her visit to the estate office brought fiery color to her cheeks, but since Beth's maid, Moira Sinclair, was the only other occupant of the carriage, Lynn did not care. She had learnt three very important things as a result of that visit. First, that not all confrontations resulted in angry words and actions; David had not been the least bit vexed, nor had he even raised his voice. Second, that he regretted that they had not spent more time together the past three weeks, but that after the wedding on Wednesday, his afternoons and evenings would belong to her and Isabelle. Third, and possibly most important, he had shown her again that even when *quite* aroused, he would do naught but kiss and caress her. She had not felt the slightest tinge of fear, or even wariness, in his arms. On the contrary, she had felt the stirrings of desire—desire she thought Frank had killed forever years before. And she'd enjoyed its resurgence.

When the coachman halted the team halfway along the row of shops in Watlington's High Street, Lynn accepted the footman's assistance and stepped out of the vehicle. Intent on her quest, she was unaware that in her blue woolen gown, new Clarence blue pelisse, and sky blue kidskin gloves that perfectly matched the ribbons of her new chipstraw bonnet, she was the very picture of a blushing bride.

Moira joined her, studying the signs on the nearest shops. "Where do ye wish to go first, ma'am?"

With a wave of her hand, Lynn indicated their destination. The two women strolled down the street, glancing at the contents of the shop windows they passed. Although disappointed that Beth felt too fatigued to accompany her this afternoon, Lynn was grateful that Moira had volunteered to come in her mistress's stead. Lynn had difficulty understanding the maid's brogue, but the petite, reserved Scotswoman was a far more pleasant companion than Caro's haughty French dresser.

Lynn resolved to resume her search for a lady's maid after the wedding, despite her singular lack of success thus far. Six very proper dressers recommended by a London employment agency were intent on turning her into a fashionable Society matron, whether she wished it or not, but the four maids in the household who might be trained for the post had chattered almost without pause when she'd given them a day's trial. The former were intimidating; the latter, fatiguing.

As they entered the shop and began examining the items displayed, Moira inquired, "Is there something I can help ye find, ma'am?"

"I am looking for a wedding gift for Lord David, and for Isabelle. I daresay I can't call Isabelle's present a wedding gift, but . . . In a way, I feel like I am marrying both of them."

"Aye"—the maid nodded—"the three of ye will be a family."

"Exactly so, Moira. I want to celebrate the occasion, and honor them, with a gift for each that will be a symbol of my love and show my gratitude to them for including me in their family."

"What sort o' presents do ye hae in mind, ma'am?"

Lynn huffed out a sigh. "I don't have any ideas, really. I was counting on Lady Weymouth's assistance in choosing, since she has known Lord David and Isabelle longer than I have."

"I dinna know Lord David well, but I can tell ye that Miss Isabelle likes dolls and books. Verra fond of faery tales, she is."

"She already has several dolls, and there is quite a collection of books in the nursery."

"I dinna think any lassie would complain that she has too many dolls or books."

Chuckling, Lynn conceded, "Probably not."

"When my lady married Lord Weymouth last year, she gae him a watch inscribed with their names and the date of the wedding. His lordship liked it verra much."

"That is an excellent idea, if the price is not too dear."

"Do ye want to look at the dolls, ma'am? They are in the corner near the window."

There were several very fine dolls, but Lynn could not decide which one Isabelle would like best. Nor could the maid. After dithering for several minutes, Lynn said, "We need a child's opinion. A girl close to Isabelle's age."

She glanced around the shop, but the only girl there was Rebecca Brady, the brewer's daughter, a young miss of eleven or twelve. Despite the gap in the two girls' ages, Lynn crossed to the counter, where Becca and her mother waited while their purchases were wrapped.

After greetings were exchanged, Lynn explained her problem. "I want to buy a doll for Lord David's daughter, but I can't decide which one she would like best. Becca, would you be so kind as to give me your opinion?"

Smiling, Mrs. Brady granted permission, and Becca accompanied Lynn across the shop to examine the dolls. Several minutes of intense scrutiny, as well as a bit of play, were required for the girl to reach a decision. "The doll in the blue velvet dress. I like her the best, and I think Miss Isabelle will, too."

"Thank you very much for your help, Becca." Lynn escorted the girl back to her mother. Turning to the shopkeeper, she asked, "Mr. Watkins, do you think a penny's worth of candy is a suitable reward for a girl who helped me make a difficult decision?"

The old man's eyes twinkled as he pretended to consider the question. "Aye, ma'am. For a difficult decision, a penny's worth sounds just right."

Lynn smiled at the wide-eyed girl. "Choose your favorite, and thank you again for your help."

"Thank *you*, Mrs. Graves."

As she paid for her purchases, Lynn put her method to the test again. "Mr. Watkins, if you were choosing a present for Lord David, what would you pick?"

"Hmmm . . . I don't rightly know, ma'am. But when my Ellen was alive, God rest her soul, every year at Christmas and her birthday, I'd ask myself, 'What does she want most in the world?' Sometimes I couldn't afford the thing she most wanted, so I'd buy her something she wouldn't have bought for herself. A necklace or a brooch, so she'd think of me when she wore it."

He handed her the gaily wrapped parcel containing the doll. "Just ask yourself what Lord David wants most and then do your best to give it to him."

"Thank you, sir. That is very good advice." Leaving the shop, she pondered the old man's words.

What does David want most in the world?

Lynn knew one thing David wanted very much, although perhaps not most in the world, but she did not think that she could give it to him yet.

As the footman took the parcel from Moira, Lynn inquired, "Thomas, which shop has the best selection of watches and cravat pins?"

"Carruthers, I reckon. 'Tis where his lordship buys christening gifts and the like. And Lady Richard's birthday earbobs." He pointed to a shop on the other side of the street. "'Tis a bit past the dressmaker's."

The jeweler's selection of watches was fine, indeed. Lynn required only a few moments to make her choice. "Oh, this one is perfect!"

"A wedding gift for Lord David, is it?" the jeweler guessed. "I can engrave your names, a few words, and the wedding date inside the lid, if you'd like. You just write down"—he handed her a piece of paper and a pencil—"what you want to say. Come back in an hour or so, and I'll have it ready for you."

Although she felt certain the watch was beyond her means, hope springs eternal. "How much is the watch?"

"Fifteen pounds."

Lynn did not gasp or burst into tears, but it was a near run thing. To give herself time to recover, she fumbled to untie the strings of her reticule. "I fear I don't have enough money for the watch. Perhaps a fob, instead?"

"You don't have to pay me today, my lady. I'll send a bill at the end of the month."

After a brief but hard-fought battle between her conscience and her pride, she mustered a smile for the rotund jeweler. "Thank you, Mr. Carruthers. But you must send the bill to me, not to Lord David."

"Yes, my lady. Now, you write down the inscription you want, and I'll have it done in an hour."

Studying the inner surface of the lid, Lynn considered the limited space available and the sentiments she wanted to convey. Her decision made, she wrote quickly and passed the paper to the jeweler. "Is that too long?"

"No. That will fit nicely."

"Thank you, sir." This time her smile required no effort.

They browsed through several other shops, but Lynn's attention was not on the items displayed; she was still worrying over her decision to buy the watch. As David's wife she would have a generous allowance—more than twice as much each quarter as her current yearly income—but it did not seem right to use even a portion of that money to buy his wedding gift. Buying a new gown, as well as the necessary accessories, for the wedding had taken nearly all of her meager funds, and she'd spent most of the rest on Isabelle's present, but she did want to give him a gift, and if she'd limited herself to the three pounds, sixpence in her reticule, she could not have bought a present that was nearly so nice.

By the time they went back to pick up the watch, Lynn had a pounding headache. And she still was not convinced that she had made the right decision.

Monday afternoon, two days before the wedding, David was coming downstairs when Lynn returned from a shopping expedition to Watlington. She was accompanied by his sister-in-law's maid, although Beth was not with them. He greeted both women, then crossed to Lynn and bent to kiss her cheek, wondering why her features were taut with strain.

"My father and my cousins arrived while you were gone. They are looking forward to meeting you at tea." He helped Lynn remove her pelisse.

An expression he could not interpret darkened her beautiful eyes before she bent her head to tease off her gloves. "I am glad they arrived safely. I—" Her hands stilled, then gripped together tightly. "Do you have a few moments, my lord? I need to talk to you."

His stomach lurched at her tone; she sounded like a woman desperately trying to keep her balance in a world that was spiraling out of control. A woman who would do anything to stop its careening. "Of course, my love." He handed her bonnet, gloves, and pelisse to the butler, then escorted her to the estate office, knowing they would not be disturbed there. He also hoped the location would remind her of the discussion they'd had a few days ago, and her vow to tell him all her concerns.

The moment he closed the door, he took her into his arms. If she needed to hold on to something until the world's mad spinning ceased, he would be her rock. "What is the matter, sweetheart?"

Her arms tightened around his waist. "Oh, David—" A sob choked off the rest of her words, increasing his alarm.

Bending his knees slightly, he lifted her in his arms and carried her across the room, then sat down in a wing chair, with Lynn on his lap. Cuddling her to his chest, he stroked a hand up and down her back. "Hush, love. Whatever has upset you isn't worth your tears." Nuzzling his cheek against the softness of hers, he murmured words of comfort, and of love, until her sobs eased to sniffles.

He pulled his handkerchief from his coat pocket, but since one of her hands was fisted on his lapel and the other was clutching the back of his coat collar, he could only drape the linen square over her clenched fist. A second later, it dropped into her lap, but she would have it when she was ready to employ it.

He smoothed a lock of hair away from her face. "What is wrong, my love? Please tell me who or what upset you so."

She drew in a ragged breath, then mopped her tears with his handkerchief. "David, I did a horrible thing."

"I find that very hard to believe." *Impossible, actually.*

"Moira and I went to Watlington so that I could buy a wedding present for you, and one for Isabelle. But because I'd already bought a new gown for the wedding, I didn't have enough money for the second present after buying the first."

She burrowed deeper under his chin, resting her head in the curve of his neck and shoulder. "When I told the shopkeeper I didn't have enough money, he said I didn't have to pay today, that he would send a bill at the end of the month. I agreed because I really wanted that present for— that present. But the more I think about it, I know it was wrong. I shouldn't use the allowance you will give me when we are married to pay for your wedding gift.

"Oh, David—" Tears again clogged her voice, and he felt one fall on his neck. "I love you with all my heart, but I should not marry you. I fear I will never be a credit to you."

Fear—deep, gut-churning fear—paralyzed him for a moment, then every muscle in his body tensed to fight. To fight for his life. For their life together. "Lynn, you did not do anything wrong. And your worry that you might have done so indicates that you will always be a credit to me."

He tilted his head, but he could not see her face. "Have you forgotten that I wanted to give you the allowance for this quarter weeks ago? Or that I wanted you to purchase some new gowns and whatever else you might need?"

"I haven't forgotten, but you shouldn't have to buy things for me before we are married."

"I *wanted* to buy them, sweetheart. You spent money to feed me when I was a guest in your home for all those weeks, so why can't I buy a few fripperies for you now?"

"It is not the same thing," she insisted.

"Yes, it is. Both are gifts, offered freely." He stroked his hand over her hair. "Will you please sit up, my love, so that I can see you?"

When she complied with his request, he cupped her face between his hands and, with his thumbs, wiped away her tears. "Please tell me you were not serious when you said you shouldn't marry me." His heart was lodged in his throat, but he managed to choke out the question. Then he prayed.

Lynn sighed, wondering how she could possibly explain her conflicting feelings on the subject of their marriage. "I think it would be best for you if we did not marry. I am the impoverished, widowed daughter of a country squire, and quite beneath the notice of a marquess's son. I lack the social graces to impress anyone—"

"You caught my notice and impressed me."

"Given the circumstances in Berkshire, you could not fail to notice me. But if other women had been present, you would not have noticed."

"I would," he contended, gallant as ever. "You give yourself too little credit. And me, not enough."

She placed her hands on his shoulders but did not shake him, even though he clearly needed a good shaking to rattle his brain back into working order. "It was not my intention to disparage you, David, merely to state a fact. Men ignore me when other, more desirable women are present."

"There is no woman more desirable than you. Not in my eyes."

"You are—" *Blind. Foolishly, endearingly blind.*

"I am the man who loves you, heart and soul. The man who wants to share the rest of his life with you. Surely that ought to count for something?"

Lynn's heart—and, it seemed, her bones—melted at his words. She slid her arms around his neck and rested her head on his chest. "It counts for a great deal, of course. I love you, David, and I want to share my life with you. But I fear that my lack of social skills, especially my near deafness, will not redound to your credit. There are many women far better suited than I to be your wife, and it would be better for you if we did not marry."

"Look at me, Lynn." It was more command than request. Especially since he grasped her shoulders to ensure her compliance.

He locked his gaze with hers. "Do you honestly believe I would be better off married to a woman who did not love me? That I could possibly be happy married to a woman who was only interested in my title and my family's wealth and social position?"

"No, of course not." Despite the nobility of her intentions, her suggestion sounded impossibly stupid when put in those terms.

He lifted her in his arms and stood, then deposited—almost dropped—her in the chair before stalking to the window. With one arm rigidly braced against the window frame, he stood in silence for more than a minute, looking out. As she wondered what had caught his attention, he turned and crossed his arms over his chest. "Yet that is what you just suggested, is it not? Or perhaps I misunderstood. Did you or did you not say that I would be better off married to a woman who did not love me, merely because her hearing was more acute than yours?"

Hearing his clipped tones, seeing the muscle jumping in his cheek, she realized that he was angry. Not just mildly annoyed, but furious. Blazingly, teeth-grindingly livid. And all of that anger was directed at her.

Lynn swallowed, hard. "That is not what I said, nor what I meant." With shaking hands, she pushed herself upright.

Then, although it was undoubtedly the most difficult thing she had ever done, but also, quite possibly, the most important thing she would ever do, she crossed the room and stood in front of him.

"I am sorry, David." Not wanting to see the scorn in his eyes, she studied the pattern of the Oriental carpet. "I did not mean you should marry someone who doesn't love you, only that there are other women—women who would love you—who are better suited to be your wife."

"So you were going to nobly step aside, sacrificing your happiness for mine?" His voice was not as curt as before; instead, he sounded almost . . . amused.

"Yes."

"But I love *you*," he said with gruff tenderness, "not one of those imaginary women."

Relief that her foolishness had not destroyed his love swamped her, causing her limbs to tremble. "And I love you."

"I am in the devil of a quandary, sweetheart. More than anything right now, I want to hold you, but I am afraid to move lest I frighten you."

She raised her gaze to his face and stepped forward, eliminating the short distance between them. "You will not frighten me if you move. I know you would never hurt me."

His arms encircled her, holding her tightly against his chest. Almost as tightly as she hugged his waist. In the warmth of his embrace, listening to his heart beat beneath her ear, her tremors eased. "I am sorry that I hurt you with my imprudent words."

"As long as you will marry me, it doesn't matter. I can live with occasional thoughtlessness, but I cannot live without your love."

Sliding her hands up his chest, she looped her arms around his neck and pulled his head down for a kiss. "I will marry you, David Winterbrook. You had your chance to escape, and you did not take it. You won't get another."

"I don't want another," he muttered between kisses. "I want you."

After several moments—and several kisses that declared his love as clearly as the words he'd spoken—David scooped her up in his arms and carried her to the chair, resuming their previous cozy position.

"I am very proud of you, my darling. You did not run away today. Indeed, you approached me, even though you had to know I was displeased."

"Displeased?" She looked askance at him. "Irate is far more accurate a description, is it not? Or seething?"

"Hmmm, yes. Does that bother you?" he asked, with considerable anxiety.

"No." Lynn was more than a bit surprised by the realization. "My foolishness was just cause for your anger."

"But—"

She placed a finger against his lips, stilling his protest. "As I said before, I know you will never hurt me. No matter how angry you are."

"Good." He rewarded her with a kiss.

Having successfully overcome her fears of confrontation and of a man's anger—or, at least, of David's anger and confrontations with him—Lynn dared to broach her final fear. "A few days ago, we promised each other that we would discuss our concerns before the day's end."

"Yes, we did." He straightened, seeming suddenly more alert. "What is troubling you, my love?"

"I—" *Oh, this was almost as hard as facing his wrath.* "I do not know if I can ever be a true wife to you. I need to know how much that bothers you."

Cupping his hand against her cheek, he guided her head to his shoulder, then stroked his fingers over her hair. As he pondered, Lynn wondered if the gesture soothed him as much as it did her. "I am not sure I know the answer to your question, sweetheart. I hope that, in time, you will love and trust me enough that we can physically express our love—and replace your bad memories with more pleasant ones. But if—"

Astounded, Lynn jerked erect. "Do you think it is possible to replace bad memories with good ones?"

David's lips twitched, then curved into a rather wry smile. "Perhaps replace isn't the correct word, since memories never completely disappear, but I do think we can create enough happy memories that the bad ones will be pushed into a dark, cobwebbed corner in the attics of your mind."

Lynn laughed at the image, as he'd undoubtedly intended. "A dark, cobwebbed corner of the attics is the most fitting place for them." Cupping his face between her hands, she brushed kisses against his mouth and along his jaw. "It never occurred to me that good memories would supplant the bad ones."

"Of course they will, sweetheart. How could they not?"

Could it really be that easy to rid herself of the bad memories? Did she have enough courage to find out?

Chapter Eighteen

Standing amid the Winterbrooks and Middlefords, Lynn felt like a tiny, gnarled sapling surrounded by proud, ancient trees. Unlike a sapling in the forest, however, she knew she need not struggle to find a ray of sunlight to survive. Within moments of her entrance into the drawing room, each and every one of the tall, handsome men gathered around her had beamed his approval, and it was clear they would willingly sacrifice their lives to protect and defend her and the other women in the room. The Earl of Weymouth, or George as he insisted she call him, was the tallest at six feet and four inches. Andrew Winterbrook, the Marquess of Bellingham, was a slightly shorter, gray-haired version of his heir—or, rather, 'twas Weymouth who was a younger, slightly taller, dark-haired image of Bellingham. George and David's cousin, Theodore Middleford, the Viscount Dunnley, was six feet tall. With his tawny hair and gray eyes, he stood out among his blue-eyed relatives with their dark brown or reddish brown hair, and in a room full of exceptionally good-looking men, he was the handsomest. Although Lynn knew he was one of the leaders of the *ton*, he was not at all high in the instep. His brother, Captain Stephen Middleford, was an inch shorter and bore a marked resemblance to David, except that Stephen's hair was the color of ginger. The rather bashful hussar captain was recovering from a leg wound and, despite the aid of a sturdy blackthorn cane, walked with a bit of a limp. An inch shorter than Stephen, David was, as he'd laughingly insisted weeks ago at Larkspur Cottage, the runt of the litter, but Lynn well knew his beautiful, loving heart and would not have traded him for one of his taller, more striking relatives for all the tea in China.

Even among the ladies, Lynn was the shortest—about five inches shorter than Beth Weymouth and Lady Matilda Elliott, and two inches shorter than Caro. But Lynn had no reason to repine her lack of stature; it was clearly the size of a person's heart that determined his or her worthiness to be a member of this family. Frank had bruised her heart, along with other portions of her anatomy, and although it may have shriveled during her marriage, her heart was blossoming and flourishing now in the sunshine of David's love. Despite her fears, Lynn's difficulty hearing troubled David's relatives not a whit, nor did they seem to think she lacked social graces. Indeed, a woman would be hard-pressed to show to disadvantage when surrounded by the gallant gentlemen and well-mannered ladies of David's family, and Lynn basked in the light of their approval.

Bellingham asked the butler for a bottle of champagne, and when everyone had been served, he cleared his throat to get their attention. "I would like to propose a toast to my lovely new daughter. Lynn, it is my very great pleasure to welcome you to the family." Smiling at her, he drank, then bent and kissed her cheek.

"Hear, hear," one of the men said.

"To Lynn," said several others.

Blinking back tears, she smiled at them all. When she could control her voice, she raised her glass. "I know ladies generally do not propose toasts, but I hope you will indulge me tonight. I would honor all of the Winterbrooks and Middlefords. There can be no kinder, more loving family in the realm, and I thank you all from the bottom of my heart for the warm welcome you have accorded me."

On Wednesday, the ninth of March, Lynn woke with a smile on her face, well aware that this, her wedding day, marked the start of a wonderful new life as David's wife and Isabelle's stepmother. Contemplating the future as she bathed and dried her hair, her heart overflowing with love, Lynn hoped that the three of them would always be as happy as she was today. She would do everything she could to ensure that they were. Starting today.

Her first visitor was Lady Matilda, or Aunt Tilly, as she'd asked to be addressed. A widow in her mid-fifties, Tilly had followed the drum with her soldier husband for years, and after his death had returned home to Bellingham Castle to care for her widowed brother and to help raise his children. Interspersed between Tilly's anecdotes of David as a boy were tidbits of wisdom about marriage—including some advice about a wife's more intimate duties.

Although sometimes blunt in her speech, Tilly had a kind heart. "Lynn, I do not know the circumstances of your first marriage, but I sense that it was not altogether a happy one. Nor a particularly loving one. Remember, always, that the past is the past. It changed you from a young girl to a woman, but it cannot affect the future unless you allow it to do so.

"I don't know how people who marry again avoid comparing—consciously or unconsciously—their second spouse to the first. But for people like you and David, whose first marriages were . . . um, less than ideal, it is essential to avoid such comparisons. You should not expect David's behavior in any situation to be like your first husband's. David loves you heart and soul, and you love him as deeply. Start with that certainty and build a new life."

Lynn hugged the older, wiser woman. "Thank you, Aunt Tilly."

Lady Richard was Lynn's second visitor. Caro also told stories about David as a boy, and offered advice about marriage. All aspects of it. Since she had overheard part of Lynn's and David's conversation the day they arrived at Greendale Manor, Caro knew more about Lynn's first marriage than Tilly did. But as a diplomat's wife, Caro's conversation was less direct.

"Lynn, I know your late husband was not a kind man. His behavior undoubtedly affected your life together in ways I cannot imagine. Your decision to marry again was a difficult one, I suspect. But given the little bit I know about your first marriage, I think David is the perfect husband for you. And you are the perfect wife for him."

Lynn looked askance at Caro, who smiled. "You don't believe me? You need a kind, gentle, compassionate, loving husband, and David has all of those traits in abundance. He needs a kindhearted, sweet-tempered, caring, loving wife—

characteristics with which you are richly endowed. He will never hurt you, Lynn, and he will be fiercely protective of you. Those are just a few of the reasons I think the two of you are perfect for each other."

Rising, she shook out her skirts, then kissed Lynn's cheek. "Be happy, my dear. Marriages succeed when a husband and wife love one another, try to understand each other, aren't afraid to speak their minds but tread gently when emotion colors a discussion, and think of each other before they think of themselves. You and David already do all of those things, so I believe you will find great joy in your marriage."

A few minutes after Caro's departure, Beth arrived, with Moira trailing a pace behind. Smiling wryly, Beth explained, "As your friend, I am here to provide a third opinion in the event that Tilly and Caro gave you conflicting marital advice, as they did me. Moira's assistance is more practical. She will fix your hair and help you dress."

"My thanks to you both." Waving Beth to a chair, Lynn sat at the dressing table so Moira could style her hair. "Tilly and Caro have been here, but their counsel was much the same. What conflicting advice did they give you?"

"Since my great-aunt is a spinster, Tilly and Caro explained the intimate aspects of marriage. Tilly said that if I . . . um, enjoyed conjugal relations and actively participated, then George would get more pleasure from them and, thus, would be less likely to stray. Caro, on the other hand, said that ladies never enjoyed the marital act, they merely served as a . . . um, vessel for their husband's seed."

"Conflicting advice, indeed! What did you do?"

Beth's smile was a bit mischievous. "I told George that I was confused because his aunts had given me diametrically opposite advice about marital intimacies, then I asked his opinion."

Lynn could not imagine having such a conversation with a man. Not even David. "Lud, Beth! You are a great deal braver than I." Then, because her own experience did not allow her to judge which of David's aunts was correct, "Did George confirm that one of his aunts was correct, or was his opinion different still?"

"He said that Tilly was correct—that he would find more pleasure in . . . um, our marriage bed if I enjoyed it, too.

But he also said that he would never be unfaithful to me, even if I did not."

Casting a curious look at her, Beth said, in a tone that was half amazed and half amused, "I cannot imagine why I am giving you advice. As a widow, you know far more about lovemaking than I do."

Lynn hesitated for a moment, then decided to confide, at least a little bit, in her soon-to-be sister-in-law. "No, my dear, I don't. My late husband did not love me, and what he did in our marriage bed was far from pleasant."

In a flurry of silk skirts, Beth knelt and hugged her. "I am sorry, Lynn. I did not mean to dredge up bad memories—"

Lynn returned the embrace. "You didn't. Not really. Besides, as Tilly pointed out, the past is past, and it can only affect the future if I let it. Which I will *not*."

Beth's mischievous smile returned. "Well, tonight you will find out how wondrous lovemaking can be. Because David does love you. Very much."

Perhaps I will. If my fears do not overwhelm my resolve.

Standing at the back of the church, watching his bride as Caro twitched a wrinkle from the skirt of Lynn's seafoam green silk gown and Beth handed her a prayer book, David wondered if there would, in fact, be a wedding today. If someone did not do something to ease Lynn's agitation, she would bite through her lip before the ceremony. If she didn't faint first. Or bolt from the church.

She was so nervous, or so engrossed in her thoughts—second thoughts, perhaps—that she had not noticed him, even though he was no more than ten feet away. Although David was not at all certain that he was the best person to calm her fears, Caro and Beth seemed unaware of Lynn's anxiety, so he squared his shoulders, sent a quick prayer winging heavenward, and crossed to his very nervous bride.

"Good morning, my love." He bent to kiss her cheek. "You are, undoubtedly, the most beautiful bride in the history of the parish." And she was, indeed, a vision of loveliness in her fashionable new gown.

Fortunately—blessedly!—she did not bolt. Instead, she grasped his hands like a drowning man grabs the rope that will pull him to safety. "Oh, David."

Her hands felt like ice, even through the gloves they both wore. Though he feared the answer, he had to ask, "Are you having second thoughts, sweetheart?"

Her astonished expression answered his question before she spoke. "Second thoughts about marrying you? No."

Relief swamped him, threatening to buckle his knees, followed by a wave of jubilation. "Good." He raised her hands to his lips.

"Are *you* having second thoughts?"

"No," he said adamantly, smiling at her. "Nary a one."

She returned his smile. "Good."

If she was not having second thoughts, why had she looked so worried? Deciding this was not the time or place to ask what troubled her, he slipped his hands from hers and tucked her hand in the crook of his arm. "Then shall we say our vows and formally join our lives, and hearts, and futures?"

"Yes"—she squeezed his arm and offered another brilliant smile—"oh, yes."

Despite her earlier agitation, Lynn spoke her vows clearly and confidently, her gaze locked with his. David had never been happier in his life than the moment when the vicar pronounced them husband and wife. George, who was serving as best man, clapped him on the shoulder, and Beth hugged Lynn. His heart overflowing with love, David took Lynn's hand and turned to face their relatives, all of whom wore joyous smiles.

As he and Lynn stepped into the aisle, Isabelle popped up from her seat beside Caro and asked, "Miss Lynn, can I call you Mama now?"

Tears sparkled in his bride's beautiful eyes—bluish green today, matching the color of her gown—as she slipped her hand from his and bent over to pick up his daughter. Hugging her tightly, Lynn kissed Isabelle's cheek and said, "Yes, darling, you can. I am as proud and happy to be your mama as I am to be your father's wife."

Then, still holding Isabelle, Lynn smiled into his eyes and took his arm. And the three of them—a newly formed family blessed by the Church and the Crown—walked down the aisle together, eager to begin their new life.

The moment they stepped outside, David wrapped them both in an embrace and kissed his beloved bride, hoping

to convey with his lips the emotions that he was too overcome to put into words.

Someone plucked Isabelle from Lynn's arms, allowing
David to hug his wife more tightly. He rested his forehead
against hers and, after a time, found enough voice to ex-
claim, "God, but I love you, Madeline Winterbrook."

She cupped his jaw, caressing his cheek with her thumb.
"And I love you, my dear husband. More than I can say."

"Ahem!"

The exaggerated, extremely loud sound recalled David
to his surroundings, and brought a delicate flush to Lynn's
cheeks. With one arm around his bride, he turned—and
was startled to see that only his father and the vicar were
present in the churchyard.

"The vicar is waiting for you and Lynn to sign the register, son," Bellingham explained. "Then we will return to
Greendale Manor for the wedding breakfast your aunts and
sister-in-law have prepared."

Leading them to the vestry, the vicar indicated where
they should sign the register, and, as they did, he completed
their marriage lines, then handed them to Lynn. Noticing
that George and Beth had already signed as witnesses,
David wondered just how long he and Lynn had been lost
in oblivion. It did not matter, he decided; surely it was right
for a couple to feel so emotional on their wedding day.

After thanking the vicar, David escorted his bride to the
carriage. His father, smiling proudly, walked on her other
side and kept up a spate of inconsequential chatter on the
drive home.

When they entered the house, all the servants were lined
up in the entry hall, waiting to greet their new mistress.
Finch, the butler, stepped forward and bowed deeply.
"Lady David, my lord. On behalf of the staff I extend to
you both our best wishes. May your life together be filled
with joy and happiness."

"Thank you," David replied as Lynn said, "I thank you
all very much."

The tweeny, after a nudge from the chambermaid standing next to her, stepped forward and handed Lynn a bou-
quet of spring flowers. "These are fer you, m'lady."

"Thank you, Mary." Lynn bent her face to the blooms,
no doubt to hide the tears sparkling in her eyes.

As David sought a way to distract attention from Lynn until she regained her composure, his father clapped his hands once. "Now, we have a wedding to celebrate!"

That night, after changing into her nightrail and dressing gown, Lynn sat at the dressing table in her new bedchamber and brushed her hair, feeling strangely unsettled. No bride could hope for a nicer wedding ceremony, nor a more joyous wedding breakfast or a more welcoming, loving new family. The celebration had continued, in one form or another, throughout the day. Even after dinner, when Bellingham convinced his sons and Beth to join him in performing a lovely, and very moving, musical tribute to the newlyweds. David had argued that, as the groom, he should not have to participate, but his father had laughingly overruled him, since David was the only violist.

Lynn had enjoyed every moment—until they'd come upstairs. David had escorted her to this room, kissed her and told her that he loved her, then left. She wanted, very much, to talk with him, but she had not the slightest idea where to find him. Until this morning, this had been *his* bedchamber. But no matter how much she wished to talk with him and to give him his wedding gift and, perhaps, to enjoy more of his kisses, she was not about to make a cake of herself by wandering up and down the corridor in her nightrail, knocking on doors in search of him.

To make matters worse, she was all too well aware that her current dilemma was entirely her own fault. If only she had realized sooner that what she wanted most in the world was to be David's wife, not just in name, but in truth. Lynn still was not certain if she was brave enough and strong enough to confront the demons that haunted her first marriage bed, but she wanted to try. Because she knew, absolutely and without a shadow of a doubt, that she trusted David completely—with her heart and with her body.

Unfortunately, she had not had a chance to tell him. That, too, was her fault, for she had not realized it until Monday night, and yesterday and today had been so busy that she'd had no opportunity to talk privately with him.

A quiet knock interrupted her reproaches. As she turned toward the door, she saw a flash of movement across the room. David, clad in a nightshirt and dressing gown, entered through a door in the far corner that she had not, until this moment, seen. Despite the fact that she'd been wishing to talk with him, his unexpected appearance startled her so that she dropped her hairbrush.

"David!" she exclaimed, her voice far from steady, "what are you doing here?"

Crossing the room to his beloved wife, David found himself, for the second time today, hoping that she would not bolt. "I want to talk to you, sweetheart."

Her eyes widened, so he quickly added, "I am not reneging on my promise to you. We won't consummate our marriage until you are ready."

He picked up her brush and began plying it, stroking her silky tresses from crown to tip, which dangled past her hips. "Your hair is longer than I thought, and it looks so lovely down. Like a gleaming cloak surrounding you."

"It is straight as a poker!"

He grinned at her reflection in the mirror. "Is there a rule that says straight hair cannot be pretty? If so, I take exception to it. Your hair is beautiful, just like you are."

"Thank you, David. I think you need spectacles, but—"

"There is nothing wrong with my eyes, sweetheart."

Although his attention was intently focused on his purpose, some corner of his mind noticed her lace-trimmed muslin nightrail and robe. The gown was a far cry from the long-sleeved, high-necked flannel one she had worn at Larkspur Cottage during her illness, and it showed her curvaceous form to advantage. That was a distraction he did not need at the moment. At least, not until he explained the reason for his presence. "Lynn, I know you need time to accustom yourself to marriage, and to trust me completely, but the best way—"

"David—"

"Please let me finish, my love. Then I will listen to whatever you have to say."

When she nodded her agreement, he continued. "The best way to develop that trust is for us to spend time together. Not just in the drawing room or the estate office—you do not fear my behavior there—but here as well. I propose that we share this bedchamber, and the bed, which is quite large. But we will not consummate our marriage until you are ready. Until you trust me in this room as completely as you do in any other."

He gulped in a breath. "I believe that the best, and the most convincing, way to build that trust is by example. By letting my actions, or the lack thereof, prove to you that I am a very different man than Frank Graves."

Reaching up, she grasped the brush, pulled it from his hand, and laid it on the dressing table, then stood and turned to face him. "David, I have known for quite some time that you are a kinder, gentler, and far better man than Frank."

Taking his hand, she led him to a wing chair in front of the hearth. Putting her hands on his shoulders, she pushed him into it, then sat on his lap. "I think your suggestion has merit, but will it not be . . . difficult for you? To share a bed but do nothing more than hold me and kiss me?"

Surprised by the question, he glanced at her, but could see only the top of her head, which rested on his shoulder. "I hadn't expected that you would want me to hold you and kiss you there. At least, not for a while."

"Yes, I will. Won't that be difficult for you?"

"I don't believe so. And even if it is, the eventual reward will be worth any discomfort I might suffer."

It is now or never, my girl. Lynn inhaled deeply, gathering her courage, then sat up so she could see her husband's beloved face and brushed a kiss against his mouth. His hands circled her waist, his thumbs stoking her abdomen, and she hoped he could not feel her body's inner trembles. "Do you remember asking me, weeks ago, what I wanted most in the world?"

"Yes, sweetheart, I do. When I first put the question to you, you said you needed time to consider it. Then, several weeks later, just before we left Berkshire, you told me that what you wanted most was to marry me and share my life."

"Yes"—she nodded—"that is true. But now I know that I want a bit more. What I really want, more than anything in the world, is to be your wife in truth, not just in name."

A sharply indrawn breath indicated David's surprise. He smoothed her hair away from her face, cupping his hands at the crown of her head to hold it back as he studied her features. "Are you certain, my love?"

"Yes, I am quite certain that is what I want, but . . ." She dropped her gaze, seeking the words to explain her doubts.

"But?" he prompted, his voice as patient and gentle as ever.

"I am absolutely certain that I want to be your wife, but I do not know if I have truly banished all my fears."

"Sweetheart, I am not sure I understand what you are telling me."

"That is because I am not explaining it very well." Lynn sighed, wondering how to clarify her qualms. "I want to be your wife, to consummate our marriage, but even though I know you are not at all like Frank, I cannot be sure that my old fears will not rise up to haunt me. And if they do . . ."

"*If* they do, then we will deal with them. Together." He drew her close and kissed her, and the gentle caress of his lips against hers was as much a declaration of his love as the vows he'd spoken this morning.

Cuddling her against his chest, he stroked his fingers through her hair. The tender touch comforted Lynn to the depths of her soul, and she thanked God for the strange sequence of events—twists of fate, perhaps—that had brought this wonderful, gentle, loving man into her life. Whatever problems they faced, including the one currently occupying his thoughts, she knew their love was deep enough, and strong enough, to overcome any difficulty.

When he finally spoke, David's tone was pensive. "I wonder if it might be better not to set expectations."

She tilted her head back against his shoulder so that she could see his face. "What do you mean?"

"I mean that we should let our relationship—our intimate relationship—deepen naturally, in stages that are comfortable for us both, instead of expecting it to develop according to a predetermined schedule." He rubbed his thumb over the puzzled frown creasing her brow. "In other words, we will start with hugs and kisses and proceed from there. Maybe we will consummate our marriage tonight, perhaps not until tomorrow or the night after or next week, but when it occurs, it will be a natural sequence in, and consequence of, our lovemaking. That should help to keep your old fears at bay, don't you think?"

Marveling at his wisdom, she nodded. "Yes, I think it will."

"Now, my darling wife"—he rose and carried her to their bed—"shall we see where our hugs and kisses and caresses lead us tonight?"

"Yes, indeed."

Although he had slept very little, David awoke at his customary early hour. Lynn was snuggled against his side with her head on his shoulder, her hair draped across his arm and chest like a blanket. *God is in His heaven, and all is right in the world.* Or, at least, in *my* world, David amended, counting his blessings and giving thanks for each one.

Gentleman farmer or not, he was not at all inclined to rise before Lynn woke. Surely even the lowliest farmer lingered abed the morning after his wedding! Through a slight gap in the blue velvet draperies, he watched as sunrise brightened to morning, lightly stroking his hand along his wife's spine. And he was well rewarded for his vigil when she stirred, then pressed a kiss to the underside of his jaw.

"Good morning, my love."

"Good morning," she replied, her voice husky with sleep. Then, "I am sorry, David."

His stomach lurched at the softly spoken apology, his euphoria vanishing like the morning mist. *Please, God, no! Please don't let her regret last night.* With an effort, he managed a light, almost jovial tone. "When a man awakens the morning after his wedding with his beloved wife in his arms and the first thing she does is kiss him, he, quite naturally, feels elated. But when she then apologizes, his elation quickly turns to dismay, and he cannot help but wonder if he made a grievous error in judgment the night before. Or if his words or deeds somehow offended his love."

Propping herself up with one arm, she used her other hand to push her hair behind her shoulders, seemingly unaware that her actions offered him an incomparable view of her bosom. "What *are* you nattering about? I was apologizing for waking you."

"Ah." He pulled her on top of him and kissed her, using both hands to caress her back. "I was already awake, sweetheart."

She fisted a hand on his chest and rested her chin upon it. "Have you been awake very long?"

"For a time."

"And you did not feel the urge to get up and milk a cow or two?" she teased with a sleepy smile. "I had the impression, from our time at Larkspur Cottage, that you do not linger in bed once you are awake."

"Ah, but I did not have you in my bed there." Grinning, he kissed the tip of her nose. "This morning I suddenly developed a penchant for lingering abed."

"Did you, indeed?"

"Yes, my darling, I did."

"Whatever will your tenants and workers think, Mr. Estate Manager?"

"They will think, and rightly so, that I am utterly besotted with my bride."

She stretched to kiss him. "That is quite wonderful because she, too, is besotted."

"Did any old ghosts rise up in the night, love?"

"No. Last night you banished the ghosts, exorcised all the demons, slayed the dragons, and buried the old memories so deeply they will never again rise to the surface. And for those wondrous feats, O Gallant Knight, you have my heartfelt thanks. I shall devote my life to ensuring that you are properly rewarded for your endeavors." She kissed him again, a longer, more lingering, and quite rewarding kiss.

"Speaking of rewards . . ." He rolled her to his side, then sat up and looked for his dressing gown. Espying it on the floor beside the bed, he grabbed it and pulled an elegantly wrapped gift from the pocket. "This is for you, sweetheart. A wedding present. I intended to give it to you last night, but you . . . um, distracted me."

Instead of an apology, she offered him a saucy smile. "Is that what I did?"

"Among other things, yes."

"Well, you distracted me, too. I want you to open your gift first, but you will have to fetch it from my dressing table."

"*I* will have to fetch it?"

"You don't want your wife exposed to the cold morning air, do you?"

"Somehow, I doubt that exposure to the cold morning air is your primary concern, my darling. But"—he threw back the covers—"I will get it for you because I am a good husband."

When he returned to bed, she greeted him with a kiss. "A wonderful husband."

Propping the pillows against the headboard, he leaned back against them and cuddled her to his side. "Why don't you open it for me, so that I can hold you?"

She removed the foil paper, then handed him a small, square box. "You must open this."

Inside, on black velvet, was a simple but elegant gold watch. The inner surface of the lid was engraved

To David,
with all my love,
Lynn
09 March 1814.

"Thank you, sweetheart," he murmured between kisses, "for the watch and for the gift of your love. I will think of you whenever I check the time—and many, many moments in between."

He handed Lynn her present, watching her expressive features as she unwrapped it, then opened the crimson velvet case. "Oh, David, it is beautiful!" Her eyes darted from the sapphire and diamond necklace to his face, then to her engagement ring. "And it matches my ring!"

"Yes." He lifted the necklace and held it in front of her. "Sit up and let's see how it looks on you."

"But—"

Anticipating her objection, he said, "Clothes aren't required to wear it, only a neck."

"But—"

"Bend toward me and pull your hair to one side so I can see to fasten the clasp. . . . There." He cupped her chin in his hand, raising her face for a kiss, then leaned back to admire the jewels and the woman they adorned. "Beautiful. Breathtakingly beautiful."

"Thank you, David." She threw her arms around his

neck and kissed him.. "It is the loveliest necklace I have ever seen, and I will treasure it always."

Tumbling her on the bed, he braced his hands on either side of her head and brushed a kiss against her rosy lips. "Since the necklace did not permit an inscription, allow me to demonstrate, once again, how very much I love you."

And he did.

About the Author

Susannah Carleton discovered Regency romances at the ripe old age of thirty-three and promptly fell in love, since life among the *ton* in Regency England is such a diverting change from that of an engineer. She lives in Florida with her husband and teenage son, and when she isn't reading or writing, she enjoys solo and choral singing and needlework. Visit her Web site at www.susannahcarleton.com for information about Susannah and her books.

Also by
Susannah Carleton

THE MARRIAGE CAMPAIGN
0-451-20802-1
Robert Symington could have any girl in London. Many a
marriage-minded maiden has swooned in the presence of this
strikingly handsome, charming rake, especially since his father's
will named him Marquess of Elston. But of the bevy, not one has
enchanted Robert. Every miss he meets has her eye on his
fortune—and his patrician nose can smell a gold-digger a
mile away.

A SCANDALOUS JOURNEY
0-451-20712-2
Few people know that George Winterbrook is a hopeless romantic
who will only marry for love. His plans are thwarted when a crazy
widow kidnaps him, but fate sends him a breathtaking savior.

**Available wherever books are sold, or
to order call: 1-800-788-6262**